RAVES FOR JAMES PATTERSON

"Behind all the noise and numbers, we shouldn't forget that no one gets this big without natural storytelling talent—which is what James Patterson has, in spades."

—Lee Child, #1 *New York Times* bestselling author of the Jack Reacher series

"Every once in a while, a writer comes along and fundamentally changes the way people read...With his mission still unfolding, James Patterson is the gold standard by which all others are judged."   —Steve Berry, #1 bestselling author of the Colton Malone series

"James Patterson is the boss. End of."   —Ian Rankin, *New York Times* bestselling author of the Inspector Rebus series

"Patterson boils a scene down to a single, telling detail, the element that defines a character or moves a plot along. It's what fires up the movie projector in the reader's mind."

—Michael Connelly

"When it comes to constructing a harrowing plot, author James Patterson can turn a screw all right."

—*New York Daily News*

"James Patterson knows how to sell thrills and suspense in clear, unwavering prose."   —*People*

REVENGE

For previews of upcoming books and information about the author, visit JamesPatterson.com or find him on Facebook, Twitter, or Instagram.

REVENGE

JAMES PATTERSON
AND ANDREW HOLMES

GRAND CENTRAL
PUBLISHING

NEW YORK   BOSTON

Copyright 2020 by James Patterson

Hachette Book Group supports the right to free expression and the value of copyright. The purpose of copyright is to encourage writers and artists to produce the creative works that enrich our culture.

The scanning, uploading, and distribution of this book without permission is a theft of the author's intellectual property. If you would like permission to use material from this book (other than for review purposes), please contact permissions@hbgusa.com. Thank you for your support of the author's rights.

Grand Central Publishing
Hachette Book Group
1290 Avenue of the Americas, New York, NY 10104
grandcentralpublishing.com
Twitter.com/grandcentral pub

First North American Edition: April 2020

Originally published in the United Kingdom by Century, a division of Penguin Random House, August 2018

Grand Central Publishing is a division of Hachette Book Group, Inc. The Grand Central name and logo are trademarks of Hachette Book Group, Inc.

The publisher is not responsible for websites (or their content) that are not owned by the publisher.

The Hachette Speakers Bureau provides a wide range of authors for speaking events. To find out more, go to hachettespeakersbureau.com or call (866) 376-6591.

ISBN 978-1-5387-1541-3 (trade paperback) / 978-1-5387-3437-7 (mass market premium edition) / 978-1-5387-0071-6 (hardcover library edition) / 978-1-5387-0072-3 (ebook) / 978-1-5387-5212-8 (large print)

LCCN 2019948234

Printed in the United States of America

LSC-H

10 9 8 7 6 5 4 3 2 1

FOR LITTLE BERTIE, and all his kisses on
the colored squares.

—A.H.

PROLOGUE

SHE LOCKED THE door, double-checked the gun was in place, and took up position on the bed, drawing the laptop toward her, ready for her next customer.

She sat with her legs folded beneath her, wearing an off-white tank top and short denim skirt. Her lips were dark crimson, cheeks thick with blusher. And as she regarded herself in the tiny communication window of the laptop—dispassionately, as though it were some other twenty-four-year-old staring back at her—she remembered a time when she wouldn't have dreamed of slathering on the makeup. Not unless it was for a student costume party. *Rocky Horror* theme, tarts and vicars, something like that. *Uh, gross*, she'd have said. *How obvious.*

But those days were history. She didn't go to costume parties anymore. Although she often invited men "to party."

Fixed to a tripod at the foot of her bed was the camera, its impassive eye trained on her, ready to take her image to screens in hotel rooms and upstairs studies and man caves; to laptops opened furtively in back rooms or maybe in the living room if the wife and kids were out, where she'd be appraised as though she were stock options, or a good deal on beef at the supermarket, or a bargain on Amazon. *Yes. No. Dunno. Maybe.*

Again, it was a thought that should have disgusted her, and once upon a time it had. The thought of all those unseen eyes on her body. The mortal dread of being recognized. But not anymore.

The camera light turned green, which meant that somewhere out in the world of the internet a man was looking at her right now, assessing her, sizing her up, deciding if she was worth it.

Her laptop cursor blinked. In the office sat her supervisor, Jason. Right now he'd be peering at his own monitor through a cloud of weed smoke and wondering why she wasn't typing, so she stitched on a smile for her audience and reached to the keyboard: *Hi, I'm bored, want to play?*

They hardly ever wanted to play. Mostly they came here via triple-X pop-ups and knew that "play" meant "pay." All they wanted to do was ogle for a few seconds and then click off in search of free porn elsewhere.

But sometimes they did want to play, and this was one of those times.

What did you have in mind? came the reply.

She smiled, licked her lips, and wrote, *I can show you something you've never seen before.*

Hidden beneath the duvet, the gun dug into her thigh.

Great, wrote the punter.

There was a pause. Payment details were entered. Plenty balked at this stage, but not this one. He was on the clock now.

Get in! wrote Jason on the IM. He always did that. In a funny way, she was going to miss Jason.

How about we lose the top? wrote the punter, emboldened, wanting to hurry things up, knowing the score. Most likely he was an old hand at cams. They were the worst, the regulars. Treated the girls like cattle, like slaves. No manners.

She turned and dipped a shoulder, dropping a strap of her tank top. Trying to smile, she found she couldn't. Instead her mind went elsewhere—to her parents, to whom she said a silent "sorry"; to the man in the hat from when she was little, her SAS man, her very own special forces, who'd protected her from the bad guys but couldn't protect her now. Wishing she could have heard his voice one last time and told him what she knew.

Why are you crying?

She hadn't even realized. But yes, a tear had slipped down her face.

Babe, WTF? What's up? wrote Jason, but she ignored him, writing to the punter instead.

What's your name? she typed.

For a second or so she thought he might not respond, things getting a bit weird for him, maybe. But then it came back. *Peter.* That was probably a lie, but as one who'd been living under a false identity for so long she could hardly judge. Either way, it felt better knowing his name, alias or not.

I'm sorry for what's about to happen, Peter, she wrote.

What's about to happen? wrote Peter.

It isn't your fault, she typed.

What isn't? came the reply.

This, she wrote. And she pulled the gun from under the duvet, using two hands as she put the barrel upside down into her mouth. She closed her eyes, and for a moment or so she paused in order to look for the courage inside, trying to find the strength to do what she needed to do.

And she found that strength. She found it because she had no other option. Because she had no choice. She said something around the barrel of the gun, two final words, and then pulled the trigger.

PART ONE

CHAPTER 1

THE STREET IN Finsbury Park was much like any other residential London road: rows of terraced homes bunched up on either side, cars nudged into every available space, each house telling its own story. This one: home to a retired couple, well kept, tidy and house-proud, wheelie bins neatly arranged out front. This one: student digs, overgrown patch of yard out front, windows dirty, shabby curtains that never seemed to open. This one: stickers in the window, paper chains hanging off the frame, home to a noisy family of four.

There was one particular house, however, where things weren't quite so easily delineated. Neighbors knew that a family of Eastern Europeans lived there—Bulgarians? Russians? Nobody was sure—and that they had a lot of visitors. The woman always had a smile, and the husband—if that's what he was, no formal introductions had been made—was a big chap, no stranger to the tattooist, and maybe not the sort you'd want to meet in a dark alley on a foggy night. But always perfectly pleasant if you saw him in the street.

And that was it. If you passed and looked into the front

room, often you'd see a much older man who whiled away the hours watching TV, and you'd probably think it was heart-warming that the older members of their family were being looked after in their dotage. Not like the British, who're happy to let them rot in an old folks' home.

One of the regular visitors to the house was Sergei Vinitsky, now walking along the pavement, hunched up against the chill of the pre-dawn, his hands thrust into the pockets of the hooded parka he wore, feeling dog-tired.

He opened the low gate and let himself into the yard. Raising his hand to knock, he noticed that he still had blood beneath his fingernails and he made a mental note to wash his hands thoroughly before he slept, which would, with any luck, be very soon indeed.

He knocked at the front door—one, two, pause, one, two, pause, one, two. As he was knocking, he glanced into the front window of the house. Sure enough, sitting in his favorite chair in the front room was the man they called Grandfather, glued to an episode of some TV program, cup of tea at hand. To look at him you'd never know that this particular old man had killed and killed again, and that his favored method of execution was to remove body parts one by one, literally to cut his victims to death.

The door was opened by Dmitry's English wife, Karen. A welcoming smile dropped from her face like falling bricks as she closed the door behind Sergei and indicated for him to make his way along the hall.

He remembered himself, stopped and called to Grandfather in the front room, "Hello, *Ded*," he said, *Ded* being the name reserved for those unrelated to Grandfather. Dmitry, his actual grandson, called him *Dedushka*. Karen too.

At the sound of the greeting the old man turned his head in Sergei's direction and grinned toothlessly, his beady eyes gleaming. He inclined his head in reply, then switched his attention back to the TV.

"The Skinsman," they called him. Just to say his name made men beg for mercy. But his ways were the old ways. Sergei and Dmitry were seeing to that.

Venturing into the bowels of the home, Sergei was struck afresh by the marked contrast between the front of the house and what lay further inside. Leading off the hall was an adequately furnished kitchen with the full complement of washing machine, dishwasher, fridge, and stove, but otherwise all semblance of domestic normality was absent, the pretense so carefully projected for the benefit of neighbors and passersby abandoned. There were no photographs on the wall, no lamps or light shades where a listening device might be concealed, ditto no carpet. Just a stretch of corridor—bare, as though awaiting refurbishment—which led to a door and the lair of the man who to the neighbors seemed a pleasant enough fellow.

This was Dmitry Kraviz, and he spent the bulk of his days peering through spectacles at a mosaic of computer screens arranged above his desk.

Sergei knocked, walked in, and stood close to the door, just as Dmitry preferred. He had called ahead to warn his boss that he had news of some importance, but of course the information itself had to be delivered in person.

"So, what do you have to tell me, Sergei?" asked Dmitry. He swiveled in his seat in order to give his second in command his full attention. A gold tooth gleamed, but there was no malice in his smile, not like his grandfather.

"There has been trouble, Dmitry, at one of our studios," explained Sergei, and he told Dmitry about the girl.

When he had finished, Dmitry processed the news without comment or even apparent emotion, turning lazily in his chair, his eyes flicking over the screens. On one a young girl was removing her bra. Another showed men gambling in a dimly lit room. Another displayed a list of what Sergei took to be prices, but of what he couldn't say, while yet another rested at a Google search screen. Who knew where Dmitry's interests might take him? As head of the organization's London operation, Dmitry had excelled in numerous areas of business: drugs, pornography, prostitution, gambling, protection, and trafficking among them. Having the family connection to the Skinsman had certainly done him no harm, but Dmitry had also earned a reputation as a thoughtful tactician in his own right. Ruthless, maybe, but never willfully cruel. Again, not like his grandfather.

"Is Karen aware?" he said.

"She didn't mention it when I arrived."

"Is that so? I thought it was her job to look after the girls."

Sergei gave him a look that he hoped would convey at least two things. One, that Karen was not exactly conscientious when it came to those duties. Two, that Sergei did not consider it his place to say so.

Dmitry understood. "Stupid bitch," he said. "But you, Sergei. You have done well."

"Thank you, Dmitry," said Sergei. He recalled the clean-up operation with a barely restrained shudder: calming down Jason, trying not to spook the other girls, keeping a lid on the whole thing during a process that had gone on into the early hours of the morning until, finally, they had deposited the body in a hostel in Clapham then left via the fire exit, stepping over an unconscious junkie on their way out.

Oh yes, it had been a very, very long night indeed.

"Which one was she, the girl?" asked Dmitry.

Sergei gave a small half-shrug. "Her name was Faye. She was only with us for a couple of weeks."

"How did she come to us?"

"From our street people."

"Good-looking?"

Sergei kissed his fingers, Italian chef style.

"Such a shame. I'll have to refresh my memory." Dmitry indicated his screens. "But a junkie, though, yes?"

Sergei nodded. "She owed us money. Our boys referred her to me and I put her to work."

"I see."

"Will you tell Grozny, Dmitry?"

Dmitry thought a moment then asked, "It is all taken care of, yes? No comebacks?"

"I believe so."

He considered. "Then there is no need to upset Alexander," he said.

Moments later Sergei was excused, and on his way out he bid farewell to Karen and then to Grandfather, who returned his goodbye with a curt nod and a strange and malevolent smile.

Briefly, Sergei wondered if there was anything more to that smile than an old man losing what few marbles he still had left. But then he decided he was way too tired to care.

CHAPTER 2

HE DIDN'T KNOW why, but that morning Shelley had been thinking about the guard in Iraq—specifically what Lucy had done to him.

This particular guard had been posted in what they called an "interrogation suite." It wasn't a particularly accurate name for it, not unless you substituted the word "chamber" for "suite," and "torture" for "interrogation." And from the intel they'd been given they had known he wasn't just an ordinary screw doing his duty—he enjoyed the work.

Lucy had slit his throat. It was either that or let him raise the alarm.

It was the sound that Shelley remembered most—blood sheeting from the new mouth in the sentry's neck as Shelley stepped from the shadows to help Lucy ease him to the flagstones, holding his mouth closed and his legs still until it was over.

It was nothing personal. An operational kill. Even so, nobody deserved it more than that guy. Never was there a bloke who had it coming more than him.

That was what had been rattling around Shelley's brain

that morning; one minute you're thinking, *We need a new light bulb for the kitchen*, the next you're remembering the sound that blood makes when it gushes from a slit throat.

Shelley and Lucy had left the military. He'd been forty-five, chucking-out time for 22 SAS. She'd been just forty. The idea was to apply what they'd learned in the field to the world of commercial security and make pots of cash.

But there was a wrinkle: they wanted a quieter life, which in turn meant avoiding "the Circuit," the international commercial security pool where ex-soldiers like Shelley and Lucy usually wound up plying their trade. While the activities of any private security company—a PSC—on the Circuit could involve asset tracing, employee screening, security audits, and risk analysis, overwhelmingly the most common service was close protection in hostile environments, which Shelley had had more than enough of during his time in the military.

Shelley had given the SAS a quarter-century of service. But for the last twenty of those years, he'd been teamed with another SAS officer, Cookie, and Lucy—who was in the Special Reconnaissance Regiment—to form a three-blade Special Projects patrol. Operating under the banner of the 22 but otherwise unaffiliated, they were a patrol without portfolio, specialists in deep-cover, covert operations usually carried out under a cloak of plausible deniability: hostage rescue, target acquisition, disruptive incursion, assassination. They were so clandestine that even within the 22 and the SRR, two of the most secretive military organizations in the world, they were thought to be a myth.

The silver lining of all that secrecy? It had made keeping the secret of his relationship with Lucy and their subsequent marriage a lot less difficult.

The bad news? They'd spent twenty years in hostile environments. Two decades of eating ration packs and using baby wipes to wash; twenty years of considering a night in a military cot to be the height of luxury.

Yes, there was the buzz. They'd spent many hours talking about that elusive 5 percent of the time when they weren't freezing cold, boiling hot, or bored out of their minds, when the adrenaline kicking in made the job worthwhile. But that was eventually outweighed by a desire not to get killed, not to see another kid with his foot blown off by an IED, another rape victim left for dead, her genitals deliberately mutilated.

Of the two, Shelley was keener to turn his back on that world. He never wanted to step in another Chinook as long as he lived. Lucy was ambivalent. "It's what we do," she was fond of saying. But Shelley had persuaded her to try it his way first. See if they could go it alone and set up a PSC with no Circuit connections. Maybe it could be the route to a quiet, comfortable life.

Sure enough, a quiet life was exactly what he had. On their books so far was precisely one job, which fell under the category of "information security." Shelley had to ferry a TV script from a producer to an actor, wait while it was read, and then ferry it back. Literally, that's all he had to do.

Otherwise? *Nada.* The problem he had was getting the word out. After all, you couldn't exactly advertise yourself, not in the accepted sense, because the kind of clients you wanted to attract (i.e., the rich ones) required a discreet, anonymous service. They weren't going to google "kickass bodyguard" and hope for the best.

Shelley tidied away the dishes from breakfast, lit a scented candle, and sat himself opposite his wife, who wanted to have what she called "a brainstorming session" in order to come up with ideas for generating work.

"A what?" he said.

"You heard."

"I heard what sounded like a load of trendy management-speak."

She rolled her eyes. "'Trendy management-speak' twenty years ago, maybe. Nowadays, just a way of getting ideas out of our heads and into the fresh air, so that, oh, I don't know, we can maybe get this PSC off the ground and start earning some actual money?"

He sighed but went along with it. However, their brains remained unstormed. After a while of getting nowhere, Lucy picked up her phone. She was a fan of the *Mail Online* website, a "guilty pleasure" that she part justified by claiming that if you dived past the trashy Kardashian-and-sensationalist-headlines stuff at the top, then there were some interesting tidbits in the uncharted depths beneath.

"Hey," she said, "didn't you once do some work for a bloke named Guy Drake?"

The name took Shelley by surprise. "Uh, yeah. Before we were married, well over ten years ago. More like fourteen. I had extended leave and . . ." He trailed off, feeling his cheeks warm.

"You were saving up for our secret wedding." Her smile was fond but it was tinged with sadness and he could sense that whatever she'd seen on her phone wasn't good news.

"What is it? He's not dead, is he?"

"No," said Lucy, "Guy's not dead—"

That was when the phone rang.

CHAPTER 3

On the other end of the line was a Scotland Yard copper, Detective Inspector Gary Phillips: "Who am I speaking to, please?"

"Why do you ask?" Shelley looked across at Lucy, who bit her lip and placed her phone carefully to one side.

"This number is registered to a Mr. David Shelley of Stepney Green, London. Would that be you, sir?" the detective pressed, doggedly, the way detectives are supposed to press.

"Yeah, that would be me. What can I do for you?"

"Do you know a woman named Emma Drake?"

For a moment Shelley struggled to match the word "woman" to the name Emma Drake, but then it came to him. "Yes, years ago," he said.

"So you know her?"

"Well, yeah, I guess."

"And in what sense do you know her?" the detective asked.

"In the sense that I was employed to provide close protection for her and her family. She was just a little girl then."

"I see," said Phillips. "Then I'm sorry to have to inform you that Emma Drake took her own life two nights ago."

Sadness descended upon Shelley like a heavy blanket. "How?" he said. "How did she do it?"

"I'm not at liberty to say, Mr. Shelley. I must ask, though, when was the last time you saw Miss Drake?"

A wariness crept over him and he pushed his grief to one side for the moment, ready for inspection later. "Why do you ask?"

"Could you just answer the question, Mr. Shelley?"

"Or . . .?"

"Or maybe you'd prefer to come to the Yard, and we could talk about it there."

"Okay, I last saw her fourteen years ago," answered Shelley. "Like I say, when I was working for her family. I've had no contact with her since."

"No contact of any kind?"

"Not that I know of."

"You didn't speak on the phone?" the detective persisted.

"I'd call speaking to her on the phone 'contact,' and I've just told you that to my knowledge I've had no contact with Emma for over fourteen years. I've had no need to."

"I ask because she called you a couple of days ago, on the day of her death."

That hit Shelley hard. "Uh . . ." he floundered. "Come again?"

"As I say, Mr. Shelley, Emma Drake called you shortly before she took her own life."

"She called me?" repeated Shelley.

Shelley tried to think, then he remembered it was about two days ago when the phone had rung during *Game of Thrones*. He hadn't recognized the number and because it was evening, and thinking it was probably a cold-caller trying to sell him a better phone package, or loft insulation, or something to do with PPI—whatever that was—he'd ignored it.

"If it's important they'll leave a message," he'd told Lucy, which was his standard response whenever he didn't feel like answering a call.

But whoever it was hadn't left a message, and Shelley had felt vindicated, thinking, *Yeah, dodged a bullet there*, before returning his attention to Westeros.

He told the cop about it, listening out for a note of disbelief but not hearing one. He guessed the facts supported him.

"How did she get your number, Mr. Shelley, do you know?"

"It's the same number. I've had it donkey's years."

"And she remembered it, all these years later? Sounds somewhat unlikely if you don't mind me saying so, sir."

"I was with the Drakes for close protection. I made her memorize my number. She was ten. You remember stuff like that."

"Yup," agreed Phillips. "I hear you. It's the stuff you did yesterday that you forget. Lastly, then, have you got any idea why she'd call you, Mr. Shelley? Like you say, it had been a long time."

"No," Shelley replied. "I've got no idea."

But more than anything, he wished that he'd paused *Game of Thrones* and taken the call.

CHAPTER 4

SHELLEY USED THE Saab's rearview mirror to check his short hair was army-neat and his black knitted tie straight. Lucy sat beside him in the passenger seat, gloved hands in her lap, gazing out across the near-empty car park.

She hated sitting still, doing nothing. Usually she'd have had her phone out, checking emails, puzzling over a never-ending game of Scrabble, or playing those brain-training games she loved so much. But not now.

The funeral cortège appeared from over their shoulders, winding its way along the approach road to the entrance of the crematorium. The Rolls-Royce hearse stopped. Two black Daimlers cruised past and stopped. Their doors opened, decanting black-clad figures.

"Looks like that's our cue," said Lucy, and they stepped from the Saab with the wind whipping their clothes. They linked arms and crossed the car park to watch the coffin unloaded and carried into the crematorium.

There were just a handful of other mourners present, all of

whom looked somber and shivered with cold: aunts, uncles, and sundry scattered family, by the looks of it.

From what Shelley could recall, the Drakes weren't an especially close or affectionate clan. Guy Drake considered Susie and Emma his true family and everyone else as just relations. Guy's attitude to his "relations" had changed when huge wealth entered the equation. Always the way. With money comes resentment, distrust, and entitlement. A whole bunch of shit you never considered when you bought your lottery ticket.

Guy and Susie stood slightly apart from the other mourners, drawn pale features accentuated by their funeral attire. Susie, tall and slim, as swan-like as ever, caught sight of Shelley, took a moment to recognize him, and then offered a weak smile in thanks.

Guy had put on weight over the intervening years. His jaw clenched and Shelley saw that his habit of moving his mouth as though chewing seemed to have become more pronounced over time—or perhaps it was just the stress of grief. He gave Shelley a short nod of recognition and gratitude, but it was a formal gesture, and something about the way his eyes slid away struck Shelley as odd, given how friendly they'd once been.

Shelley became aware of two new arrivals, a pair of bodyguards who wore suits in keeping with the occasion. They stood erect with their hands clasped in front of them, jackets cut so as not to reveal whether or not they wore shoulder holsters, which Shelley had a feeling they would be.

What's more, he knew one of them—the older of the two, who had graying hair and a short salt-and-pepper beard and wore large, studious-looking spectacles. His name was Lloyd

Bennett and, like Shelley, he was ex–special forces—a Para, in Bennett's case. Like Shelley he'd sought new opportunities in security after being put out to pasture. Unlike Shelley, he'd joined the Circuit.

The two men acknowledged one another with nods, and Shelley wondered why he felt uncomfortable. Was it something as simple as professional jealousy? After all, there was a time when he was the one the Drakes called upon for close protection.

Or was it something else? Like why, when your daughter has just taken her own life, do you feel the need to employ security? Ex–special forces security at that.

The man next to Bennett was taller and younger, with close-cropped hair. He gazed over at Shelley but made no attempt to greet him, just stared, and for a moment their eyes locked, the guy trying to stare him out. *Have it your way*, thought Shelley, breaking the stare. *I'm not playing.*

A short while later, attendees filed into the crematorium. On their seats was an order of service, "A celebration of the life of Emma Jane Drake," bearing a recent photograph of her. The small news piece Lucy saw on *Mail Online* had been little more than a headline, "MILLIONAIRE'S DAUGHTER FOUND DEAD IN HOSTEL," and a couple of paragraphs of text. This girl he had known as a child had grown up to be a beautiful young woman. She'd had her mother's fine features, her father's determined eyes, an innate intelligence that was all her own.

Neither Drake nor Susie was in any state to give a eulogy, so the service was conducted entirely by a celebrant. Mourners chuckled and nodded in recognition at her descriptions of Emma as a bright, curious little girl, in love with life, ponies, and Destiny's Child, in that order, as besotted with

Mommy and Daddy as they were with her. No doubt about it, she'd enjoyed her only-child status, but rarely letting it tip over into spoiled-child territory.

Shelley had been curious to hear what she'd done next, and by all accounts she'd continued to show promise at her all-girl public school. Head girl, no less, she'd discovered a passion for theater. So much so that when she'd moved on, it was to York University and a BA in Theater: Writing, Directing, and Performance.

She'd never completed the course. And here the mourners' chuckles died in their throats and the fond reminiscences ceased as the celebrant tactfully skirted the details of her last years, saying only that, like many of us, Emma had her demons, and that despite the love and support of her parents, Guy and Susie, who had reached out to her many times over the years, those demons had eventually claimed her.

Drake and Susie sat ramrod straight in the front row, the backs of their heads betraying nothing of their grief—nothing until the coffin disappeared behind the curtain, when Susie's shoulders dropped and Drake did something that was extraordinary and yet perfectly forgivable in the circumstances: he let out a long impassioned wail, a sound dredged from the very depths of his soul.

As the service ended, Susie took him in her arms. His shoulders shook as he wept, his head buried in her so that at least he was spared the sympathetic looks of the mourners as they filed out of the crematorium quickly to escape the weight of his grief.

Outside they stood making small talk. When the two grieving parents eventually appeared, Drake was red-eyed but composed. Shelley shot Lucy a look—*Would you mind waiting?*—and was about to move over to them when he found himself intercepted by Bennett.

"Captain Shelley of the SAS," said Bennett with a smile appropriate to the occasion. He held out a hand, and for a childish moment Shelley considered refusing to shake it. "It's an honor to meet you," continued Bennett.

"It's nice to meet you too, mate," said Shelley, although he wasn't so sure about that. "Bennett, isn't it?"

"In one," said Bennett, glowing a little.

"You on close-protection duty, are you?"

"Something like that. I've got a man on the perimeter keeping the press at bay. Couple of paps he's needed to chase off but that's about it. Just general security, you know?"

Shelley nodded, trying to keep it casual. "That's all, is it?"

"That's all, yes," replied Bennett, throwing up a barrier.

"Fair enough," said Shelley, acting as though he bought it. But when he walked across to see Susie and Drake, he could sense the eyes of Bennett and his minion upon him.

He and Drake shook hands and he could feel the grief radiating off him like heat from a fire.

"Thank you so much for coming, David," said Susie. They kissed and she enveloped him in a cloud of the same scent she'd worn all those years ago, the smell of it taking him straight back there—back to their home, excursions out with her and Emma, those shopping trips . . .

"I'm so, so sorry," he said, trying to find the words. "Emma was really something. I think you know how fond I was of her. I only hope that she did too."

"She did, David, she did." Susie was one of the few people who had ever called Shelley "David." It sounded strange and slightly incongruous, and another time he might have laughed. But not now.

He found himself wishing he could ask how she had done it, how Emma had killed herself. He wanted desperately for Susie simply to surrender the information. Indeed, it was almost as though there was a gap in the conversation waiting to be filled with that piece of information, and maybe Susie sensed it, too. He saw her lips part, words forming . . . and then her husband spoke instead.

"We appreciate you coming, Shelley," said Drake, his Manchester accent undimmed by the years in London. "I know it's normal to invite everybody for a drink and a bite to eat to remember Emma, but we've decided we'd rather say our goodbyes here. I hope you understand."

"Of course, mate, of course," said Shelley, at the same time unable to rid himself of the idea that there was something odd about it.

Standing some way off, Lucy had been talking to some of the mourners. He'd seen her embrace a girl who would have been about Emma's age—a friend or a cousin. He couldn't help but notice that Drake was keeping an eye on things in that corner, too. Bennett and his mate drifted across, hoping to achieve Shelley had no idea what. If it was to try to intimidate Lucy then good luck with that.

Lucy was wrapping up her conversation as Shelley finished saying his goodbyes to the Drakes and stepped away.

She took his arm as the funeral-goers dispersed.

"Did you ask how it happened?" she said. They reached the Saab and climbed in.

"I chickened out," admitted Shelley ruefully. He picked his hat up off the back seat and fitted it back on his head. A

Christys' newsboy cap. Like him, it looked like a worn relic from another age, and just wearing it made him feel more himself again.

"Thought you might. So I asked for you. Well, I didn't ask outright. I dug."

His fingers dropped from the ignition key. "Yes. And?"

"She shot herself, Shelley. Took herself off to that hostel and ate a bullet. And if anybody knows anything more than that, they're not saying."

For a moment he simply sat in silence, absorbing that fact, thinking, *She shot herself. But before that, she called me. Why did she call me?*

He reached for the key to start the car. "Did you see any paparazzi hanging around?" he asked Lucy.

"No," she said.

"No, me neither."

CHAPTER 5

THEY ARRANGED TO meet in a coffee shop in Islington, close to where they used to make contact on another job.

It was funny, thought Shelley, how you never really left your old life behind. You just added to it, like the old masters reusing a canvas. You painted over it, but it was still there underneath all those layers, and at some point it would make its presence known again.

Already installed at a table, wearing a pinstriped suit and looking incongruous among the yummy mummies and retirees, was his appointment: the man from MI5, Simon Claridge. He was slouching a little, reading the *Daily Telegraph* as he sipped his coffee, but he looked up as Shelley turned from the counter and made his way across the coffee shop. "Hello, Shelley," he said.

Shelley placed his coffee down, removed his newsboy cap, and dropped it on the table, running fingers through his hair and dragging his scarf from around his neck.

Claridge watched it all with a half-smile. "Looking good there, Shelley," he said, raising an eyebrow. "In fact, you're looking like a man who's enjoying a well-earned rest in the company of the beautiful Lucy." He laid his *Telegraph* to one side and pulled up his chair, ready to talk.

"Careful," replied Shelley, "or I'll tell her you said that."

Grinning now, the MI5 man held up his hands. "I beg you, anything but that. How is she? Well, I hope?"

Claridge knew Lucy, but they hadn't seen each other since the three of them had worked together to bring down the Quarry Company, a sick hunting-game organization that had murdered their friend and comrade Cookie.

After leaving the Regiment, Shelley and Lucy had retired to their cute Stepney Green terrace in order to look after their dog Frankie and cook up ideas for their fledgling PSC.

Cookie, however, had fallen on hard times and taken to living on the street. Then a bunch of blokes with too much money and bad taste in high-powered weapons hunted him down and killed him for sport. The Quarry Company. The bastards had killed Frankie too.

After taking down the Quarry Company, Shelley and Lucy had to spend time on the run—just over a year—until Claridge had been able to assure them that the coast was clear. With that they'd returned home to resume their lives, which meant renewing attempts to get the business off the ground. Their low-profile period, while proving to be a wonderful holiday, hadn't exactly done much to advance their plans in the PSC department.

"She's fine," Shelley answered. "Mostly."

"Mostly?"

"Yeah. Mostly."

"I see, and what about you?" asked Claridge. "How's life treating you?"

"Well, you know," shrugged Shelley, "can't complain."

"Hmm, not much of an answer, is it? Okay, but if you were to complain, what would you be complaining about?"

Shelley felt one side of his mouth lift in what he knew would be a somewhat wintry smile. "I guess things could be a bit more comfortable. Financially, I mean. It's not like the work is flooding in."

Claridge nodded. "And that's why Lucy is 'mostly' fine?"

"She misses life in the forces more than I do. She'd be happier back in Iraq, I reckon, as long as she had something to keep her occupied."

"And you've got nothing in this country to keep her occupied?"

"Like I say, the work isn't flooding in."

Claridge frowned. "The last time we spoke, I told you that if you had difficulty finding work then you were to get in touch. Now you tell me that you are having difficulty finding work but that's *not* the reason you got in touch, is it?"

"I like doing things on my terms," sighed Shelley. "As soon as I start accepting work from someone, even someone I trust, I'm surrendering that luxury. I stop being the one who says yes or no, and I start being the one who says 'thank you, I'll do it.'"

Claridge rolled his eyes. "Welcome to the real world, Shelley. It's called commerce. And really, it's no great hardship. You decline work if you don't like the sound of it, wait for something more suitable to come along, and if you put a few noses out of joint doing that, well, who cares, frankly. None of those noses will belong to me, of that I can assure you. What does Lucy say?"

"If Lucy was here she'd be nudging me in the ribs right now, going, 'See? I told you so.'"

"There you go."

"Look," said Shelley, "I'm really grateful for the offer, you know I am. Let me just try it my own way first, see if I can make a go of it, and if I can't, then I'll try it your way, the Lucy way. How does that sound?"

"Can't say fairer than that, I suppose," said Claridge. "So, let's get to the matter that brought us here today."

Shelley nodded slowly, his mind returning to Emma Drake.

"Okay, before we start, there is one thing I need to get clear." Claridge had laid his hands on the table, palms down, fingers spread. "Have you told the police everything you know?"

"You're talking about the phone call."

Claridge nodded.

"My phone went. I ignored the call. That's it."

"That's it?" Claridge offered him an appraising look, his head cocked slightly to one side. "You're asking me to believe that you just 'ignored the call.'"

Shelley looked away, across the coffee shop, where moms tended to babies in strollers and gossiped with other mums, where older gentlemen sat with newspapers, looking like relics from another time. In the old days when phones had handsets, and even dials, and no little readout to tell you who was calling, you just picked the fuck up. Nowadays you got to "screen" your calls. And that was what had happened. He'd ignored her call because he was screening.

He returned his attention to Claridge. "I get the occasional cold call," he explained. "I didn't recognize the number so I chose not to answer. I figured if it was important—"

"Somebody wanting to hire you, for example," pushed Claridge.

"Somebody trying to hire me," conceded Shelley, "then they would leave a message."

"And?"

"No message. And now I feel like shit and wish I'd taken the call. Happy?"

Claridge lowered his eyes. "My apologies. I'm being insensitive."

Shelley leaned over and pretended to give Claridge a slap. "Don't be daft. No, you're not. Christ, people die. Even young people, sometimes. That's the way the world is—we know that better than most. It's just that she was a great kid. So much spirit."

Claridge was sipping his coffee. He placed his cup to the saucer before he spoke again. "So what are you saying? You're surprised she killed herself?"

Shelley thought. "No, not really. People change, don't they? Nobody can look at a ten-year-old kid and predict they're going to kill themselves. But there's something up about this one—something a bit more than usually *off* about it all. For a start, she called me, out of the blue, for no good reason I can think of. Why would she do that? Secondly, her dad's employed security. Three guys. *Three.*"

"All right," said Claridge, "I'll tell you what I've got. Victim: Emma Drake, twenty-four years old. Cause of death: self-inflicted gunshot wound. But you know all this already."

Shelley nodded. "Do we know where she got the piece?"

"No, we don't."

"What sort of gun was it?"

"Nine millimeter, semi-auto. Croatian Parabellum. The sort of thing you can buy in a pub, which is probably where she got it."

"Stolen?"

"No doubt. Originally. Serial number hasn't given us any-thing yet."

"Right," said Shelley, seeing something pass across Claridge's face. "What?" he asked.

"Did you know that she had a history of intravenous drug use?"

Shelley screwed up his eyes in a wince. "Ah, shit. Really?"

"I'm afraid so. She was a user, Shelley, of some vintage. My apologies if that comes as a shock."

It did. But then again it didn't. He would have hoped that Emma, of all people, might have stayed away from hard drugs, but he knew how easy it was to fall into. He, Lucy, and Cookie had carried out operations against the cartels. He'd seen the pain and suffering drug addiction inflicted indiscriminately. It was a scourge with no respect for gender or class. It didn't look at a bright young girl from a good and loving family and decide to walk on by. It didn't work like that.

So no, shock wasn't exactly what he felt.

It helped explain her taking her own life suddenly. He doubted she would have been able to go home and admit her addiction to her parents. Guy was a good father, but he was the doting, overprotective sort, and probably not nearly as approachable as he liked to think. Susie? Shelley was sure Emma would have got a good hearing there, but even so, anything serious would likely have got back to Guy sooner or later.

"She obviously meant something to you," said Claridge.

Shelley nodded. Yes, she did. But in that moment he was mainly thinking, *Why, if she was a user, didn't she just use smack to check out?*

CHAPTER 6

TWO DAYS LATER, Shelley found himself in the living room of the home of a thirty-something actor in Berkshire, having completed the first phase of the one and only job on his books by safely delivering a supposedly top-secret script.

"So you're the SAS man, are you?" the actor said, leading him into the house. He wore jeans and a tight T-shirt, his hair shaved in a number two or three. He stared hard at Shelley. "You don't look much like an ex-SAS man."

"And how do we normally look?" asked Shelley, feeling old and out of shape, and also thinking the guy was a weapons-grade arsehole.

"I don't know," laughed the actor, dropping onto a large sofa and propping bare feet on a glass coffee table before pulling the brown envelope onto his lap, "like Jason Statham, I suppose. You're more stylish than I expected." He pointed to Shelley's boots. "Nice Red Wings, by the way."

"Thank you."

The actor cocked his head. "What's that accent?"

"My accent?"

"Yes, what's that? Where are you from, originally?"

Shelley shrugged. "Originally? Limehouse."

"Limehouse in London?"

"Yeah, Limehouse in London."

"Do you work out?"

"Not as much as I should," said Shelley, thinking of that rarely used gym membership. "I stay mobile, that's the important thing."

"I stay mobile," repeated the actor, trying to approximate Shelley's rasping voice. "That's the important thing. Limehouse. In *Lahndahn*. South of the river. Do you smoke?"

Oh, Christ, you're a dick. "No, mate, no, I don't."

"You sound like you smoke."

"Look, mate—" started Shelley, and then, belatedly, feeling like a man who'd only just understood the punch line to a bad joke, he realized why he had been asked to do this particular job. It wasn't just a delivery for this guy. It was research. "Don't tell me," he sighed, "your script involves an ex-SAS man."

Grinning, the actor gestured with the envelope. "I hope you haven't had a peek."

Typical. Guys like this thought the world revolved around them; they couldn't imagine it any other way. "It was sealed," said Shelley. "It's still sealed. I didn't look at your script. That's *your* job. I'm just supposed to wait while you read it and then return it."

He swiped the hat from his head and began to shed his woolen overcoat, indicating an armchair, all black leather and steel tubes, the kind that was popular in the 1970s but must have come back into style. "If it's all right with you I'll take a seat while you get on with it."

"*Mi casa su casa*," quipped the actor, and Shelley sat down in order to wait.

He was sitting watching the actor—who read his script while at the same time being supremely aware of Shelley's presence, as though the process of reading the script was in itself a performance—when his phone buzzed. Claridge. Shelley excused himself and moved out of the living room to a quiet corner of the house.

"Good to see you the other day," the MI5 man said. "I hope I was of some use."

"I guess," said Shelley, who still hadn't decided what, if anything, he planned to do with the information he'd been given. It was like some bad movie tagline: he'd gone to Claridge in search of answers but all he'd got were more questions.

"Something else has cropped up since we spoke," said Claridge. "I left a flag on the file and an old friend got in touch to let me know there's been a development. Two developments, to be exact."

"Fire away."

"Well, the first thing is that you're not the only one who's been making inquiries about the death of Emma Drake. Don't ask me who, I don't have names. All I know is that, according to my contact, interest has been shown by party or parties unknown."

Bennett, perhaps? thought Shelley. Was that it? Was Bennett doing investigative work for Drake? Could be, although an ex-Para wasn't the first person you'd call on to do some detective work. Not unless there were other, related, duties you wanted performed.

"Right. I see. And this third party, are they being supplied with information?"

"That I couldn't possibly say with any degree of authority. Ask me what I think, however, and I'd say yes, because . . . well, why not?"

"Okay. Well, thanks for that. And what's the other thing?"

"The cops are working on a theory," said Claridge. "Not that she was murdered. As far as they're concerned it's beyond doubt that she killed herself. But they seem pretty sure that the body was moved to the Clapham hostel. And if that is the case, then the body was moved complete with bedsheets. Wherever she killed herself, it was also on a bed. But not, they think, in that hostel."

"I see," said Shelley.

"One final thing, about the gun. It only had one bullet in it."

"What, like one round remaining?"

"No," said Claridge, "what I mean is that she only ever used one bullet. The bullet that killed her."

"So she only loaded one bullet?"

"Exactly. But the odd thing is that there were no other bullets recovered. It seems that she bought a gun and one bullet. Or she bought a gun and several bullets but discarded all but one."

Shelley considered. "Maybe she didn't want them falling into the wrong hands."

They fell into silence, knowing it was an implausible scenario. Shelley filed it away for later use.

"That twitching antenna of yours, what's it doing now?" asked Claridge.

Shelley swerved that particular question. But he decided that the Drakes' home in Ascot wasn't too far away, and while he was in the area he might as well pay Guy Drake a visit.

CHAPTER 7

AS HE DROVE—ELVIS on the stereo—Shelley thought about the man he was on his way to see.

Guy Drake had launched Drake Electronics in 1980, when microchips were still making the journey from science fiction to everyday mundanity. It was because of entrepreneurs like Drake that chips dropped in price and became smaller. And then, as a result of their size and availability, came to be used in every gadget in every room in every house in the developed world.

But where Drake had prospered more than others was in spotting the military applications for this new, smaller, and less expensive microchip and being quicker to offer them for sale to the British Army. That had made him very rich, very quickly.

What's more, Guy Drake had a great backstory. He'd been laid off from an engineering job in Salford, Lancashire, "victim of the bastard Tories," he liked to say. But instead of retiring to the nearest pub and drowning his woes in cheap bitter, he'd used his redundancy payment to launch his new enterprise. What had previously been a spare-bedroom hobby had become Drake Electronics.

With his success had come a taste for publicity. Credit to him, it was usually for the right reasons. He donated to charity and he cultivated a reputation as a generous employer, often treating his staff to lavish parties—even, on one well-reported occasion, a holiday, en masse, for all his employees and their families.

But then came the begging letters. Followed by the threatening letters. And when the letters started to become more menacing, Drake made use of his military contacts and employed a security consultant, Gerald Mowles, an old friend of Shelley's, to decide whether any of them constituted a credible threat.

Gerald was one of the few people entrusted with the information that Shelley and Lucy were a couple and were planning to get married. Knowing Shelley was due a sabbatical, as well as being in the market for a bit of extra cash for his impending nuptials, he'd got in touch. With good reason. Take a map and pin the world's kidnap hot spots—Afghanistan, Iraq, Somalia, Nigeria, Yemen—then pin the places Shelley had served. You wouldn't need two sets of pins.

"Kidnappers don't usually call ahead," Shelley had told him.

"This isn't Mexico. There's more than one way to profit from a kidnapping threat," Mowles had said. "It could be that it works more like extortion, like some kid offering to look after your car when you park it on the street. You pay the money because it's easier than *not* paying the money; because it's cheaper than having to pay guys like us."

"False economy."

"Exactly. And Guy Drake's one of the smart ones. He

knows that if he pays up once, they'll never stop asking for money. They might also decide that what's needed is a display of power. Just something to say 'you're vulnerable, we can get you.' We need to make sure nobody gets that idea into their heads."

"That's where I come in?"

"That's where you come in," Mowles had agreed. "Bit of easy money."

CHAPTER 8

MEMORIES, THOUGHT SHELLEY as he drove. *They'll kill you. Just like a blade or a bullet.* Even the journey back there was like time travel. Still, at least it took him further away from the actor.

Reaching the Drake residence meant driving past Tittenhurst Park, the house once owned by John Lennon. Passing, he found that the road was clear so he took the opportunity to slow down and gawp at the famous gates, a living bit of Beatles memorabilia that never failed to move him. He wished that he'd known he'd be passing; he'd have brought *Sgt. Pepper's* to play. Elvis would have to do, he thought, imagining the Beatles meeting the King at Graceland, treasuring those connections as he pulled away to continue his journey.

The thought kept him going until he reached another set of gates, beyond them the Drakes' grand Georgian home.

The sight of it jolted him back—back to the person he'd been then: a soldier, starchy but battle-scarred, a nervous fiancé stressing over cash. It was just a job babysitting an anxious entrepreneur, but he'd resolved to bring to it the same level of professionalism he brought to soldiering.

That was what he'd told himself at the time.

He pulled up, got out of the car and approached, aware of a camera mounted on the gates. Through the wrought iron he could see the house, with a Jaguar and a Porsche parked out front on a vast pebble-covered driveway, as well as a Mercedes, an electric-blue BMW, and a VW Golf. Drake's house had always had various people in and out all the time: PAs, gardeners, men who came to clean the pool, upkeep the tennis courts, or install gym equipment. That was rich people for you. They filled their homes with strangers and then bleated about wanting privacy.

He looked at the entry pad then pressed the intercom button, heard it ring, and imagined it going off inside. A woman answered.

"Hello?"

"My name is David Shelley, I'm here for either Guy or Susie. An old friend."

"One mo—"

She was cut short by another voice: "What can I do for you, Shelley?"

He'd had warmer greetings. "Who's that?"

"We met at the funeral. Name's Gurney. Sergeant James Gurney of the Parachute Regiment."

Jesus, thought Shelley. *And you thought the actor was a tool.* "Yeah, I remember you," he said, "giving me the skunk eye at a funeral. Classy move. They teach you that in the Paras, did they? Or were you too busy getting daggers tattooed on your arm?"

Gurney chuckled. "Not got a regiment tattoo of your own, then? Don't tell me, scared of needles?"

"Don't you believe it. I can put up with any number of little pricks. Right now, for example."

"Yeah, yeah, good one," sneered Gurney. "Very funny coming from the man on the wrong side of the gate. Tell you what, mate, I'll let Mr. Drake know you came to say hello. Why don't you leave your number? Better still, write it down on a piece of paper, gob in it, screw it up, and throw it in the bin. Save me the bother."

Shelley sighed, casting his eyes to the heavens as though looking for divine inspiration. "Listen, mate, I've got no argument with you, precisely because I have no business with you. I'm here for Guy or Susie. Put one of them on or let me in."

His only answer was Gurney's laughter, rendered metallic by the intercom system, and then a click as the line went dead.

Shelley stepped to one side and looked at the keypad thoughtfully. *Surely not?* he thought, and then on a whim punched in the code he remembered, Susie's birthday. *1606.* The gate hummed and began to swing open.

Some protection. They hadn't even bothered to change the security code.

"Fucking idiots," muttered Shelley, and stepped through.

CHAPTER 9

IT ALL CAME back to him as he crossed the pebble drive. The lawn on one side, perfectly trimmed and just the right shade of succulent green, hedges clipped neatly but not ostentatiously, a thoroughbred horse peering incuriously at him over a five-bar gate.

And on the other side the house, which wasn't so much a house as a mansion, its flat frontage a luxurious shade of cream, the window frames gleaming white, sparkling glass reflecting the winter sun. No two ways about it, it was a gorgeous-looking pad.

Only problem: the short-arsed, red-faced bloke in combats and a camo top who'd just appeared from the front door. Not Gurney but cut from the same cloth. Sure enough, Shelley saw the tip of a Para tattoo peeking from beneath his T-shirt sleeve as he strode fast toward him, all spit and snarl, boots laced up tight and looking for action.

"Where the fuck do you think you're going?"

He held a short-range walkie-talkie in one hand and had a Glock in an unsecured molded holster at his hip, the sort you wore for a quick draw. As he advanced he indicated the holster as though to say, *What do you think of that?* but Shelley wasn't impressed because there was no way in the world this bloke was going to start firing off rounds right now. And what kind of dickhead made a show of a weapon he had no intention of using?

Shelley didn't break stride or slow down. He sped up.

The other guy saw. His eyes widened and his moment of feeling as if he had the upper hand evaporated in the time it took him to realize Shelley wasn't in the slightest bit intimidated by the weapon and even less by the hard-man act.

Preparing to defend, the bloke took a step back, aligned his core, ready to use the walkie-talkie as a weapon and reaching for his Glock.

What he didn't expect was for Shelley to go for the Glock, too, which is exactly what he did.

It all happened in the time it took to blink. Shelley knocked the Para's swinging walkie-talkie hand out of the way, drawing the guy's sidearm at the same time as he dropped and swept his legs from under him, sending him sprawling to the stones with a shout of pain, surprise, and outrage.

It was messy, and it was ugly, and Lucy would have criticized the angle of Shelley's arms, his stance, his breathing, whatever. Most of all she would have said that he'd used force when he should have been diplomatic, and she would have been right about that, because as Shelley rose with the gun held two-handed and trained on his opponent, he saw the hurt, humiliation, and hatred in the other man's face and knew he'd made an enemy for life. The Glock was dull, aged, probably a treasured weapon, and the fact that it had so easily found its way into Shelley's fist was bound to enrage its owner even more.

But fuck it. It was done. It wasn't as though Shelley could apologize, return the gun, and compliment him on a well-kept weapon. He had to see things through.

"One question. What are you lot doing here?"

"Go fuck yourself," rasped the bloke in response.

For just a second—and thank God he restrained himself—Shelley considered adding insult to injury by putting a bullet in his leg. See how the little fucker liked that.

But he thought better of it.

"I'll ask again, what are you doing with the Drakes?"

"Go fuck yourself," repeated the guy on the ground. Beached on the stones, he looked like a red-faced and bested bully wanting to run for his mother. Shelley wasn't sure he'd ever seen a man look so pathetic.

"Would somebody mind explaining just what on earth is going on?" came a raised voice.

It was Bennett. He'd appeared from the front door of the house, smart in a navy suit, shirt collar open. He, too, held a pistol. Also a Glock. But he held it loosely, almost casually trained on Shelley, as though he'd be just as happy casting it aside.

"I wanted to see Guy or Susie," said Shelley, "but Pinky and Perky here had other ideas."

"*My men* were just doing their job, Shelley," said Bennett firmly. "Now stand down, or I'll consider this an aggressive trespass and be forced to take appropriate action."

"I don't think so, if it's all the same to you," said Shelley.

"Oh, come on, Shelley," implored Bennett. He was well spoken, but with an underlying London twang, and he held forth with the confidence of an expert orator. "Neither of us is going to use these, are we? We're on the same side, remember? It serves us no purpose to start taking shots at each other."

Shelley thumbed the safety, shoved the gun into his coat pocket but held it there. It was on the tip of his tongue to ask if it was Bennett who had been making inquiries about Emma Drake, but some instinct told him it was best to keep his powder dry on that score. Instead he said, "So, tell me what you're doing here."

"As I've already told you, we're here to provide security for the Drakes following the loss of their daughter—" began Bennett, only to be cut off by a derisive laugh from Shelley. "And yes, you're right," he resumed, "we need to improve if a guy can enter the premises and disarm Johnson as easily as you did." His smile was wintry. "Lessons will be learned. Admonishments given. But that doesn't change the fact—"

"Oh, come on. Security my hairy arse. You didn't even change the gate code."

Bennett looked amused. "Are you charging for this advice, Shelley? Or is it a freebie?"

"Drake wants payback. That's it, isn't it?" said Shelley. "And you're here to do that for him. Or at least that's what you're telling him—that you'll be able to help heal that broken heart of his. Is that what you're pouring into his ear? Are we going to find drug dealers turning up dead?"

If Bennett was surprised that Shelley was so well informed then he hid it well. "Does it matter?" he said. "Do you really care? If Guy was standing here he'd tell you that the scum who sold drugs to his daughter deserve to die, and I think you'd look into his eyes and agree with him."

"I'd tell him that's not how it works," said Shelley.

"You won't get the chance," said Bennett. "It's time for you to leave, I'm afraid."

Shelley gave the matter some thought, wondering what was to be gained by staying put for longer and deciding the answer was nothing, except for more beef. "Don't follow me," he told Bennett. "I'll drop the piece by the gate."

As he went to leave, Shelley glanced up and saw a figure at the window of the house. It was Susie Drake, tall and willowy, her face framed by straight blond hair cut in a bob. She was watching him, and for a second or so he considered raising his hand to wave, but decided against it.

Instead he turned, and the only sound in the bright winter morning was his feet crunching over the stones as he crossed to the gates, wiped Johnson's Glock clean of his prints, dropped it to the stones, climbed into the Saab, and left.

CHAPTER 10

SHELLEY WASN'T THE kind of bloke who made friends easily. He was what you might call a slow burner.

So it had been when he'd first met the Drakes: Guy, Susie, and their daughter, Emma. Guy was still only in his midforties then. He'd packed a lot into his life thus far, but the threats against his family had found their way deep beneath his skin. Newly etched into his face were lines born of concern and paranoia, maybe even a little fear, feelings that weren't going anywhere soon.

Even so, he was "bluff northern businessman Guy Drake," as the newspaper profiles always seemed to describe him. He didn't like to think he needed help from anyone, and so at first he'd treated Shelley as though he resented having him there, as if Shelley was somehow evidence that he couldn't take care of his own family, even though Shelley's presence was in fact evidence that he was doing exactly that.

Shelley hadn't taken offense—he knew it was complicated. He soon understood that his job wasn't just to protect the family, it was also to deal with their individual expectations. He had to make them feel at ease with his presence there.

The way he did that was to keep himself busy. Rather than just hanging around with his registered weapon out of sight he decided to make himself into something of a family right-hand man. He took over driving duties, he ran errands, he suggested shooting trips with Drake and won his employer's trust by bonding over clay pigeons and paper targets. Most rewarding of all, he started to teach young Emma martial arts. Shelley's own style of fighting was partly learned in the regiment and partly self-taught, a combination of Filipino Kali, Krav Maga, and Jeet Kune Do, with a bit of street fighting thrown in for good measure. And although at first he'd thought that something a little more formal would be appropriate for Emma, and he'd tried to get her started on Taekwondo, she'd soon sussed him out and insisted that he teach her to fight the way he did it.

"The street way" was what she called it. Like all privileged children, Emma was fascinated by the tough kids—those who spent their time hanging around town centers instead of tending to their horses. Back then she had all the qualities of someone who was destined to make her mark on life, whether life liked it or not.

Then there were the trips out. Susie Drake was that rarest of things: a multimillionaire's wife who enjoyed a visit to the supermarket. She liked to choose her own fruit and got excited about the twofers.

Shelley had advised the family that they should carry on as normal: if they changed their behavior then the threat-makers won. So it was that he found himself chauffeuring Susie and Emma on trips to Waitrose. As far as was possible he tried to maintain the normal rules of protection—never use the same routes, never keep to a schedule—but it was only Berkshire and they were only going to Waitrose, and besides, Shelley had started to think that it was time the threat status was downgraded. Plus there was another, more delicate, issue . . .

All of which meant he was not being as vigilant as he should have been the day the kidnappers struck.

CHAPTER 11

THEY WERE IN the family BMW, halfway between home and Waitrose, when Shelley first spotted the car following them, a Peugeot 307 in nondescript navy blue, one of the most common cars on the road.

He wouldn't even have given it a second look were it not for the fact that there were two men sitting up front.

Might be nothing, he thought. The two guys could be mates on their way to the pub, or job center, or picking up a car from the garage.

On the other hand it might be something. They might—just might—be part of the crew that had contacted the Drakes. And maybe that crew had decided to make good on their initial threat and show they weren't to be messed with.

And if that's what they were, then they'd have scoped out the Drakes already; they'd know that Shelley, Susie, and Emma were on their way to Waitrose. Which meant that Shelley had missed their surveillance runs, too busy yakking. He swallowed, perspiration prickling his forehead, cursing himself as an amateur, thinking, *You fucking idiot*.

At the lights, the Peugeot eased out from behind and drew alongside. Shelley kept up his conversation with Susie and Emma in the back, surreptitiously checking out the Peugeot at the same time: two guys, one in a navy sweatshirt, the passenger wearing a black puffa coat. They didn't look across. They, too, were deep in conversation: neither of them seemed to pay the BMW much attention.

Even so, Shelley remained alert, thinking things over. It could be that they were just a couple of blokes arguing over last night's football.

Or it could be that they were good at their job, and didn't want to show their hand.

He leaned forward as though to scratch his thigh, eased his SIG Sauer from its holster, checked the safety, and tucked it underneath his buttock.

The lights changed. The Peugeot beat Shelley off the line and then tucked in front of them. Right, thought Shelley, if they were kidnappers, then there'd be a second team. And the second team would be behind.

His eyes went to the mirror, scanning the traffic: VW Passat, one lady driver; behind that a Vauxhall of some kind, again a lone driver. But sure enough, behind the Vauxhall there was a white van, the builders' sort, or at least that's how they wanted it to look, dashboard stuffed with yellowing copies of *The Sun*, crumpled Burger King wrappers, and discarded coffee cups.

The van. That was the second team. And if Shelley was right they'd make their way up the line of traffic to come up behind the Drakes' BMW. Once in position the BMW would be boxed in.

When? was the question. They might wait until the

supermarket. If they'd been carrying out surveillance—and Shelley thought so—then they'd know that Susie Drake was on a shopping expedition. The supermarket would be the perfect place. That's where Shelley would choose.

But he was wrong about that.

CHAPTER 12

REACHING THE NEXT set of lights, the Peugeot was first in the queue, Shelley behind, the white van a few cars back.

His hands were tapping on the steering wheel as he continued a conversation with Emma, fielding her latest inquiry about what he'd done "in the war." That's what she always said: "in the war."

"Which war, Emma?"

"Any war. Did you kill anybody?"

"Emma!" chided Susie. Shelley's eyes flicked to the rearview to check the status of the van behind. Still there. Biding its time.

The lights changed. The Peugeot in front began to move off. Shelley lifted the clutch and inched forward. The Peugeot jerked to a halt.

He tensed. Cars to the right of them, the pavement to the left, teeming with pedestrians. His eyes returned to the rearview but nothing was happening at the van. Maybe he was wrong. Maybe the Peugeot had simply stalled. Even so . . .

"I don't like this," he said out loud, cutting Emma's chatter dead, the edge in his voice letting Susie and Emma know he was serious. Emma had been told: there might be a situation, and if there was, then Shelley was in charge. Don't question. Don't hesitate. Just do everything he tells you. And this was one of those times.

Still no activity from the van. The guys in the Peugeot seemed even more animated than before, behaving like a couple of blokes trying to get a recalcitrant car restarted. Shelley was on a knife-edge, ready for something to happen, ready for it not to happen, hoping, praying that he'd be able to tell Susie and Emma, "False alarm, guys," and go back to bantering about what he'd done "in the war."

Eyes to the van. No movement. The indistinct shape of the driver looking bored. Eyes in front, the Peugeot double act still going strong.

And then came a movement he only saw in his peripheral vision. At the same time Susie, with fear in her voice, said, "Shelley . . ."

It was the woman from the VW Passat. She'd got out of the car and now stood by the BMW. In the next instant the locks to the BMW flicked open, the door was yanked wide, and she bent into the car, looking for all the world as if she was loading something into the back seat.

Except for the gun that she lodged into the back of Shelley's neck, making him freeze.

"Awright, hero?" she said in a strange put-on northern accent. "Face front, hands through the steering wheel and flat on the dashboard." Her short hair was ill-fitting, probably a wig. "Move your hands again and the last thing you'll see is your teeth hit the windscreen."

In the rearview he saw that in the other hand she held

a lock remote, some kind of universal access, and with that hand she reached for Emma. "Get out of the car, honey," she ordered. At her neck was the furry nodule of a microphone. Eyes front, Shelley saw that the two blokes in the Peugeot had put on headsets and were monitoring the situation behind. One of them turned to show him a handgun but made no move to leave the car. They wanted to do this discreetly, with the minimum of fuss.

Time stood still inside the BMW. Susie sat frozen, eyes round with fear, parental instincts kicking in, but at the same time abiding by Shelley's instructions to let him take charge.

"I won't tell you again," said the short-haired woman. "Get out before I paint the car with your bodyguard."

"What shall I do, Shelley?" asked Emma. The fear in her voice cut through a symphony of angry car horns from behind. The entire junction was locked, the whole street brought to a halt.

"Just do as she says, Emma," replied Shelley, very aware that his words were being relayed to the car in front and wanting to put them at ease. "Just go with the lady. She won't hurt you, I promise."

"You heard the man," said the woman in her awkward northern accent, like something she'd learned off *Coronation Street*.

Reluctantly, Emma moved across the seat toward the kidnapper, who took hold of her.

"Be lucky, sweetheart," Shelley told Emma.

It was the signal they'd worked out in advance: *If I say "Be lucky, sweetheart," it means that the bad guy's grabbed you and I'm ready to make my move and I want you to bite the hand he's holding you with. And I mean bite. I don't mean nibble, or chew.*

I mean bite, like you're biting down on the biggest, toughest bit of steak you've ever eaten. You understand me?

Emma did as she had been told and bit down hard on the woman's hand. The woman screamed and pulled the trigger in the same moment as Shelley twisted in his seat, praying the gun barrel wouldn't follow.

It didn't. The shot singed a sideburn and cost him the hearing in his right ear for a week, but it missed and struck the center of the steering wheel. Shelley heard another explosion and felt an almighty punch to the torso as the airbag deployed.

Pinned but half twisted in his seat, he grabbed the woman's arm and with a shout of effort snapped it across the BMW's midsection.

Her gun dropped and she screamed like a wounded animal as she yanked herself away from Shelley and free of Emma's teeth, rebounding off her Passat and then running toward the Peugeot with her snapped arm cradled. Shelley saw red-tipped bone poking through torn flesh. She dragged open the rear door of the Peugeot and threw herself inside.

The men in the Peugeot were half in, half out of the car. Shelley saw a sawn-off shotgun, but so did pedestrians. Someone screamed. With that the guys in the Peugeot knew the game was up, the element of surprise lost. They decided to cut their losses, clambered back into the car and sped off.

Susie didn't make it to Waitrose that day.

CHAPTER 13

A FEW DAYS after the attempted kidnapping Shelley was in his room at the top of the house, stooping in the eaves as he packed his few belongings into an open suitcase on the bed, when there came a small knock at the door.

He stopped, a white T-shirt in his hand, held as though he were about to serve it for dinner, and squeezed his eyes shut. Thinking, *Oh no, not this.*

"Come in, Emma," he said, and cleared his throat of a crack that had appeared in his voice.

She entered, owning the room. Its tiny dimensions seemed to suit her. She was so small, but so resilient. While Susie had yet to recover from the attack and had taken to her bed as though physically ill—not that you could blame her, mind you—Emma had relished the extra attention. She'd told her story to anyone who'd listen, even given painfully accurate demonstrations of her great and fearsome biting technique, basking in the adults' proclamations that she was "so brave, such a little warrior." Maybe that was all kids. More likely it was Emma being Emma.

She cast her eyes over his folded clothes. "You're very neat," she said brightly as she perched on the edge of Shelley's bed and let her sneakers swing. "Don't tell me, 'old habits die hard'?"

It was one of his catchphrases. Apparently.

"Exactly right, sweetheart," he said, placing the folded T-shirt into the case. "And from what I've seen of your playroom it looks like you could do with a spell in the forces yourself."

She sniffed as though to say *Not likely*, and then seemed to take stock, leaving a suitably significant pause and watching him expertly fold and pack a shirt before she next spoke. "Daddy says you're leaving."

"That's right," he said without looking up from the suitcase.

"Were you going to say goodbye?"

"I wouldn't have left without saying goodbye," he told her, which wasn't strictly true, but wasn't exactly a lie either. The truth was that he hadn't decided. Neither option appealed.

"Why?" she said.

"What do you mean?" he replied, knowing exactly what she meant, of course. Just wanting to delay talking about it.

"Why are you going?"

"I made a mistake. The kidnappers had been scoping us out for days—they must have been. They got the better of me, Emma, and if they did it once, they can do it again. I got complacent." *That, and the other thing I can't tell you about.*

Funny thing with Emma, he was never sure if she was being a genuinely curious kid, or was in fact a super-intelligent puppetmaster, using advanced psychological techniques to get her way. Whatever the truth—probably somewhere be-tween the two—she was shameless when it came to being cute. She was doing it now.

"But they didn't get the better of you, Shelley," she said.

"You won. The bad guys went away and Mommy and me are still here. I came home to my own house with you and Mommy and Daddy and my ponies and all my teddies and my messy playroom. And all of that happened because of you, because of what you taught me and what you did. Your job was to be a bodyguard, Shelley, and you did that job."

He'd been down, no doubt about it. He'd been way harder on himself than he needed to be. But now, even though Emma's words came from a place of not knowing the whole truth, he felt a kind of relief, a knowledge that although he had not done his job to the best of his ability, he had not failed. And that, at the end of the day, was the most important thing.

"That's good of you to say, sweetheart," he said. "It means a lot to me, it really does."

"Good," she said with finality. "Then you'll stay?"

"No."

"But . . ."

"I'm afraid it doesn't change anything," he told her. "I still have to go. I'm going to talk to my contact, Gerald, ask him to employ someone else. That's what the post needs. A fresh pair of eyes on the job."

"But what if I don't want you to go?" she asked. Her eyes were wet with tears.

"I'm sorry, Emma."

She came to him, beckoned him to bend, which he did, and received a kiss on the cheek for his efforts. "Then thank you," she said, and a wave of emotion threatened to engulf him, a strange mixture of gratitude and guilt.

A couple of hours later he was gone, and the next time he saw Emma Drake was in a photograph at her funeral.

CHAPTER 14

DAYS PASSED AFTER Shelley's stand-off with Bennett in front of the house in which he'd once been like one of the family. Shelley called the house again to be told the Drakes were unavailable. He left messages but the calls went unreturned. He called Susie's mobile and left messages, but she didn't answer.

He tried Gerald Mowles, the security consultant who'd hooked him up with the gig all those years ago. Gerald was warm and friendly and they chewed the fat for a while until Shelley started asking questions about the Drakes.

"I can't tell you anything, I'm afraid," he told Shelley, drawing a curtain across the conversation.

"Why is that?"

"Because it would be a breach of client confidentiality."

"So the Drakes are clients?" Shelley said.

"If I were to tell you that, it would be a breach of client confidentiality."

"So the Drakes are clients, but you didn't refer them to me?"

"My job is to match clients with the appropriate operator depending on the service required," Mowles said.

"So whatever service Guy wants, you knew I wouldn't touch?"

"If I were to tell you that, it would be a breach of client confidentiality."

And so on.

In the end Susie rang him, a hurried conversation: "I'm so grateful and touched by your concern, David, but you must stop calling."

"*Concern.* Exactly. You know that's what it is, don't you? I'm worried that you're getting into something you'll regret. Is it Guy, Susie? Is he driving this?"

She paused and he could sense that she wanted to tell him something, just as she had at the funeral. "I can't," she said at last, and the phone went dead.

He tried to ring her back. There was no answer.

CHAPTER 15

"I DON'T THINK I understand, Sergei," said Dmitry. Canyons formed in his brow. "You told me that everything was sorted. You said to me, 'She's just a junkie, Dmitry. The police will not investigate.' You told me this and I believed you."

Dmitry glared at Sergei, who held his gaze, aware that his conduct and performance were being appraised.

"The inquiries are not being made by the police, Dmitry. If they were, they would get nothing."

"Then who?" snapped the boss. "Who is making these inquiries?"

"It appears that the girl's father is rich. Very rich. Perhaps he has bought people to make these inquiries on his behalf."

Dmitry reached for the spectacles that hung on a cord around his neck. "Name? What was the girl's name?"

"The name she gave us was an alias . . ."

Dmitry shook his head in frustration. "*What was her real name?*"

The air crackled. "It turns out her real name was Emma

Drake, and she was the daughter of a man named Guy Drake."

Dmitry held up a finger instructing Sergei to wait, then replaced his glasses and turned his attention to the screens before him.

After some minutes of peering and tapping, Dmitry once again removed his spectacles, and sat back with a low whistle. "Wow. Rich guy."

Sergei nodded. He looked at his boss, seeing gears shift.

"This changes things," said Dmitry.

"Should we close the studio, Dmitry?" proposed Sergei.

Dmitry looked at him sharply, both knowing that "the studio" was an idea beloved of Alexander in Grozny, who would not take kindly to its closure. Alexander liked things to run smoothly. As Dmitry often said, his least favorite word was "complication."

"Are you really suggesting we close the studio, Sergei?" asked Dmitry carefully.

"I'm saying we should take such measures into consideration, Dmitry."

"Could they connect it to the dead girl?"

"If they do, nobody will talk. I'll make sure of it."

"Good," said Dmitry, "then let's keep business as usual. Perhaps this rich microchip man will realize no amount of asking questions can bring his junkie daughter back. What do you think?"

Sergei thought that a father's grief might not recede quite so easily, but said nothing. Instead he bid Dmitry farewell, turned, and left the office.

On his way out he passed the doorway to the front room, where Grandfather sat watching television. For a moment he considered simply not paying his respects. After all, if the old man's behavior the other day was anything to go by, then he was already touched by dementia.

Then again, it wasn't worth the risk. What if the old bastard was to have a sudden attack of lucidity and report back to Dmitry?

"Good day to you, *Ded*," said Sergei, hand on the door handle about to let himself out.

Grandfather remained immobile, but his eyes swiveled slowly, as though unsticking themselves from the television screen in order to regard Sergei in the doorway.

"He squealed, you know," said the old man in a sand-paper voice.

Sergei had been about to open the door but he stopped, rendered statue-like by a feeling that ran through him like fingers of ice. "Who squealed, *Ded*?"

The malevolent smile returned.

"Your brother," said Grandfather.

CHAPTER 16

SHELLEY STOOD INSIDE the gates of the Drake house in the cold night. He crossed the grounds at the rear of the house, careful not to activate any of the security lights. The house had a basement gym and swimming pool area, and he took a chance that a window there remained the possible entry point it had always been.

It was. He hunkered down, hearing cartilage in his knees crackle, a sound like snapping tinder in the silence of the night. *Old man*, he thought. *Too old for all this.*

Through the glass he saw the blue shimmer of the swimming pool and skeletal shapes of gym equipment in an otherwise empty room. The window was the double-glazed type with an internal sliding door. In thirty seconds' time he was standing by the indoor pool.

Noiseless. The water still, like a mirror, glimmering at him. Almost eerie.

He left the room and climbed the stairs that led up to the ground floor. There he glanced in an open door and saw that the Drakes had redecorated one of the downstairs bathrooms.

In the reception hall a grand staircase led up to the first floor. For a moment or so he stood and allowed the shadow to claim him, eyes adjusting as he reacquainted himself with the house, fixing the layout in his head.

Next he trod the stairs to the first-floor landing and took stock. If Bennett had a man on duty then he wasn't alerted. Nor was he making rounds of the house.

A second or so later Shelley was slipping into the master bedroom which, like the downstairs bathroom, had been given a makeover in the intervening years: the dressing table was new, the sofa, easy chairs, a huge television the size of a snooker table that looked like part of the wall. All were new.

In the bed slept Guy Drake, alone, fitfully, a prisoner of his nightmares. Shelley watched him for a moment or so until it became uncomfortable, gazing at this rich, powerful man in a state of such profound vulnerability. He cleared his throat. "Guy," he whispered, steeling himself for Drake waking up alarmed and grateful when that didn't happen. Instead, Drake sat up slowly and blinked hard, absorbing the sight of Shelley standing in his darkened bedroom at 3 a.m. and taking it in his stride, as though compared to his fortune lately, this was the least life could throw at him.

"What the bloody hell are you doing here?" he asked, even more woozy than Shelley might have expected. His eyes went to the bedside table but he saw no medication. Or was it just that Guy had been duffed up by events? He looked jowlier than Shelley remembered. The whole lower half of his face seemed to wobble when he moved his head. There were dark bags beneath his eyes, the skin hanging loose, almost as though the flesh on his face had begun to melt. Was this what a nervous breakdown looked like modeled by a recently bereaved CEO?

Not for the first time, Shelley thought gratefully of the fact that he'd never had kids and never planned to. All that worry. The knowledge that life might snatch out your heart just when you were least expecting it. *I'll pass, thanks.*

"I wanted to say again how sorry I was to hear about Emma," he said. Here and now, as a night-time intruder, his words sounded ridiculous, but he thought they needed saying all the same.

"Didn't you already say that, pal?" drawled Drake. "Didn't you say that at the funeral?"

"There's something else."

"Oh yeah?" Drake picked sleep from his eyes. You had to give it to him, he'd handled it well, the fact that he'd woken up to find Shelley standing in his bedroom. Who knows, perhaps he'd been half expecting it.

"I'd like to know why you've hired Bennett," said Shelley quietly, the dark and silent bedroom making each utterance significant.

"That's why you felt the need to break in, was it, chief?" growled Drake.

"The normal approach didn't work. You've been avoiding me."

Drake's mouth was set. "I've been avoiding the fucking gardener, but that doesn't give him the right to break into my house."

Fooking was how he pronounced it.

"What if you had some new gardeners? And the first gardener thought the new gardeners were going to kill your lawn and destroy all your flower beds. Wouldn't you expect him to say something?"

"Oh, bugger off, Shelley, clever dick. Fucking gardeners."

"At least tell me what's going on. Better still, let me see Susie. Let her tell me what's going on. Where is she?"

Drake looked up at him with dark-ringed eyes. "I'll show you," he said.

CHAPTER 17

DRAKE WIPED HIS face with his hands and then swung his legs out of bed, reaching for an old gray sweatshirt that he pulled on over his pajama top. Wordlessly he beckoned Shelley to follow, looking baggy and ancient as he led the way to the landing and then along to Emma's old bedroom.

At the door he stood for a moment, gathering himself, and then they both went inside.

Pony Club rosettes, that's what Shelley remembered. She used to have them all over the walls. Pony Club rosettes and pictures of pop bands.

But there were no rosettes now. The bedroom belonged to a young lady. Or had. There was an Apple Mac on a desk and a TV on the wall. The Destiny's Child posters had been replaced by collages of club flyers. Shelley found himself wondering what age she'd been when she left home. *When did the heroin take hold?* he thought. *How long was she an addict? Did she smoke or shoot up in this very room?*

All questions that would have to wait. For now his attention went to Susie Drake, who sat on the edge of Emma's bed.

Her head was raised and she stared emptily, at nothing in particular, hands fretting in her lap. She didn't acknowledge the fact that Guy and Shelley had entered. She just sat, in her dead daughter's room, staring at nothing.

"Susie . . ." prompted Guy. "It's Shelley."

"Yes," she said, "I know. I can see him." She turned her face slowly to Shelley. "Hello, David," she said. "I had a feeling you wouldn't be put off so easily. You want answers."

He nodded. "I'd like to know why she did it, Susie. Was it the drugs?"

"I suppose you could say that. That's where it all started."

Drake sat down beside her and exhaled in exasperation. "We're doing this, are we?" His jaw worked, and a little muscle on the side of his face jumped. "We're telling him everything?"

Susie ignored the question and continued, "We knew about the drugs—"

"We didn't know about the drugs," Drake interrupted. "We would have bloody done even more if we'd known about—"

"We didn't know about the *heroin*," corrected Susie, voice rising, "but we knew about the drugs, whatever drugs they were. Party drugs." She indicated the club flyers decorating the wall. "We knew what she was into."

"We thought she was going through a phase," argued Guy. His voice dropped. "That was all."

Neither of them knew which side was up. They both wanted someone to blame and couldn't find that person in the mirror so they chose the nearest target.

Susie continued, "Emma liked to go out. She liked to live it up. Parties abroad, that kind of thing. We gave her a lot of money, enough to live on, but it wasn't enough."

Shelley saw the pair of them share a look and knew there was another bone of contention lurking there, so he quickly moved the conversation forward. "She needed more," he pressed.

"For her lifestyle," said Susie. "For drugs."

"And this is what you found out since she died, is it?" he asked them.

Susie looked away. Guy folded his arms nodding, averting his eyes.

Which brings us to your new security detail, thought Shelley.

"Investigations for you conducted by Bennett, Gurney, and that other muppet, I guess?"

Again came the nods and averted eyes.

"Why didn't you come to me?" he asked them, although he already knew the answer.

"I wouldn't have known how to contact you." Guy's answer was a little too quick and not at all convincing.

"I still have the same number."

Guy gave a little exasperated sigh. "How was I to know that?"

"I know plenty of folk who've had the same number for decades. You've kept the same gate code, for God's sake. Besides, Emma knew it."

They both looked at him sharply, and he returned their gaze evenly. He hadn't known whether or not he planned to tell them about the call, but there it was, out in the open for all to see.

"What do you mean?" asked Susie. Her eyes narrowed, body language changing.

"She tried to call me. Correction, she *did* call me. I didn't pick up."

"And now you wish you had," said Susie. It wasn't a question, just a bald statement of fact, arrowing right into the heart of all that had been haunting Shelley these past few days.

"More than anything I wish I'd picked up, Susie," he said.

For a moment or so, the three of them lapsed into silence, each enduring a period of private grief, lost in a world of what-ifs and what-might-have-beens. Until at last Susie broke the silence, voice low but raw and husky with tears already shed and more to come. "Are you going to tell him?"

Drake made a noise, twisting away like a kid in a huff.

"You tell him or I will," she pressed.

Drake shook his head but then spoke anyway. "I employed Bennett and Gurney to do some detective work, to find out about Emma's final movements, that's all," he said. His words sounded watery and weak.

"How did you get them? Did you go to Gerald Mowles?" Again, Shelley knew the answer but wanted to hear it from them.

"As a matter of fact I did."

"But Gerald would have recommended me. Gerald knows full well that I've left the Regiment and set up on my own and that I've got a history with this family. I'm in no doubt he would have put me forward."

"He did," said Susie simply. "He told us all of that."

Shelley nodded. Guy was about to say something but Shelley stopped him. "But you wanted more than just investigative work, didn't you? And when you put that to Gerald, he told you I'd have nothing to do with it, didn't he? Because it's not just information you want. It's payback."

Guy's face was hard. His eyes lost their misty grief and became flinty once more—the hard-nosed businessman. "Yes," he growled. "Yes, that's exactly what I fucking want."

CHAPTER 18

SHELLEY SHOOK HIS head in frustration then turned his attention to Susie. "And you?" he asked her. "Is that what you want, too?"

She looked at him and said nothing, but Shelley thought he saw it there too, that desire—no, that *need*. An eye for an eye.

"Susie," pleaded Shelley, "you can't go down that route."

She looked away from him. He saw all the indecision within and knew that if there was any way to reach the Drakes it was through her. "Susie—"

She rounded on him. "David, you don't understand. It wasn't just the drugs . . ."

"She was in porn," Drake said with a trembling voice.

"They groomed her, David," added Susie. "They made sure she owed them thousands and then put her to work when she had no other choice."

Shelley's fists clenched, dreading the answer to the question he asked next. "What kind of porn?"

"Cams. Do you know what they are?"

"I think so," he replied cautiously. "Like peep shows for guys with an internet connection."

"Yes, just like that," said Susie. "That was what they had her doing. Working for them, stripping, doing God knows what else."

"Where?"

"We don't know," Drake answered.

"Well, who are these people?"

"We don't know that either."

"But you're trying to find out?" said Shelley.

"That's what Bennett has been employed to do."

"And this is what they turned up so far, have they?"

Drake nodded.

"But none of that information came from the police," said Shelley.

"How would you know?" asked Drake.

"Because I've done a little digging of my own. And the cops don't know anything about any cams. Not yet anyway. So where did they get that information?"

"They hit the streets, Shelley," said Drake.

"Using your money to open doors."

"It's worked, hasn't it?"

Shelley considered for a second. Was it possible that Bennett and Gurney were lying, that this was some kind of shakedown? Well, yes, of course it was possible—but *probable*? He didn't think so. Their sources, on the other hand . . .

"Desperate people will say anything if you wave a few quid in their face," he told the Drakes.

"I'm afraid it's all true, David," said Susie. "We wish more than anything it wasn't."

"She was . . ." Drake trailed off.

When Shelley looked at him he saw that the older man's face had gone red but not with fury, or at least not just with fury. Written all over his features was a disquieting mix of rage, grief, frustration, and impotence, all feelings that millionaire businessman Guy Drake, MBE, had never expected to have to suffer again.

"She was working," Susie completed her husband's sentence for him. "She was working the night she killed herself."

"Doing one of those cam things." Drake had found his voice. It shook with suppressed rage.

"She did it on camera, David," said Susie, "there's film of it. Somewhere out there on the internet is film of our daughter killing herself."

There was absolute silence in the bedroom. Shelley took in the news, not knowing what to think or how to react, certain only that what he'd just learned was an obscenity. For a moment or so, before he tamped it down, what rose to the surface was a desire for vengeance so clean and bright and pure that he could almost touch it.

And of course he understood the Drakes and their need for prairie justice. He understood it perfectly.

"So that's what Bennett and Gurney are doing for you, is it?" he said. "Giving you information that's only going to make your grieving worse?"

"They're telling us the bloody truth, man!" exploded Drake.

"Or telling you things that you as parents don't need to hear."

"Oh, you're talking out of your arse, Shelley. You don't have kids, do you?" He made it sound like an insult. "If you did, and you had a daughter and she killed herself, I guarantee you'd want to know exactly what happened to her.

You'd want to know why she killed herself. You'd *need* to know. And, having found out what we now know, are you honestly telling me that you wouldn't go after the people responsible?"

"I wouldn't," Shelley lied. "It would solve nothing."

"Fucking bollocks!"

"Language, Guy," chided Susie. "Not in here. Anywhere but here."

"Sorry, love," said Drake, "but this just isn't on. He comes breaking into our house, that much I can just about take, even if he is demanding answers to questions he has no right to ask. But standing there and lying to our faces? That's an insult to our intelligence, and to her memory. So now I'm going to ask you to leave, Shelley—get out of my bloody house, before I pick up that phone. And don't you bloody well come back here. Ever. Do I make myself clear?"

"Guy . . ." started Susie weakly.

"You've made yourself perfectly clear," said Shelley.

He felt no anger or animosity toward Drake. If anything, what he felt was even more sadness, even more sympathy. "I'll leave you. And I suppose you're right, it's better to know the truth, even if you don't like it, rather than be kept in the dark. I can understand that. But you also have to know when to leave well alone. You have to know when you're out of your depth."

"Yeah, well, I'll let you know if I need my water wings, Shelley. In the meantime I'll thank you to sling your hook before you upset Susie any further."

Before he turned to go, Shelley looked across at Susie, wondering whether to appeal to her better nature. But all he saw on her face was desolation.

Then, just as he reached the door, she spoke up. "Help us, David" was all she said.

Shelley stopped.

"Susie," started Drake, "have you gone—"

"Help us, David," she repeated. "Instead of standing in judgment, help us."

His shoulders rose and fell. All of a sudden he felt very tired. He felt all that pain in the room, and knew that his own was there, too. But the other thing he knew was that to pursue revenge would only add to that pain.

"I'm sorry," he told her, and left.

CHAPTER 19

IT WAS THE following afternoon when the Shelleys' door-bell rang. There on the step stood an uncomfortable-looking Lloyd Bennett, who seemed to have left something behind in Berkshire. At the Drakes' he'd been every inch the commander in front of his men. Now he wore the fish-out-of-water look of an awkward suitor.

"I come in peace," he said with a lopsided smile.

Shelley eyed him up and down suspiciously. "You're not about to give me a bunch of flowers, are you?"

"No flowers," said Bennett, inclining his head so that he peered at Shelley over the top of his glasses. "Just a chat, one soldier to another, about this Drake business."

"Yeah, well, I didn't think you wanted to talk about foot-ball," sighed Shelley, standing aside. "You'd better come in." He called up the stairs, "Luce, we have a visitor. You want to join us?"

"Be down in a sec, hon," she said.

If Bennett disapproved of Lucy sitting in, he made no sign. Instead he stood in their small lounge with his hands in his pockets, squinting at photographs and looking at the bookshelves while Shelley busied himself making coffee.

Bennett was still studying the pictures when Shelley reappeared with a cafetière and three mugs. He didn't need to ask Bennett how he took his coffee. Like all those who'd spent time in the field, he'd take it black, no sugar.

"Dog," said Bennett simply. He pointed to a photograph of Lucy and Frankie that rested on the mantelpiece, and then looked around the room. "But no sign of a dog. Do I take it he's no longer with us?"

"Frankie. Somebody shot him."

"Oh, I'm sorry." There was a pause during which Bennett seemed to ruminate, looking at the coffeepot as Shelley set it down. "And what did you do to the person who killed Frankie?"

"I killed the bloke. Look, I know where this is going, Bennett, I know exactly what you're going to say, but the circumstances are totally different."

"But still."

"'But still' what?"

"There are certain impulses that can't be denied."

"Maybe. Maybe not. Whatever, things are a whole lot different where the Drakes are concerned. They have more to lose and they're much more likely to lose it."

Lucy appeared and Bennett acknowledged her with a smile. "Lucy Shelley, I presume?" He raised a finger, slightly theatrically. "No, let's do that again, I mean the *legendary* Lucy Shelley of the 22nd. It's an honor." He spread his hands. "Just a shame I couldn't have met Cookie for the full set."

Shelley cleared his throat, and Lucy shifted awkwardly.

Bennett acknowledged their loss with a tip of the head.

"I mean, you three. Bloody hell. I don't use the word *legend* lightly, you know. It's only in the last couple of years that them upstairs even admitted you exist. The only three-man patrol in all of special forces? The top blades of the 22nd for twenty years." He looked at Lucy. "Not to mention the SRR."

Lucy grinned. She wasn't immune to a bit of flattery, especially when it concerned her military record.

The three of them sat down to drink coffee, and Shelley was taken by the sense of how surreal a situation this was: three ex–special forces, God knows what kind of body count between them, reminiscing over coffee in the cozy front room of a terraced house in London.

"Why are you here?" he said at last.

Bennett placed his coffee cup on the table and then raised his eyes to look first at Lucy and then at Shelley. "I know what happened last night."

Shelley shrugged. "Then you'll know I'm out. I gave Susie my answer then."

"I'm here to ask you to reconsider."

Shelley pulled a disbelieving face. "Oh, come on. You don't want me on board, looking over your shoulder."

"Really? What makes you say that?"

"Because . . . look, I don't mean to be rude, but instinct tells me you're one kind of animal and I'm another, and you don't put us in a pen together."

Bennett nodded, eyes going from Shelley to Lucy as he picked up his coffee for a sip and once again replaced the cup on the table. "Because of the Circuit?"

Shelley sat back and folded his arms. "Maybe," he said. From the corner of his eye he caught Lucy's amused look. She'd never really understood his antipathy to the Circuit. He wasn't sure he fully understood it himself. But when he met blokes like Johnson and Gurney it all came flooding back.

"I see," said Bennett with a wry smile. "Look, we're not all bad news on the Circuit, you know. You watch the news, you see some reporter doing a stand-up in a war zone, who do you think is escorting that reporter? Who gets them in there and keeps them safe? Who's supporting the troops on the ground? Who's providing protection for the workers trying to build an infrastructure? Circuit guys. Guys like me."

"And guys like Gurney and Johnson?"

"Okay, look, I'll be the first to admit they're a bit rough around the edges, but you'd want them at your back."

"I'll have to beg to differ, mate."

"They're my men, Shelley. They were doing their job. In the case of Johnson he didn't do his best, and we've had to have a word about that, a little refresher, you might say, regarding unnecessary confrontation. In Gurney's case, he simply wound you up, and while I can understand you might not like him as a result, he wasn't at fault. He was simply proceeding as per his orders."

Not that he'd show it, but Shelley was impressed with Bennett's loyalty to his men. It would have been easy to sell them out and win brownie points with Shelley, especially as this was so obviously Operation Schmooze. But he hadn't.

"Sounds like you got a tight little unit there," said Shelley. "All the more reason why you don't want me hanging around like a fart in a trance."

Bennett shook his head. "Look, here's the thing. You knew Emma. I didn't. But from everything I've heard about her, she was a great kid who didn't deserve what happened to her. Neither did her parents because they're good people, too.

Susie wants you on board with us. That's why I'm here. Man on a mission. It was Susie who asked me to come. Message: please join us." Shelley sighed and Bennett held up his hand. "Just consulting if you want. Same fee as me—and I can tell you it's a good fee."

"I've already given her my answer," said Shelley. "I'm not getting involved in any revenge deal. End of."

"If Susie was here she'd tell you that it's not about revenge, retaliation, payback, whatever—you can pick your synonym. She'd say that it's about making sure these people don't do to any more girls what they did to Emma."

"Who? What people?"

"Well, for a start, the cam channel operator, where girls are forced to work to pay off their drug debts. There's a word for that, Shelley: slavery."

Shelley felt his jaw clench. "You know who they are?"

Bennett nodded. "Name's Foxy Kittenz, would you believe. With a Z. And we know where they're based."

"Where are they based?"

"Ah, well, *that* I can't tell you just yet. Are you in or out?"

Shelley cast a sideways glance at Lucy. Her face was unreadable. "I need time to think it over."

"Then I'll leave you to it." Bennett went to stand. "In the meantime, I've got something else for you. Susie would like you to call her after you've watched it."

"Watched what?"

Bennett reached into the inside pocket of his jacket and withdrew a small USB stick that he placed carefully on the coffee table.

CHAPTER 20

AS THEY CLEARED away the coffee cups neither Shelley nor Lucy mentioned the USB stick, which remained on the table where Bennett had left it. They needed to visit Sainsbury's anyway—those food cupboards weren't going to fill themselves.

"What is it about the Circuit?" she asked him. "What do you have against it?"

He sighed. "Haven't we been over this?"

"But Shelley, it's what we do. It's what we are."

"Is it?"

She stood with the empty cafetière in her hand, looking solemn all of a sudden. "Yes. Like it or not, yes. That's the path we chose."

"And we can't try a new path, a little bit off the beaten track?"

"You know what I think it is?" she said. "It's that moral compass of yours. When you were in the army you could tell yourself that you were on the side of the angels, but the job of a security company isn't to do good in the world, it's to make money, and that's what you can't take, isn't it? You want to be noble, Shelley. You want to be doing right."

"Is there anything wrong with that?"

"No, of course not, and that's exactly what I'll tell myself when I'm starving to death: thank God for my husband's sense of personal integrity."

They washed up the cups in silence and then, just before they left, Shelley moved the USB stick to the mantelpiece, placing it beside the photo of Lucy and Frankie.

Later, with the trip over, the shopping bought and packed away, Lucy broached the subject they'd been avoiding. "Well? And before you say 'well, what?,' you know exactly what I mean, so don't say it."

He scratched his head. "I don't know."

"You'll have seen worse."

"That's not really the point."

"Sure," she conceded. "Okay, then, how about you take yourself upstairs, go have a shower or something? I'll report back."

He retired to the bedroom, where he closed the door and sat on the bed, waiting.

When Lucy called he returned downstairs to find her closing the laptop lid, eyes wet with tears that she brushed away.

"Well?" he said.

"She was tough," said Lucy, nodding in admiration. "Brave."

"Is it brave, killing yourself?"

She shook her head, not wanting to go there. "Where did he get it from? The film. Can anybody see that?"

"Online, I guess. There's some fairly shady shit out there."

Hanging in the air between them was the knowledge that Cookie had been the guy in their patrol who took care of all the tech stuff.

"There's something else," said Lucy.

"What?"

"She said something, just as she pulled the trigger."

"What did she say?" said Shelley.

A short time later he rang Susie.

"Thank you for seeing Mr. Bennett," she said. "He tells me you were most welcoming."

"He seems all right." Shelley heard the begrudging note in his own voice.

"Did you watch it?" she asked him.

"Yes," he lied. "Did you?"

"No," she said. "Nor did Guy."

"Emma's last words before she pulled the trigger . . ." he began, and then stopped.

"Yes. Mr. Bennett told me that she said something," said Susie. "He couldn't quite make it out, because . . ."

Because of the gun barrel in her mouth.

"I know what she said, Susie. I could make it out. She said, 'Be lucky.'"

"I see," said Susie.

"You remember . . ."

"Yes, I remember."

He took a deep breath. "Listen, Susie, if I'm on board nobody dies, nobody gets hurt. We're after justice, not revenge."

"Maybe justice *is* revenge," she said softly.

"Maybe."

There was a pause before she asked, "Well?"

PART TWO

CHAPTER 21

"WHAT IS THIS place?" the man with the cropped hair demanded to know.

Sergei looked around at the cars parked either side of them, at the sign that said "MOT & Service Center," and at the open roller doors of the garage through which they could see cars on ramps and men in overalls, and said, "This place? This is a tanning salon."

"Very funny," growled his passenger. "You people do have a sense of humor after all, then."

Sergei decided to ignore the "you people." After all, simply by coming here his passenger was placing his head into the lion's mouth. So if he wanted to kid himself that he held the upper hand, then let him. Saying otherwise would be like telling a kid there's no tooth fairy.

They made their way to the entrance, a frosted-glass door that needed a bit of persuasion to open, and then stepped into the front office. Sergei was a regular visitor, of course, and usually there'd be a young woman called Sofia there to greet him, a receptionist who booked in cars, took payment, and behaved as though the garage really was a garage.

Which it was. Partly. But given that the owner was Dmitry— not the registered owner, but the owner all the same—it was also concerned with another sort of business. Dmitry business. Company business. Whatever that might be.

Except today Sofia was absent. Everything else was normal—the smell of dirty carpet tiles, ancient cigarette smoke, instant coffee, and a cluster of cardboard Christmas tree air-fresheners that dangled from her terminal—but in her place sat the Skinsman, his hands interlocked across his chest, head cocked to one side, watching a television mounted on the opposite wall.

It was a strange sight, enough to prompt a derisive snort from Sergei's companion that coincided with a sudden lull in the TV volume. In response, Grandfather's eyes slid from the screen to the visitor. For a moment they gleamed with malice and Sergei didn't like to think what the old man was imagining. Instead he simply greeted Grandfather with a respectful nod and then hustled his guest—oblivious to the malevolence of the old man's gaze—through the reception area without introducing him, escaping through a second door to an administrative area and more offices.

"Wait here," he told his visitor, and a moment later he was inside one of the offices, taking a seat opposite Dmitry, who sat at a desk.

In contrast to Dmitry's home set-up, the office was sparse, desk bare but for an open laptop and two smartphones. Dmitry wore a Harley Davidson T-shirt, one that best displayed his tattooed and muscly upper arms, the way he liked, and his spectacles dangled at his chest.

"Have you been keeping an eye on the internet, Sergei?" he asked glumly.

Sergei thought he knew what was coming, but even so. "It's a big thing to keep an eye on, Dmitry."

"Yes, but if you were hoping to see footage of a stupid hooker blowing her brains out, where might you look?"

Sergei shook his head. "I honestly don't know, Dmitry. I've never been tempted to look before."

"The dark web, have you heard of that?" sighed Dmitry.

"I don't think I have, boss."

"That's where you go for the bad stuff, my friend. Cocaine by post, child porn, and bitches blowing their brains out. Instead of 'dot com' they use 'dot onion,' did you know that?"

"No, I didn't know that, Dmitry."

"In the onion is where I found it. I've watched the bitch's brains go all over our studio," he waved his hands around, "over and over again. Well done for managing to clean it up, by the way, you did a good job. But it doesn't change the fact that this film is in . . . the public domain." He chewed over the words. "It is possible, is it not, that somebody might see it and put two and two together? A nosy policeman. Somebody who knows the girl or who saw her picture in the papers?"

Sergei made noncommittal noises, sensing that whatever the decision, Dmitry had already made it.

"There is no doubt about it," continued Dmitry, "we must be cautious as always, and cautious in this case means closing the studio."

"I see," said Sergei. "Alexander will be unhappy."

"Alexander is in Grozny and need not know immediately. Besides, he'll be even more unhappy if the operation is crawling with cops. No, my mind is made up, and you know me, Sergei: when my mind is made up then that is what we must do."

Sergei understood Dmitry's reasoning. Admitting failure was bad. But if it was discovered that they were neglecting to admit their failure, maybe even caught trying to *cover up* that failure, then that was really bad, no matter how you tried to justify it.

"Can I leave that to you? Can I leave that to you and my beloved wife?" said Dmitry, savoring the satire of the words "beloved wife" as though they were a sip of fine wine.

"You can, Dmitry," replied Sergei.

"Good, good. Now, this other matter. This informant. Have you brought him?"

"He's outside now, boss, looking forward to making your acquaintance."

Gold glinted as Dmitry smiled. "Then by all means bring him in. Let the squealer start squealing." He snapped his laptop shut, stood, and then came around from behind the desk. "Perhaps this Emma Drake did us a favor, eh, Sergei?"

Maybe, thought Sergei as he got up to go to the office door.

"Oh, Sergei," said Dmitry from behind him. "Your wallet."

Sergei turned to see Dmitry lifting his wallet from the seat where it had slipped out of his back pocket. As Dmitry picked it up it flipped open and he saw inside, his brow clouding briefly before his smile returned and he handed it back.

"Thank you," said Sergei. He pocketed the wallet and then turned, opened the office door, and beckoned his visitor inside. "This is my boss, his name is Dmitry," he said.

"Please, sit," said Dmitry, indicating a chair. "Sergei has told me much about you. You used to be in the Parachute Regiment, is that right?"

"That's right," said the new arrival. He took a seat and sat with his knees together and his shoulders square.

"Good, good." Dmitry gave him an askance look, just for comic effect. "Are you sure that our operation has no interest in you? Perhaps it is *you* that we should be taking as a prize, and not this other man, yes?"

The new arrival sneered. "Nah, I don't think so. As far as I know my lot never had any argument with the Russian Mafia."

Dmitry's smile froze. His eyes flicked to Sergei, who cleared his throat. "The Chechen Mafia," corrected Sergei.

"Yeah, yeah, whatever," said the guest. "The SAS, on the other hand . . ."

Dmitry threw up his hands and made a disgusted spitting noise. "Ah, the SAS, they think they're the Avengers, Bourne, and Bond all in one. They're like Tom Cruise going round the world and doing good, all at our expense. And you can give us an SAS man, can you? So that we may exact a little payback?"

"Oh yes," said Corporal Johnson, ex–Parachute Regiment. "Too fucking right I can."

CHAPTER 22

JASON HAD QUITE enjoyed his job. No, in fact, he'd *really* enjoyed his job. Apart from the antisocial hours it pretty much ticked all the boxes. Those boxes being, one, he got to smoke a lot of weed, and two, he got to see loads of naked girls (and not just naked, but "doing stuff").

Also great was the fact that the girls mostly looked upon him as a kind of "big brother" figure, which meant they were always dead nice to him and there was never anything sexual to make things awkward.

Jason and another guy, Dan, split the duties between them. Dan was a bit more full-on with the girls; he'd had a couple of relationships, well, if you could call them relationships, but Jason had never gone that way. Never exchanged so much as a kiss with one of them. The whole "big brother" thing was important to Jason. He prided himself on it. He liked to think that the girls relaxed more around him as a result. And because of that he got to see even more "stuff." Win–win.

These weren't unattractive girls either. Most "normal" cam

girls just filmed the shit on their laptops, in between baby feeds and arguments with their other half.

This operation was different. For a start, his Russian bosses called it a "studio"—studio! ha!—and secondly they claimed to offer superior quality. Not just picture and sound quality, either, but the most beautiful and willing girls—beautiful, willing girls who would do practically anything the punters asked, providing the price was right.

And Jason, being a man of small or, to be perfectly honest, zero ambition, could quite happily have kept that particular job for the next, oh, until-he-retired number of years. He was as happy as a clam in that job.

And then it all came crashing down around his ears, when poor old Faye blew her brains out, live on camera.

He'd been first on the scene, and he knew that the brief glimpse he'd had of the room—splattered with blood, gobs of brain matter, and weirdly bright skull fragments sliding down the walls—would stay with him forever.

Thank God for Sergei, insisting that he concentrate on reassuring the other girls that things were fine while the clean-up operation took place.

And then there was Karen. She had a gammy arm, but even so, you wouldn't kick her out of bed for eating toast. She seemed to quite like Jason as well. She often spent time with him in the office during her visits, just chewing the fat. They shared an unlikely passion for *Downton Abbey*.

It helped that she wasn't Russian herself, of course; she had an English accent. But as far as Jason could tell— you weren't exactly encouraged to ask questions—she was married to one of the Russians, a guy higher up the tree than

Sergei. It also helped that the girls never warmed to her, nor she to them. That suited Jason down to the ground.

But Karen had taken a particular interest in Faye from the start. "What's her name? Jace?" she'd asked on one of her visits. Jason had to admit that he was quite fond of the way Karen called him "Jace."

"It's a new girl. Well, been here a couple of weeks. Gorgeous, ain't she?"

Karen was staring at the screen, staring intently at Faye, who was currently between punters, fixing her makeup, primping the bed, oblivious to the fact that she was being scrutinized.

"How did she get here?"

"One of the other girls brought her in. Precious, I think it was."

"Is she using?"

Jason had nodded yes to that one. Girls tended to arrive at Foxy Kittenz after a journey whose stops along the way included abusive parents, violent partners, and drug addiction. All three, if they were really unlucky. Every single one of those girls was living proof that good looks and a firm young body weren't necessarily a passport to getting ahead in this world. Fortune's smile and parents who weren't fuck-ups, those things were important, too.

"Faye," Karen had said, repeating the word like a mantra. "I bet that ain't her real name, though, is it?"

Jason had shrugged. All the girls used assumed names. More fool them if they didn't.

"And I bet you could find out her real name for me, couldn't you?" Fingers with red-painted nails found their way to his leg.

"How could I do that?"

Karen had a strange smile. It lifted her top lip to reveal a slightly crooked tooth below. Even so, despite that—actually, on second thoughts, maybe *because* of it—it was cute. And it did the job on Jason.

Moments later he was in Faye's room. "Fancy a quick toilet break? I've got to adjust the cam," he said, knowing Faye would jump at the chance—and do more in the toilet than just a wee.

"Thanks, sweetheart," she said, smiling at him, and he thought, not for the first time, how much he liked Faye. He hoped he wasn't helping get her into trouble with Karen.

Anyway, on with the job. Aware of Karen, in the office watching, he found Faye's handbag, rifled through it, and in seconds flat had discovered her real name. Letting himself out, he returned to the office.

"Well?"

"Her real name is Emma—Emma Drake," Jason told Karen, and watched closely for her reaction, which was a slow nod, the name evidently coming as no surprise to her. "You know her," he pressed.

"Yeah," Karen said. "You might say that. You might well say that, Jace."

A couple of days later Faye killed herself, and for Jason the days of wine and roses were over. Not only did he have the trauma of that to deal with, but the studio had been shut down. And now he was out of a job.

So what did he do? As before, he sat around, smoked weed, and watched porn, only now he wasn't getting paid for it. It was what he was doing when the buzzer went.

He crossed his small flat to the intercom. Thumbed the button. "Yeah? Who is it?"

"Jace, it's Karen, sweetheart. I've got some wages for you. Well, not just wages. A little thank-you, you might say, for all your hard work and discretion."

That's more like it, he thought. He'd been feeling a little bit taken for granted. He'd briefly considered getting in touch with Karen and dropping a hint: *Wouldn't it be awful if the police found out about Faye?* But then he'd had second thoughts.

He buzzed her up, waited until he heard her tap at the door, and then went to open it.

"Oh," he said, because it wasn't *just* Karen. With her was a tall guy wearing a leather bomber jacket.

"Oh, don't mind him," Karen tried to reassure Jason. "Just Dmitry getting jittery. Thinks I shouldn't go anywhere alone."

Jason kind of hoped she might just give him his wages at the door, but she made to come inside and he had little choice but to admit her.

"Nice place you've got here." She smiled and he was 99 percent certain she was taking the piss, but what the hell? This was Karen after all, and he liked Karen, in all the ways.

He wondered if he should offer them tea, but then remembered he didn't have any tea to offer. Besides, he really just wanted to get back to his weed and porn.

Karen stood there looking a bit like a secret agent. Black coat belted tight at the waist. Black leather gloves. "So you haven't managed to find any other work yet?" she said.

"I'm considering my options," he replied, dropping into the sofa as if to watch the TV, even though it was switched off.

"I'm sorry about the studio shutting," she said. "It was this business with Faye." He looked across at her and tried to work out what she was thinking. Jason wasn't the sharpest tool in the box but he wasn't entirely dim either, and he knew better than to ask Karen straight out whether she'd been involved in Faye's death. For a moment the curiosity almost got the better of him, but then his eyes slid to the bodyguard guy, and he thought better of it.

"I hope that you've been discreet, Jace," she said, smiling, but with a scrutinizing look on her face.

Sunk into the sofa, Jason suddenly felt vulnerable as Karen loomed over him. She moved forward a little and put one hand in her pocket. He swallowed. "What do you mean?" he said, knowing precisely what she meant but figuring it was best to play dumb. The bodyguard guy hadn't moved from the front door.

"What I say," she said sweetly. "You ain't said anything to anybody about any of the goings-on at Foxy Kittenz, have you?"

"What? No, of course I haven't. This is pretty much my social circle right here."

"Good," she said. She pulled a black-gloved hand from her pocket and swiped across his neck.

Jason saw the blood that sheeted down his front a second before he saw the Stanley knife in Karen's hand. He flailed around uselessly for a few seconds on the sofa now saturated with his blood before unconsciousness quickly faded his world to black.

CHAPTER 23

"I'M REALLY NOT sure how I feel," she told him.

Shelley looked at her. "Come again, Luce?"

"I said I'm really not at all sure how I feel about you going off to work for the Drakes under the circumstances."

"Um, right," he said. "Did I ask how you felt, then?"

Her lips pressed together. "No. You didn't ask, actually. But you were about to ask. Or you should have asked. And just so we don't get to the point where I get mad at you for failing to ask, I'm giving you my opinion anyway."

There were times that Shelley suspected he was more at home in the field than he was in his own house. This was one of those times. "Uh, right. Sorry, Luce. I should have asked. Of course. We're in this together." Deep breath. *Let's start again.* "Okay, how do you feel about me going?"

"I just said."

"Yeah, but . . ."

"I don't know. I don't know how I feel."

He spread his hands, thinking, *I can't win.* "I just want to be there. See to it they don't end up doing something stupid."

"You don't want revenge?"

He shook his head emphatically. "No. I don't want revenge. What I want is to stop this from escalating." It was the truth. He wasn't in it for payback. A whole bunch of other reasons, maybe. But not that.

She looked at him. "All right, I'll take your word for it. But listen, Shelley, if you need backup . . ."

"You're here."

"Of course I'm here. But look, don't do anything that *needs* backup, okay? Go in there, tell them not to be such gung-ho arseholes, and get back out again, all right?"

"Roger that," he said.

"You owe me a brainstorming session, remember?"

"Sure."

"Oh, and one more thing, Shelley."

"Yes?"

"Susie Drake. She's a good-looking broad."

He swallowed. "Yes."

"Anything ever happen between you?"

"No," he replied. "You and I were engaged at the time."

"I've got eyes, Shelley, and I know potential when I see it." She pursed her lips, giving him a comical look that nevertheless held serious intent. "Just you watch yourself, okay?"

He smiled, relieved the moment was over. "Don't you worry about me, Luce."

During the drive he tried to clear his mind. He knew what his job was: making sure Guy Drake's thirst for revenge didn't result in a bloodbath. He'd packed enough to stay a few nights—plenty of time to talk some sense into Camp Drake. He resolved to have a quiet word with Guy and Susie—a chance to lay down some of the ground rules—before he did anything else.

When he arrived, he saw the usual array of vehicles in the drive, although in place of the electric-blue BMW was a van with the words "Freeman Van Hire" emblazoned on the side. He looked at it for a moment, puzzling over its incongruity, wondering if it was at all significant.

The front door was ajar and he let himself in. Right away his heart sank when he saw that one of his key demands had been ignored. Last night on the phone he'd told Susie he didn't want to work with either Gurney or Johnson. As in, he *refused* to work with either Gurney or Johnson. It was either them or him.

"I'll inform Lloyd," she'd said, which Shelley had taken to mean: *I'll tell Lloyd to give them the boot.*

But although there was no sign of that Johnson turkey, Gurney was there, and still giving Shelley the skunk eye, as though he was sitting on some insults he was just dying to deliver, a thin veneer of professionalism preventing his true feelings from seeing daylight.

And so, with no sign of Susie or Drake, Shelley grabbed hold of Bennett and took him to one side, which in this case was the Drakes' pool-hall-sized kitchen.

"What the fuck is going on, Bennett?"

The other man held up his hands, a gesture Shelley was beginning to realize was as much his habit as chewing was for Guy Drake. "Well, it's nice to see you too, Shelley, good morning and all that. Have you had a coffee yet?"

"Yeah, yeah. Yadda yadda yadda. What's Gurney doing here?"

"He's here because I need him, that's all there is to it."

"Well, then, maybe Susie didn't tell you what we discussed last night, because one of the conditions of me coming was no Gurney, and no Johnson."

"And Johnson isn't here. Do you see Johnson? Johnson has the day off; he'll play no part in this operation. Doesn't even know it's happening. But I need a three-man team on this. You of all people should know that."

"What operation?" Shelley was getting a nasty feeling in the pit of his stomach. "What are you talking about?"

"We've located Foxy Kittenz, where Emma killed herself."

"And . . . ?"

Bennett's eyes did the military look left and right, a look that meant: *This is not my idea, I'm following orders here.* "And we're paying it a visit," he said.

"When? Not . . ."

"In one. Tonight."

Shelley pulled off his hat and raked a hand through his hair. "Right, look, I know where you're coming from on this. I know Guy. He's hurting. He wants revenge and he's used to getting what he wants. But Susie's worried about him. *I'm* worried about him. The point of me being here is to stop him doing anything stupid. You said so yourself last night, remember? Or did I imagine that?"

Bennett pulled his hands from his pockets, tipped his glasses up his nose, and then leaned to Shelley, taking him into his confidence. "You're right. Maybe I'm just a bit out of my depth here."

"I never said—"

"You didn't need to." He lowered his head as though finally admitting an uncomfortable truth. "Maybe you should speak to Mr. Drake. He'll listen to you." Clearing his throat awkwardly, he added, "He wants to burn the place down."

Shelley gaped. "*He what?* All right, where are they?"

Drake and Susie chose that moment to enter the kitchen, Susie in front and Drake wheeling two small suitcases just behind. Shelley's own overnight holdall was still at his feet. He hadn't yet removed his coat, and he looked from Susie to Drake as the couple joined them at the kitchen's central island.

"David," she said, coming close to kiss him. Enveloping him in a cloud of perfume. That perfume again. That same perfume.

"Susie," he said, softening, "we need to have a word."

"Of course, of course. You're probably wondering what's going on."

"You might say that." He gestured at the suitcases. "Are you going somewhere?"

"Into town," said Drake, by which of course he meant into London.

"Tonight? Right. What about this . . . *operation?*"

For a moment he allowed himself to believe that it was all a case of crossed wires, until Susie reached for him, her head tilted to one side. "Oh, David, I'm sorry it's such short notice. I had no idea about this when I spoke to you last night, but thanks to Mr. Bennett, we've found out where—"

"He told me. What I want to know is what you're planning to do."

"We're going to get those scum tonight, whether you like it or not," Drake said, defiant, angry, and commanding. "Do you understand me, chief? We'll start with this lot tonight and then we'll move on to the dealers. Now, you're in my house, on my dollar, and you'd better get your head round that or you might as well sling your hook right now."

Shelley shrugged and reached for his holdall.

"David, no," said Susie quickly. She turned to Drake. "David isn't here to stop you taking action—'revenge,' if you want to call it that. He's here to prevent you doing something stupid. Something that'll come back to haunt us. That's what *you* need to get your head round."

Bennett took a deep breath. "There's a famous proverb," he said. "Confucius, I think. When going in search of revenge, first dig two graves, one for your enemy and one for yourself."

"Who the fuck's side are you on?" Drake said, turning to Bennett. "Matter of fact, who the fuck's side are you *all* on?" He waved a hand, and for the first time Shelley noticed Gurney, who stood by the door to the kitchen and watched them with his arms folded across his chest and an amused expression on his face.

"Yours, sweetheart," said Susie to Drake. She gently calmed him and the color in his cheeks gradually subsided and the fire in his eyes dimmed. Shelley had seen Drake rattled before—the kidnap attempt for one. But he'd never seen him like this. Never seen him so close to the edge. Susie turned to Shelley. "I got tickets for a show, reservations for dinner, and booked us in at the Connaught."

"Drake's not joining the operation, then?" asked Shelley.

"You can bet your sweet peach I'm joining it," Drake cut in before Susie could reply. "A friend at the Connaught. A car back here. I'll be part of it all right, don't you fret." He cast a sideways glance at Susie. "Just you try to stop me."

Susie ignored him. "We need you there, David. You have to—"

" 'Look after Guy,' is that right?" seethed Drake. "You needn't bother, Shelley."

"You sure?" shot back Shelley. "Then what's all this I hear about burning the place down?"

Bennett winced,, glaring daggers at Shelley, who realized, belatedly, that the arson plan was news to Susie.

Oh well. There was an expression beloved of one of Shelley's old instructors at Hereford. He used to say it whenever he farted. *Better out than in.*

CHAPTER 24

"WHAT? ABSOLUTELY NOT. Absolutely *not*, Guy, is that understood?"

Susie was raging, as angry and upset as Shelley had ever seen her. Even so, Drake wasn't ready to give in. In his mind's eye he was dancing on the ashes of Foxy Kittenz and he wasn't about to part with that image easily.

"Why?" he yelled at her.

"Because we're not gangsters, Guy," she threw back. "We're not terrorists."

"*Then what?*" roared Drake. "How do we hurt them?"

Shelley was about to answer when Bennett cut in. "We smash their equipment," he said coolly.

"'Smash their equipment,'" snorted Guy derisively. "It's not exactly a mortal fucking blow, is it?"

"We do enough to put them out of action," continued Bennett, still in diplomatic mode. "Look, sir, whatever measures we take, there's always the chance this gets traced back to you. Imagine if it was, if you were exposed in the press, perhaps even prosecuted. If that happened and it turns out that you're a man who put a bunch of lowlifes out of business then I dare say you could style it out and emerge looking like a bit of a folk hero.

"But arson is a different proposal altogether. You look reckless. You look dangerous and out of control. As Susie says, like a gangster." He spread his hands, no-brainer, but like everybody else in the room he was braced for Drake's reaction. It was clear to all of them that Drake had taken the idea of fiery vengeance to his heart.

"All right," Drake agreed reluctantly. "No burning."

The quick change in Drake's thinking didn't completely ring true with Shelley, but it was the best they were going to get. The meeting broke up and Guy and Susie left for London. With the light outside beginning to fade, Shelley picked up his holdall and took it to his room.

It was the same room he'd stayed in all those years ago, and like Susie's perfume it had a transporting effect on him: the low eaves, having to stoop to avoid banging his head; even the bed linen looked the same.

He sighed and sat on the edge of the bed, painfully aware of how much time had passed. Remembering a little girl who stood in that very same room and, like Hermione from the *Harry Potter* stories she loved so much, had performed magic, showing him that his mistakes were in fact hard-won experience.

He'd thanked her by leaving.

"Is that why I'm here, Emma?" he said into an empty room. "One good turn and all that?"

And what would Lucy say if she were here, sitting beside him? She'd tell him to pick up his holdall and leave if he wanted, because nothing he could do would bring Emma back anyway. Get out, before the bad shit happens.

But he couldn't do that. He was an old soldier. He had an undiminished sense of doing his duty.

He returned downstairs. The house he remembered from years ago always had various helpers and employees hanging around: cleaners, housekeepers, gardeners, chauffeurs. But if those people still existed in the Drake household—and Shelley assumed they did—then they'd been given temporary leave of absence. Shelley, Bennett, and Gurney were the only occupants, all a little wired with anticipation and circling each other warily.

As night drew in and the three of them began preparing for the operation—reluctantly, Shelley had bought into the whole "operation" title—they gathered once more in the kitchen, the only downstairs room that was lit, where Gurney opened a laptop to Google Earth.

"Here's where we're going," he said, navigating to a location at Millharbor in Docklands, a road lined with anonymous buildings on one side, land ready for business redevelopment on the other. The buildings were squat two-story affairs, studies in anonymity, the color of soggy cardboard: storage, office units, studio space and . . .

"This one," said Gurney. His finger moved across the screen. "We can park the van here. Be out of the van and in the building in about ten seconds."

"And if it's locked?" asked Shelley.

"We fully expect it to be locked, mate," replied Gurney, "that's why we've got an enforcer in the van."

"An enforcer?"

"A sort of battering ram that the police use," explained Bennett. "They call it the big key."

"And once we're inside?"

Bennett and Gurney exchanged an uncomfortable glance.

"Go on," prompted Shelley.

"We don't know the layout of the place," said Bennett, "and as you know, it's not exactly desirable to make a nighttime incursion into unmapped territory."

"But fuck it—it's just an office building," sneered Gurney. He hitched up the combat trousers he wore, then he cleared his sinuses. "We don't expect any opposition," he added, leaving Shelley in no doubt that he considered this a terrible shame.

"Well, what *do* you expect?" asked Shelley.

Gurney shrugged. "Girls. Computers. Cameras. That kind of thing. Maybe a bouncer. We've got baseball bats in the van."

Baseball bats. Great.

"We should be keeping a watch on this place," said Shelley. "How do we even know they're still using it? If we're right and Emma killed herself in there then the most sensible thing for them to do would be to pack up before the cops show an interest."

Bennett was nodding. "We think they're continuing as normal."

Shelley looked at him. Getting it now. "Drake insisting you go ahead tonight, is he?"

"That's about the size of it, yes."

"Okay," said Shelley, seeing that he had no choice. "The girls are left unharmed. Any guys are scared off and sent packing with no serious harm done, is that clear?"

"You don't have to convince me of that," said Bennett, who if anything looked relieved.

It struck Shelley that revenge was a burden. You carried it yourself. But you made others carry it too.

CHAPTER 25

IT WAS APPROACHING eleven when Drake appeared. Shelley, who'd been trying to relax in his bedroom, received a text message to tell him they were due to proceed, and he'd pulled on his balaclava and made his way downstairs to find the others congregated outside, the van idling close by with its rear doors open.

The night was good and dark, the moon barely making its presence felt. The cold froze their breath into clouds that hung in the air, as though held in place by an icy calm that turned the sound of their footsteps into gunfire. There was nobody around to hear but even so, they spoke in a whisper, even Drake, who had arrived from London, disappeared inside, and then returned wearing black jeans and a black hoodie like the others, accepting the balaclava handed to him by Gurney.

"Are we ready?" asked Bennett, and although he said "we" it was to Drake that he addressed the question.

"It's not too late to call it off, Guy," said Shelley. And he was pleased to see Bennett nodding in agreement. Less pleased to see Drake's fists clench. The older man's eyes were at once vacant and aflame. Shelley recognized the look of a man on a mission when he saw it.

Sure enough, the go was given and they clambered into the van: Gurney driving, Bennett shotgun, Shelley and Drake in the back. They sat on pull-down seats on springs, settling in for what during the daytime would be a long journey from Berkshire to the south of London, but at just after 11 p.m. would take them little over an hour.

There were no windows in the van, which only increased Shelley's sense of being cocooned with Drake, who sat opposite with a look that was weary, doughy, and hangdog, but determined. Once again Shelley became aware of Drake's grief and how it had calcified into something far more poisonous.

"Guy," said Shelley over the throb of the engine. Drake looked sharply at him. "I meant what I said. You can still stop this."

It was gloomy in the back of the van and Shelley wasn't sure if he read correctly the look that flitted across Drake's face. It looked like contempt. Maybe even something worse.

"Do what, Shelley? You think I should chicken out of smashing a few computers, do you? I thought you had more gumption, man. I thought there was a bit more to you than that. Maybe I misjudged you, eh?"

"Did Susie? Did Emma?"

"How would I know? This much I *can* say. If not for Susie you wouldn't be here."

"You should be grateful she cares. She just wants to protect you. We both do."

Drake looked away, unwilling to accept the truth. "She

hangs on to you, Shelley. You know that? She thinks of you as some kind of lucky charm. But you're not, are you? You're just an old soldier, like them two turkeys up front. Just trying to make a bit of cash out of fellas like me. That's what it's all about, isn't it? With them two there, Susie hardly gives them the time of day. But *you*," he pointed for emphasis, "you're some kind of talisman for her. You know why?"

Shelley shook his head. He found he was holding his breath, unsure if he wanted to hear what was coming next.

"Because of what you did, saving them from the kidnap. She practically idolizes you. So did our Emma. You were their hero, Shelley, you know that?"

Again Shelley shook his head, feeling a mix of relief and fresh hurt.

"Oh yeah. You were. And what do you know? On the day she killed herself she called you. *Emma rang you.* She didn't ring us, did you know that? She didn't bother to call her parents before she put that gun in her mouth. Just you.

"That makes you important to Susie. That Emma was reaching out to you then. That's what she called it, 'reaching out.' But that's Susie for you, wanting to find the good, always looking for that positive angle.

"Me, I just feel hurt. I wanted to know why Emma needed to hear the voice of some bloke who was her bodyguard fourteen bloody years ago—*fourteen bloody years*—and not the voice of her own father."

In the dim light Shelley saw the tears of rage and frustration plotting a course down Drake's cheeks, but he couldn't find words of support or condolence. Instead he said, "Why did she call me?"

Drake sniffed, embarrassed by his tears, wiping them away. "You what?"

"You're dead right. What was she doing calling me?"

"Like I say, because she had you on a pedestal, didn't she? You were her knight in shining bleedin' armor."

"Really?" said Shelley. To his own ears he sounded as though he were playing devil's advocate, but as he spoke it began to sound more plausible. "How much did she talk about me?"

"She cried for a bloody week, mate, when you left," said Drake bitterly, but Shelley pushed on.

"No, I mean, over the years—how much did she talk about me?"

"Susie often—"

"Not Susie—Emma."

"I don't know." Drake's jowls shook. "Every now and then, I suppose."

"So not much, in other words." He leaned forward with a fizz of sudden realization. "It doesn't really make any sense, does it, her calling me? Maybe to you and me fourteen years seems like yesterday, but she was only ten at the time of the kidnap attempt. By the time she was thirteen, ten years old would have seemed like a lifetime ago. It's not false modesty, I'm sure she thought fondly of me. But enough to make *me* the one she called on the day she decided to kill herself? It doesn't quite make sense to me."

He didn't mention the gun that only had one bullet in it. He didn't wonder aloud why if Emma was a smack addict she didn't use smack to end her own life.

But those questions were still lodged in his head, not planning on going anywhere soon.

"She loved you, Guy," he said, and saw Drake bite his lip. "She did. She properly loved you and she loved Susie, and if she was going to kill herself—if she needed someone to talk to, it would have been you."

"So why wasn't it?"

"Think about it . . ."

"Stop pissing about and say what you've got to say."

"Okay," said Shelley, "maybe she wasn't going to kill herself."

"But she did—there's film of her doing it."

"Yeah, yeah," Shelley shook his head with frustration, "but there's more than one way to skin a cat, know what I mean? Or . . . I don't know, maybe she didn't plan to." He was thinking now, the idea taking hold. "Maybe she discovered something—something that she wanted to tell someone, and that someone was me—and *then* she killed herself."

Drake was looking at him with an unreadable expression. Shelley wondered what was least painful: the idea that your daughter took her own life, or that someone did it for her? Either way, it was better to know the truth. Wasn't that what Guy himself had said?

They were close to Docklands now. Had to be. Perhaps Drake realized the same. He reached down behind his feet and picked up his baseball bat, winding his gloved fingers around the handle.

"Guy," he said, trying to draw him out of his reverie. "Listen, mate, listen to me, right. Where we're going—there may be someone there who knows something about Emma's death. There might be a way of getting answers. Guy?"

No reply from Drake.

The van slowed and the engine noise changed as Gurney hit the brake and downshifted.

"We just need to change our approach here. We might be able to discover what happened to Emma . . . Guy?"

Drake looked at Shelley, a haunting, heartbreaking intensity in his stare. "I couldn't help myself, Shelley," he said.

"What do you mean? Couldn't help yourself do what?"

"I watched the film of her. I watched her do it. You're sitting there talking about what, and how, and maybe this and maybe that. It doesn't fucking matter. None of it. Because I watched her sit in that slutty room and put a gun in her mouth and pull the trigger. So you say, 'Oh, Guy, we might be able to find out what happened to her?' I know what happened to her. *That's* what happened to her. And now they're going to pay."

CHAPTER 26

THEY PASSED THROUGH tunnels. The sound of the van changed as they negotiated roundabouts.

Word came back. "We're approaching the building," called Bennett, "you might want to put on those balaclavas. Gurney will park close to a side door, just as we discussed. Let's assume we need to use the big key." It lay at Drake and Shelley's feet. The words "knock knock" had been painted on it in white. "Leave that to Gurney."

The driver chuckled. "I'm an old hand at it."

"Remember what we said," warned Shelley, telling the whole van but keeping a close eye on Drake, unnerved by what he'd just heard. "Nobody gets hurt. Damage is limited to computers and cameras."

"Roger that," said Bennett, and as Shelley rolled down his balaclava, adjusted the eye holes, watching Drake do the same, he wondered if he should be concerned that neither Drake nor Gurney had replied.

And then they arrived.

Shelley heard the sound of the front doors opening, boots

hitting the tarmac of the car park. Then the back doors were flung wide and a masked Gurney reached in for the big key. A security light had flared on, sodium dazzle picking them out, but otherwise there was no sign of alarm, no cameras fixed to walls peering down on them as they crowded around the doorway.

To one side stood Drake, holding his bat, hefting it like a proper slugger, fingers anxious on the grip. Shelley tried to find his eyes to send signals: *Calm, Guy, calm*, but Drake was watching Gurney, who was lifting the big key, ready to slam it into the door. Close by, as though deliberately positioned in order to keep their employer safe from harm, was Bennett.

And now the big key swung back, a medieval battering ram in miniature, Gurney grunting as it came forward and smashed into the door with an almighty wallop. If those inside hadn't known of their presence, they did now. And if they didn't know now, they soon would. Gurney did it again.

Bang! The door splintered.

Bang! Third time lucky. The lock separated and Gurney shouldered the door open, bursting into the building with a warrior cry.

Earlier, they'd used the words "shock and awe." "Noise," they said. "Make lots of it," the idea being to terrify the occupants, even those who were innocent. So it proved as Bennett raced inside with Drake and Gurney not far behind, the three of them making so much ruckus that at least it relieved Shelley of any obligation to do the same.

And now they were in a corridor, rooms on either side. Ahead of Shelley, Gurney kicked open a door, waved his bat, screaming, "Get out, get out, get out!"—a demented mantra as he battered the door frame side to side with the bat, like a quartermaster calling dinner with a gong, adding to the sudden, horrifying cacophony.

To the workers in the cam studio it must have seemed as if the world was ending. Wearing just a bra and panties, dark circles under her eyes and her face pale, the first girl came pelting out of the room. She ducked past Gurney as though terrified he was about to use the bat on her, and then, at the sight of Shelley, screamed again and stumbled cowering against the wall.

He reached to her. "Wait," he said. "You'll freeze out there. Get some clothes, get your stuff."

From ahead came the crunch of Gurney laying waste to equipment and the girl flinched again, but said, "Really?" in an uncertain voice. *Polish*, he thought.

"Yeah, really. I won't hurt you."

His eyes flicked to further up the passage where Gurney was kicking open another door and charging inside—*get out, get out, scream, bish, bash, bosh*—"I won't let him hurt you, either," he said more loudly, over the din of cameras being smashed and screaming.

There was no sign of either Drake or Bennett save for a door swinging open at the far end of the hallway. Gurney had moved on to a third room, wielding the bat like Jack Nicholson with his ax in *The Shining*. Further up, two more doors were flung open and women appeared, adding to the noise with shouts of surprise, fear, anger, defiance.

Shelley yelled at Gurney, "Oi, let them get their stuff, all right?" receiving a look in return that was impossible to decipher under the balaclava.

Still trying to impose authority on a situation that had been careering out of control virtually from the moment they arrived, Shelley moved forward, glanced into a room, and saw the first girl he'd encountered pulling her things from the floor, dancing as she dragged on a pair of jeans. He saw the smashed camera. A laptop almost staved in half. Another woman dashed past with a bundle of clothes in her arms. He counted five altogether, the last of them past him now. Gurney like a wild man at the other end of the building, the bat flailing.

And then from somewhere up the corridor came a terrible wail—the unmistakable sound of a man in pain. In the next moment Shelley reached the end door—marked with the word "Offices"—just as smoke started to billow from the doorway.

CHAPTER 27

AND NOW IT became clear just how fucked up things were. The office area was already on fire, and scrambling into the passageway in a bid to escape was a young guy with long hair, blood streaming down his face from a cut above his forehead, mouth already swollen. A terrified man. Rubber legs. Pinballing from one side of the corridor to the other. A man desperate to avoid not just the fire, but further beatings as well.

Behind him came Drake, bellowing insults, chasing the guy into the hallway with his bat held two-handed as if he were at home plate. He looked up and saw Shelley, but if the sight gave him pause for thought then he didn't show it, still screaming at the terrified employee who'd half fallen, half dropped to his hands and knees, trying to crawl away from further attack.

"Get on your feet, now," ordered Drake, raising the bat and, before Shelley could stop him, bringing it down hard on the small of the man's back.

"Christ, you'll break his spine!" shouted Shelley. He lunged to grab the weapon, to wrest it from Drake's hands.

"Leave me the fuck alone," Drake snapped back at him, in no way letting go of the bat, acting like a kid with a new toy.

Shelley looked up and saw orange patterns dancing on the walls. More smoke. He realized he didn't have time to play gimme-the-bat with Drake and let it go. "Just get out of here, both of you," he commanded and went in search of Bennett, stepping over the kid, through the doorway and into the heat.

Now he was in a small reception area, complete with low table, potted plant, and a framed photograph of a beach in the Maldives. There were two office doors, both open, one of which had smoke pouring from it.

Pummeled by heat, he knew there was no chance of fighting the fire. Escape was the only option now, damage limitation the new objective.

Bennett stood in the reception area. Motionless, he stared vacantly at flames as they began to curl out of the office, like orange fingers gripping the door frame, his bat dangling from his hand, only just registering Shelley's arrival.

"He went bananas!" he yelled.

Shelley could imagine. He'd seen Drake in the van. But he also knew that Drake had planned this all along. In order for the fire to get so hot so quickly he had to have had an accelerant, probably hidden in his hoodie.

Shelley grabbed Bennett. "Come on, let's get out of here," he bawled over the roar of the fire.

"This was not supposed to happen."

"But it *has* happened," snapped Shelley. "Now we deal with it. Leave the fire, come on."

Bennett nodded, shook off the torpor, and Shelley thanked God he'd pulled himself together. A temporary blip; it happened. Dealing with it was what counted, and credit to Bennett, that's what he did.

Meantime, Shelley had Drake and the worker guy to worry about. He wheeled, ran down the corridor, putting the fire at his back. His mind raced. His one objective now was to stop Guy Drake before he did any more harm.

He was too late. As Shelley burst out of the door, the sight that greeted him was Drake with his feet planted wide apart and his bat raised—then arcing down and into the prone body of the young bloke.

One. Twice. A third time.

Not the head, thank God, but Shelley was sure he heard ribs crack. At the same time Drake was screaming, "You tell them! You tell them Guy Drake was here! You tell them this is for Emma!" and Shelley knew that his main priority had been to stop Guy Drake doing something like this, and in that he'd failed miserably, because it was going to take more luck than any man deserved to walk away from this with no comebacks.

From inside the building came the dull thump of something exploding. The fire was spreading fast.

Shelley heard a screech from across the car park—"Stop it, you bastards!" He peered into the gloom, past the cone of light thrown by the security lamp to where he could just about make out the figure of a woman—one of the cam girls, brave enough not to flee. *Great*, he thought, *a witness. All we fucking need*, and he lunged, grabbed the bat on a downward stroke to prevent it from thumping into the cam worker a fourth time, and snatched it from the older man's grip with such force that Drake skittered backward, lost his balance, and sprawled to the tarmac.

For a moment that was where he lay, locking eyes with Shelley. Behind the balaclava there was no sign of shame, just the glowing embers of violence. His lips were wet, parted. His shoulders rose and fell.

Shelley knelt to the worker. The kid was in his early twenties, and he was in a bad way. Evidently Drake had got some serious digs in, at least one of them a head shot, probably delivered back in the office.

But he was alive. "Ring for an ambulance," called Shelley to the distant figure of the girl.

"You animals. You *animals*!" she screamed. "What did he ever do to you?"

"He killed my daughter!" bawled Drake as he pulled himself to his feet. "He killed Emma."

"What you talking about? Emma who?" came the shout back.

She doesn't know about Emma?

But there was no time to ask. "Get him into the van," Shelley told Bennett, who had materialized in the doorway of the office building. Smoke billowed around him. Behind its gray veil was the dancing orange of flames. Gurney was there too, escaping the fire, already clambering into the driving seat of the van as Bennett maneuvered Drake into the rear and Shelley prepared to climb aboard.

"That was my *job*." The girl stepped forward and Shelley saw that it was the same girl he'd spoken to. How come she hadn't heard about Emma? "What am I going to do now?" she wailed.

Drake was being bundled into the van by Bennett, but

over his shoulder yelled, "We did you a favor." The anguished millionaire, who would shortly be delivered to his five-star London hotel by his paid team of bodyguards, screaming how he'd done a favor for a woman who suddenly had no idea where her next meal was coming from.

Shelley felt sick.

CHAPTER 28

THINKING ABOUT IT later, Sergei really should have known all along. Why? The clue was Grandfather.

The Skinsman sat in his usual place in the front room of the terraced Finsbury Park house, a familiar comforting figure to oblivious locals passing by, a symbol of threat and terror to anybody who knew him as the Skinsman.

However, to his usual attire of baggy old-man jeans and gray sweatshirt he'd added a scarf and coat, looking as though he was waiting to be taken on an outing by a carer.

That's what Sergei saw as he peered through the window, taking the opportunity to scrutinize Grandfather a little more closely than he ever had before, remembering what the old man had said the last time they met.

He knocked in the code, waited. When Karen opened the door she wore her usual for-the-neighbors smile and, as usual, the mask slid away when she closed it. But this time, instead of gesturing for him to proceed along the hallway, her eyes scooted left and right and she leaned toward him.

"Sergei," she said very quietly, "we need to talk about Ivan."

That was all she said. But it was enough to surprise Sergei, who pulled back and looked at her askance, eyebrows knitting together in confusion. She had a finger to her lips, tilting her head back at the room in which Grandfather sat all wrapped up ready for his mystery trip but staring hard at the TV.

"Ivan? My brother Ivan?" he whispered.

She nodded. Her eyes were flint. "Not now, though," she said in a smoker's rasp. "Dmitry's on the warpath. I'll call." She fixed him with a complicitous stare. "I think you'll find what I've got to tell you very interesting indeed."

And that was how she left it. Light glinted off the gold hoop earrings she wore as she turned and walked away in high-heeled boots.

That was interesting, he thought, proceeding down the hall. *And what was all that about Dmitry being "on the warpath"?*

Sure enough, as he ventured further into the house he saw that in another room sat three men he vaguely knew as guys who worked for the organization—men Dmitry called upon when, as he put it, "things got dark." On the table were their phones, their car keys, their cigarettes. Their guns.

They responded to Sergei's greeting with the merest, almost reluctant incline of their heads and there was no warmth in their eyes, none at all. Sergei felt something in his stomach shift, a feeling of disquiet, and he wondered if it would be wiser to make his excuses, turn, and leave right now. And never come back.

But then from the back room he heard the call. "Sergei, is that you? Get your big Chechen arse in here right now." Sergei's Chechen arse wasn't big, but he recognized that tone in Dmitry's voice and knew it wasn't the time to argue.

"*Now!*" shouted Dmitry, although Sergei was already hurrying through.

"Yes, boss," he said. He wondered what was going on, eyes on Dmitry's screens, which were blank, monitors in sleep mode. That in itself was unusual. He braced himself for whatever came next.

"Did you close the studio?" asked Dmitry.

"Yes, Dmitry," replied Sergei cautiously. "All done as you asked."

"Yes, yes. Watch this," said Dmitry. Impatiently he waggled a mouse and tapped at the keyboard at the same time. As one the screens fired up, Dmitry keyed in a password. Now Sergei was looking at footage. He recognized where it had been taken, of course. The cam house. But as for what was happening . . .

"*Blyat*," he muttered in Russian. *No fucking way.*

Instead of watching a girl joylessly remove her clothes, what he saw was a man in a balaclava leering into the camera, baring his teeth, flipping the finger, and in the next instant hefting a baseball bat.

The picture died.

Another image, also the studio but a different room. Same guy, same smash-cut ending. Another room, another.

Dmitry's mouth was set. His color rose. "They attacked the studio last night," he seethed.

Sergei floundered. "But . . . I don't understand, Dmitry."

"They hit the wrong fucking studio."

CHAPTER 29

SHELLEY WOKE, RANG Lucy, told her about his fun night and that he'd be leaving shortly. Next he went downstairs into the quiet of the house, in search of the other two.

In the kitchen he found Gurney, still wearing his combat trousers and hoodie, head down over a bowl of cereal.

"You enjoy yourself last night, did you?" said Shelley from the doorway.

The Para looked up, milk spackling the stubble on his chin. "Felt good getting busy with the baseball bat," he grinned. "And good to see a few birds with their kit off."

Shelley nodded, thinking if he had a button that could call up a tactical napalm strike, he'd be pressing it and aiming the strike in Gurney's direction.

But there was no button. There was just the wild contradiction of an expensive designer kitchen and a paratrooper who couldn't eat cereal without getting it on his face. So instead he asked, "What's happened to the van?"

"Already taken care of. Me and Lloyd sorted it earlier."

Shelley nodded. "Right. Where is he now?"

Without looking up Gurney pointed outside.

Shelley found Bennett on the stones. Unlike Gurney he'd changed and now wore his suit. He stood with his hands in his pockets staring into space with a vacant expression that Shelley recognized from the previous night.

"Not zoning out on me again, are you?" said Shelley, and instantly regretted reminding the man of something he'd no doubt rather forget. "Look," he said, changing tack, "there was nothing you could have done differently last night. Don't take it bad."

"It was supposed to be my show and it was FUBAR, how else should I take it?" replied Bennett, sounding dismal.

Shelley wasn't sure about that. He was the guy that Susie had asked to look after Drake. If anybody was to blame it was him. Even so. "What are you doing now, then?"

"Waiting for Johnson to arrive."

"Then?"

"Then we're packing our shit and getting the fuck out of Dodge, Shelley. Suggest you do the same, my friend."

Shelley sighed. "Listen, mate, we used to have a thing back in the 22. 'Anti-fragile,' we called ourselves. You know what that means?"

"It means the worse shit gets the more efficient you are."

"Exactly. We're anti-fragile, blokes like you and me, but occasionally we need reminding of that fact."

Bennett nodded. "Cheers, Shelley, appreciate that."

"Things were bad last night."

"They don't get much worse."

"But we need to move on," Shelley told him. "There's no point in having a pity party about it all. We're all at fault for what happened. We all either did too much or didn't do enough. So right, yeah, we'll make plans to leave and let Guy Drake think about what he's done, like a naughty schoolboy. But in the meantime we need to be clever.

"Think about it, Bennett. Last night he told all and sundry his name. But you know what? He's the only one of us with an alibi. We need to work on making sure we can't be connected. You burned the van, did you?"

Bennett nodded. "It all went up. Bats, balaclavas, hooded tops."

Thinking about burning kit reminded Shelley of something that was bothering him. "While we're on the subject, how did the fires start? Did Drake have some kind of fuel with him?"

Bennett sighed. "I don't know. In the office I saw him with a bottle of water. Like a bottle of mineral water, you know? Only it obviously wasn't water, because the next thing I knew the fires started." He pulled off his glasses, his eyes looking tired and beady without their magnification, and pinched the bridge of his nose.

"We should have seen the signs."

"You *did* see the signs, Shelley, you were right all along."

"I'll do my gloating later," said Shelley. "Where is our glorious leader, by the way?"

"He's been in touch. He'll be here soon. Same with Johnson."

Shelley was in two minds about seeing Drake. There was no point in reading him the riot act, and yet on the other hand he wanted to look into his eyes and gauge how he felt about the events of the previous evening. He wanted to see shame, sorrow, apology.

He turned and went back inside the house in search of

caffeine. Things had changed, he knew. Not just the fuck-up of last night. Other things. He wasn't going to be tethered by some misplaced sense of duty to the Drakes. Fuck that. The mystery of Emma's death would have to remain just that.

Leave. Don't look back. That was the plan now.

CHAPTER 30

PARKED OUTSIDE THE block of flats that Corporal Adrian Johnson (ex–Parachute Regiment) called home was the only thing apart from his regiment and the men who had fought at his side that he had ever truly loved: his BMW 3 series, wrapped in matte metallic blue.

It was his pride and joy, that motor. He'd lowered it, as well as adding customized bodywork and a large sub-woofer in the rear—and when he wasn't calling it his "bimmer," he was referring to it with feminine pronouns and telling anyone who'd listen how he'd left a Porsche for dead the other day.

To make sure his pride and joy was never far from his sight, he always parked her in the space close to the entrance, the space reserved for disabled people and blue BMWs. And as he left his first-floor flat that morning and took the stairs to the car park below, he looked forward to seeing her, knowing that just to sink into her leather seats would help make him feel better about the situation at work: this ex-SAS guy Shelley coming on board.

It was because of him, *Shelley*—the word felt bitter in his mouth—that he'd missed the fun last night.

Fun? Oh yes. How did he know? He'd had a call that morning—James, not Lloyd, which was a bit weird, but anyway—only to be told that the lads had got tooled up and laid into Foxy Kittenz last night.

Bastards. Did it all without him. James and Lloyd—they got to see the cam girls, they got to rough people up, not him.

What's more, the raid on the Russkis' unit could potentially land him in a lot of trouble. The Russkis were going to think he had something to do with it. They might even think he was involved.

He'd been at home all night, having a curry and shagging Jane, who would back him up on it. If he saw the Russkis again he'd tell them that. Style it out. They were a bunch of clueless muppets anyway.

Johnson got down the stairs and exited the block, only to see some bloke leaning against his bimmer.

His immediate reaction was angry indignation. He was about to start forward and begin his day by administering a beating when he got a better look at the guy. He wore a turtle-neck sweater underneath a long dark woolen coat, and he held something in his lap, a piece of fabric. Johnson didn't recognize him but knew instantly that he was one of the Russkis.

Next he became aware of two more men, and swiveled to see them as they emerged from where they'd been standing, on the other side of the entranceway.

They were dressed similarly to their mate. Like sharks they moved in on their prey, boxing him in.

"What's going on?" said Johnson, turning back to the first guy.

In reply, the guy merely grinned and held up the piece of fabric he was holding. At first Johnson couldn't work out what it was, but then it hit him. He'd used them several times in the past. Mind you, he'd never worn one himself.

Oh shit.

It was a hood.

CHAPTER 31

THE LAST OF the fire engines had departed. Tendrils of smoke rose from the damp, blackened remains of the office units. The fire had spread from the first block, taken by wind and cost-cutting building work to gut two and a half neighboring buildings.

Detective Inspector Gary Phillips drew up to the scene and drained the last of a Starbucks. Looking around, he saw that early-bird workers had started to arrive for their day at the office, clambering out of cars and staring in shock at what once had been their place of work. Phillips, meanwhile, slammed his own car door shut and hoped he wouldn't have to go looking for the officer in charge. After all, it was Phillips who'd been called here, so it would be courteous not to make him—

"You DI Phillips?" came a voice from behind him. He turned to see a plainclothes who had peeled off from talking to one of the fire investigators.

"I am. What am I doing here?"

"I'm DS Steve Lawler, OIC," said the man. "I'm told you're in charge of an investigation involving some kind of online sex-worker setup, yes? Goes by the name of Foxy Kittenz?"

Phillips was indeed in charge of that investigation, and the name Foxy Kittenz had come up in connection with the Emma Drake case. In turn Foxy Kittenz had been linked to a much, much bigger fish.

All of which meant that he looked at the OIC with fresh interest. "I am, yes. Why?"

"Well, according to a girl who works here, this is your actual Foxy Kittenz," said the DS, waving an arm toward the first building. "Or was."

DI Phillips was confused. "Um, I don't think it is, mate. Or even was."

"Really? That's what it is according to this girl. She's a foxy kitten herself, she says, and she's making some pretty wild claims. The name Guy Drake has come up. And she's talking about a girl called Emma. Google says that could be Emma Drake."

Phillips had to admit there was something going on here. "Where is she, this girl?" he asked.

The DS indicated a car. "In there, being looked after by a WPC. Some guy, her boyfriend, I think, was badly beaten. He's in the hospital now."

"Beaten? So this is . . ."

"Arson? Oh yes, no doubt about it. This girl saw the lot. Four men in balaclavas and carrying baseball bats burst in last night, turfed out all the girls, beat up this guy, and then set fire to the place. Not necessarily in that order, by the sounds of things. They even left a battering ram behind."

"Good of them," said Phillips. He thanked Lawler and moved away, reaching for his phone. He had a call to make to his contact in MI5—a guy called Claridge who'd asked to be kept informed of any developments in the Emma Drake case.

CHAPTER 32

JOHNSON TRIED TO remain calm. He'd been bundled into the back of a van that was now on the move.

"I didn't have nothing to do with the raid," he said, his voice muffled by the hood. "I didn't even know it was happening. I was at home all night. You can ask my missus. I can tell you what we watched on telly. I had four tins of San Miguel and we ordered a curry. Fuck me, you can smell my farts if you think I'm making it up."

"They attacked us last night," came a voice. Russian, low and matter of fact.

"Yeah . . . but . . ." Johnson tried to grasp at straws but found there were no straws to grasp. "We can make it up. Come on, guys, we can talk about this."

"You are going to talk about it. Make no mistake about that."

And that was it. None of his questions or protestations were answered. Instead he was forced to sit in silence, hood on his head, his hands bound with a plastic cable tie.

His captors spoke in Russian, laughing occasionally. He wondered what they were saying, tried to make out words.

The only thing he caught was something that sounded like "kingsman."

There was a film called *Kingsman*. He'd seen it with Jane. Were they talking about that? Maybe he could engage them in conversation about *Kingsman*. There was a joke about anal sex. He'd laughed like a drain at that one. If only he knew the Russian for "anal sex." If only he knew any Russian at all.

Then the van shuddered to a halt. He heard the side doors open, then the rear doors. "Come," said the guy who'd stayed with him in the back, pulling him to his feet at the same time as he dragged off the hood.

They were outside now and Johnson recognized where he was immediately. A place he was never, ever going to bring his bimmer to for her service or MOT.

"I know this place. Why did you bother with the hood?"

But he knew the answer even as the words left his mouth. They wanted to unnerve him. Well, if they thought they were going to scare Johnson, they had another think coming, because ex-Paras don't scare easy.

Another of the big guys came to him. They grabbed him roughly under each armpit. "Oi!" he yelled as they hoisted him almost off his feet and half dragged him to the garage entrance.

On the other hand, who was he fucking kidding? He was absolutely terrified.

They dragged him through the reception area. There was no old man there today, just a woman who lifted the phone and pointedly looked in the opposite direction as he was dragged through the room to a door at the back and then into the corridor beyond. He expected them to pull him into an office but instead they went past, Johnson still held up by a Russian heavy on either side, half walking, half being dragged to another door.

"Machine Shop," read the name on the door, which was flung open, and Johnson was shoved inside so hard he lost his footing and fell painfully to the concrete floor. He stayed there for a moment or so to gather himself, and then raised his head to take stock of the welcoming committee.

There waiting for him was Dmitry, his beefy arms folded, with Sergei beside him, as well as the old guy, who sat close to a table on which was arranged a series of instruments: knives, saws, scalpels, a hand drill.

There was one other thing about the room—an extra terrifying detail. The plastic. It hung off the walls and lined the floor, clear plastic sheets.

Johnson was special forces. He'd seen all sorts of bad shit. He knew exactly what the plastic was for.

He looked pleadingly at Sergei, who had been his first point of contact in the organization, when he'd leapt at the chance of making easy money and getting one over on Shelley at the same time.

But Sergei's eyes swiveled away, and Johnson recognized that look: *Things are out of my hands. You're on your own, mate.*

"Mr. Johnson," said Dmitry breezily, "you and I need to have a little chat."

Johnson was shoved into the chair, a hand on his head. His two companions busied themselves at his hands and feet. Working fast, they cable-tied his ankles to the legs of the chair, his wrists to struts behind.

He looked up to see a CCTV camera watching over him, its green light blinking. He gazed into the lens and was wondering whether he should call for help when Dmitry said, "No sound, I'm afraid, Corporal. *Dedushka* doesn't mind though, he likes silent movies."

Dedushka? Dedushka? Wasn't that a Kate Bush song? Johnson's eyes skittered. The evil old guy, the one watching TV last time he was here, levered himself from his chair. One of the men moved forward, perhaps to help, but the old guy warded him off with an angry flick of his hand. And then, bent a little, the old man moved to the table on which the instruments had been laid. Torture instruments.

"You won't need those," whined Johnson. "I'll tell you everything you need to know. Ask, just ask."

His gaze went to Dmitry, who stood beside Sergei. Did he imagine it, or did the two of them look almost uncomfortable? Johnson experienced a brief surge of hope as it struck him that this wasn't the way these guys wanted to conduct their business. They were professionals, not sadists. They weren't like this evil old geezer.

"It is Grandfather," Dmitry told him, reading his mind. "He does insist on having his fun. And of course, we are who we are, we have a reputation to uphold." He raised his voice. "Isn't that right, *Dedushka?*"

The old man turned, a silvery line of saliva tracing its way down his chin. He was ninety if he was a day, this old boy. When his hand reached to the table it shook like an autumn leaf.

But he understood everything Dmitry was saying. He understood exactly what was required of him. The instrument he had selected was a straight razor and as he opened it and began to advance on Johnson, something almost supernatural happened: his hand ceased to tremble.

"Where would you like to start, Grandfather?" asked Dmitry. He shot Johnson an almost sympathetic look. Like a parent at the dentist's. *Be brave, it'll all be over soon.*

"The nipples," croaked Grandfather. "I always start with the nipples. That way they know we mean business."

"Very good, Grandfather. You may begin with the nipples." He gestured and one of the heavies took a kitchen knife from the table, moved forward and used it to slice the front of Johnson's T-shirt, parting it like a waistcoat. "Will he lose consciousness, do you think?" asked Dmitry.

"Not yet, not yet," replied Grandfather. Stepping in front of Johnson he squinted to get the measure of his subject and raised the straight razor. His other hand, steady as a rock, went to Johnson's chest to tauten the skin, ready for the first incision.

"Good, good," said Dmitry, "we need him to talk."

"Oh, he will talk," said Grandfather.

Light ran along the blade of the razor as it slashed downward.

And indeed, Johnson talked. He talked plenty. When the screaming was over.

CHAPTER 33

SHELLEY WAS STILL waiting for Johnson and Drake to arrive when his phone went. It was Claridge.

"Hello, mate," said Shelley.

"Shelley," replied Claridge. But the word was drawn out, schoolmasterly. "And where might you be at this very moment in time?"

"Oh, come on. Ask me no questions and I'll tell you no lies."

"Well, I have to say that I'd much rather I asked you questions and then you told me no lies. How about we try that? Or how about if you get in touch with me asking for help in the Emma Drake death, and I give you that help, then that in turn entitles me to hear the truth from you?"

"It's better for you if you don't."

At the other end of the line, Claridge sighed long and hard, a sigh of the eternally downtrodden, like an end-of-her-tether mother-of-three. "You're at Drake's house," he said.

Shelley couldn't help himself. He looked left and right, even up. "How did you know?"

"I'm MI5, Shelley, I get to know these things without even breaking a sweat. Do you know what else I know?"

"Go on . . ."

"Some people attacked a building used by an outfit called Foxy Kittenz last night. I'm assuming you would know something about that, especially as it has been reported by an eyewitness that one of the men doing the attacking—balaclavas, Shelley, baseball bats, I really thought this sort of thing was beneath you—was none other than Guy Drake. What do you have to tell me about that?"

"Nothing," said Shelley coolly. "Don't know what you're talking about."

"No, I didn't think you'd have anything to do with it, my reasoning based mainly on the fact that if you had been involved then you would have hit the right building."

Shelley's blood chilled. "What do you mean?" he asked.

"Foxy Kittenz operates two units. We believe that Emma Drake took her life in the other one, closer to where she was living, closer to where she was found, closer to the dealers she used. You hit—sorry, I mean whoever it was that did the hitting hit—the wrong place."

To take the call Shelley had wandered over to a far edge of the driveway close to the border of the lawn. Standing there, he raised his eyes to the heavens and thought of the poor beaten guy cowering on the tarmac, the girls thrown into the street. Drake would say it didn't matter, that they'd struck out at Foxy Kittenz, and so what if the wrong building was hit and the wrong guy got beaten.

Shelley knew one thing for sure. It would have mattered to Emma.

"Now, there's something else," continued Claridge. "Something that I'm afraid makes this rather more serious than it already is."

That brought Shelley back down to earth. "What?"

"Detective Inspector Phillips has been keeping me up to date on the investigation, parts of which have been handed over to us at MI5. A colleague of mine has made the connection between the Foxy Kittenz enterprise and a section of the Chechen Mafia operating in London. It seems that Foxy Kittenz is one of their many businesses."

Shelley swallowed. "Right," he said.

"You know these people," said Claridge. And yes, it was a statement, not a question. "You have caused trouble for these people in the past." Again, a simple statement of fact.

"Afghanistan, 2004," said Shelley. "We took down one of their supply lines."

"There have been other occasions but yes, that's probably the one that caused them most hurt."

"So I'm messing with dangerous people," said Shelley. "You're right, I've done it before."

"The difference is that last time you messed with the Chechen Mafia you did it with the SAS and Her Majesty's Armed Forces at your back," said Claridge. "This time you're on your own."

CHAPTER 34

WHEN DRAKE ARRIVED home shortly afterward, they stepped out to greet him. Bennett and Gurney: well, they no doubt had loose ends to tie up before they upped and got the fuck out of Dodge. Shelley, on the other hand? At first he'd been telling himself that he wanted to supervise the clean-up operation, or that he wanted to look into Drake's eyes and see if he was at all ashamed by his behavior last night.

But he'd had second thoughts about all of that. In the meantime he'd realized that what he most wanted to do was see Susie. It was her with whom he needed to make his peace.

So his heart sank when Drake's Jaguar swept into the drive and Susie was not in the passenger seat. Drake peered balefully at the three men through his windshield, and he appeared to take a deep breath before letting himself out of the car to face them.

There they stood, Shelley, Bennett, and Gurney, looking like the housekeeping staff in a period drama, and for a moment or so Drake faced them in silence, unspoken recollections of the previous night passing between them.

But no shame. No apology.

That's it. I'm going, thought Shelley. *I'm out of here.*

"I don't think much of my welcoming committee," said Drake without humor. He turned his attention to Shelley. "Surprised to find you here. I thought you'd have gone by now, taken your conscience and cleared off to give your halo a polish."

He and Shelley stared at one another, as though Drake was daring him to come back on the halo comment, but Shelley ignored the jibe. *Laugh it up, fat boy. I'm not making excuses for you anymore.*

"Where's Johnson?" asked Drake, breaking the stare and talking to Bennett.

"Due any minute," said Bennett. He thrust back his shoulders and took on the mantle of officer in charge. "We need to get rid of anything that connects us with last night."

"You think the police are going to come knocking?" said Drake, and Shelley had to restrain himself from letting out a gasp of frustration. What planet was this bloke on?

"Yes," replied Bennett with the kind of patience and calm that Shelley feared he himself couldn't possibly muster, "we anticipate the police getting involved at some point."

"Oh yeah, and who told you that?" growled Drake. "Was that our friendly local alarmist there?" He tilted his chin at Shelley.

Bennett's face stayed neutral but his eyes found Shelley, who saw the silent apology there. "The fire spread," explained Bennett. "An eyewitness heard the name 'Drake' being shouted. It seems likely they'll come and ask questions. It's an outcome we anticipated and prepared for. That's why you have an alibi."

Drake was about to say something when his phone rang. He fished it out of his blazer pocket, looked at the screen. "Number withheld."

"Don't answer it," said Bennett quickly, but Drake shot him a look.

"Don't be soft, man," he said, and lifted the phone to his ear. "Hello," he barked, every inch the gruff northern businessman, not prepared to take shit from anybody. "Yes," he continued, "this is Guy Drake." He paused. "Wait a second," he said, "before I say another word, why don't you tell me who *you* are?" And then he activated the speaker and placed the smartphone on the bonnet of the Jaguar.

"Who am I?" said the voice, and Shelley knew at once they were in big trouble because there was no doubt about it: the guy was a Russian, which meant he was probably a Chechen. "I am somebody that you have upset. You have disrupted my business and cost me money."

"That was the idea, pal," said Drake. Trying to stop him from saying anything incriminating or inflammatory, Shelley drew his finger across his throat, shaking his head at the same time, but of course, Drake being Drake, he plowed on. "You got what was coming to you. Believe you me, you can count yourself lucky."

"Wait. Am I on speakerphone, Mr. Drake? Please, introduce me to your friends listening. Perhaps these are the same men who helped you to beat up my employee and scare off my girls? Perhaps feeling very pleased with themselves. Are they as brave without their masks and bats, Mr. Drake?"

Shelley experienced an odd sensation. He felt ashamed of himself.

"Gentlemen, that was good work you did smashing that equipment," continued the caller, "and if ever I need some equipment smashing you can be sure I'll call upon your services. But you see, there's a snag. You now need to pay for all the damage you caused."

Drake snorted as though to say, *You should be so lucky*, but the Chechen continued, "I would like twenty million please. Pay this money straightaway with no arguments and there will be no more bloodshed."

Drake's chewing habit always became more pronounced in times of high drama, and his jaw now moved rhythmically, like a man battling with gristle. For a moment Shelley wondered if he might simply blow his top there and then. To his credit, he maintained composure.

"Listen, my friend, I don't know who you are, or who you fucking *think* you are, but last night was about teaching you a lesson, not the beginning of a beautiful new relationship, you get me? And I can tell you this much. Those men in the balaclavas? You've got them to thank for the fact that we didn't go much, much further. What's more, your lad who works there has got them to thank for the fact that it's only a visit to the hospital he needs, and not one to the graveyard. Now I'm going to pretend I didn't just hear your pathetic blackmail attempt and tell you to fuck right off."

There was a pause. It was as though the Chechen decided to try again. "Mr. Drake, my name is Dmitry and I work for people whose wealth and influence equals yours. But the difference between them and you is the way in which they have acquired that wealth and gained that influence. You think that you have gone over to the other side, yes? That you have become a bad man? And you have, because it's a bad thing you did, paying men in balaclavas to scare girls with baseball bats. But you probably think it doesn't matter, because you think that your bad is a good-guy kind of bad, and anyway your wealth and influence will save you from your British justice system, and it probably will, because that is the way the world works. Your wealth and your influence can indeed save you from jail.

"But it will not save you from us, Mr. Drake. Those feeble men you have, ex-soldiers, old men thrown out of the army. Maybe they are tough guys who tell you they can keep you safe. But they can't. Really they can't, Mr. Drake. All I have to do is give the order. And we won't just kill you, Mr. Drake, we'll take you somewhere, and we'll make you watch as we hurt and kill your loved ones, and then we'll kill you, and we'll do it slowly, over a period not of days or weeks, but of months."

Shelley's mind raced. This guy, how come he was telling them his name? More to the point, how did he know that Drake's men were ex-military? A lucky guess, perhaps? Or something else?

"Tell you what, mate," said Drake. His voice was rising. His cheeks had reddened. "You can fucking do one. Russian Mafia, is it? Something like that? You're a fucking joke. Something out of a bad Sylvester Stallone movie. I tell you what, mate. You send your fellas here. Send as many as you like. I'll be waiting. And I'll come back at you twice as hard with everything I've got—and that's everything I've got within the law *and* outside it, which is a lot more than you can muster, I promise you that. You think I'm underestimating you, do you? You fucking turkey. I'll fucking show you how we do things in my country."

There was a pause. Shelley wondered about the temperament of this man Dmitry. Was he going to lose it?

No. "Then let the battle commence," said Dmitry.

The line went dead.

The sound of a car engine made all four men look in the direction of the front gates. They could see through the wrought iron to the approach road beyond.

About two hundred yards away was a metallic-blue BMW, getting nearer.

CHAPTER 35

"THAT'S JOHNSON," SAID Bennett.

"Wait," said Shelley. He'd seen what Bennett and Gurney had not. A short way behind the blue BMW was a black Range Rover.

"Are either of you armed?" said Shelley to Bennett and Gurney. In reply Bennett flapped open his jacket to reveal the grip of a pistol. Gurney drew his own Glock and held it loosely at his side.

"What are you thinking, Shelley?" said Bennett. He peered into the distance, watching the strange procession as it drew closer.

"I'm thinking that they got to Johnson," said Shelley. "I'm thinking that's how this bloke Dmitry got Guy's number and how come he knows we're ex-military and how many of us there are. Guy," he said without looking at Drake, his eyes fixed on the oncoming cars, "are those gates the ones we installed when I was last here?"

"Aye, they are, more or less. Why do you ask?"

"I chose them myself. They're built to withstand a car ramming into them."

The BMW wasn't slowing. The gap to the Range Rover behind was widening fast. In fact, the Range Rover had pulled to a stop. The two front doors opened and its occupants climbed out. Shelley saw the dim shapes of men wearing dark sunglasses and overcoats. Waiting, watching.

That made up his mind. "Okay," he said, "take cover. Now." There wasn't time to run for the house; they'd be caught out in the open. Instead all four of them crouched behind the Jag. Gurney held his Glock two-handed across the bonnet. Bennett, Shelley, and Drake watched the BMW come closer, on an inevitable collision course with the gates. In the driving seat was the figure of a short guy with cropped hair.

"Rigged to blow, you think?" said Bennett to Shelley, his voice loud over the revving engine of the BMW. Never taking his eyes off the oncoming car.

And then they had their answer as the BMW crashed into the gates with a whump followed by a shriek of traumatized metal like a steam engine screeching to a stop.

A strange silence fell. Shelley braced himself for an explosion.

It never came.

Over the way, smoke issued from the crashed car. The front gates had buckled but not broken; they'd done their job.

Now Shelley's eyes went to the two men and their Range Rover. They stood watching. For what reason, Shelley wasn't sure: wanting to be seen, making their presence felt, perhaps?

Either way, it was as though they decided *job done*, and one of them raised his hand in a wave that could almost be interpreted as friendly before the two of them climbed back into the Range Rover. Still behind the Jag, the four men watched as the Range Rover performed a three-point turn and then drove away.

"Wait," counseled Shelley. "It could have a delayed fuse."

Through a windshield cracked by the accident they could make out the figure of the driver. They saw blood.

"And what about Johnson?" asked Drake harshly.

"He's dead," replied Shelley bluntly. "And if he isn't dead now then he will be when the car blows."

"*If* the car blows," said Bennett.

"Which is what we're waiting to find out," growled Shelley.

Bennett took a deep breath and peered over the bonnet. "Well," he said, "today's as good a day as any." He looked at Shelley, who knew exactly what he meant, and drew his Glock from his shoulder holster. Then, with his sidearm held low, he rose from cover and jogged across to the entranceway.

Beside the main gate was a smaller pedestrian access, untouched by the accident. Bennett's fingers tapped out a code, the gate clicked and swung open. A second later he was on the other side of the twisted metal.

They watched, breath held, as Bennett opened the driver's door, peered inside, and then withdrew. Looking over to them on the driveway, he gave a short but definitive shake of his head. Next he held up a hand—*wait there*—and they saw him hunker down to check the underside of the car and then jog around it, doing the same on the other side.

He cupped his hands to his mouth, calling, "Clear," and in seconds they had joined him at the BMW.

"Christ," said Drake, turning away with his hand over his mouth. The businessman's stomach heaved, and for a second

Shelley thought he was going to lose his Connaught breakfast right there. Even Bennett had paled.

What they saw was mutilation.

Johnson had been cut, maybe hundreds of times. His hands, taped to the steering wheel, were bloody stumps, fingers snipped off. In the well of the car, Shelley saw the same, toes removed, bloodied feet duct-taped to a breeze-block. His eyelids had been taken, his ears, nose, and lips too.

Further down, his T-shirt had been sliced open. A blood-encrusted torso was crisscrossed with knife cuts. In places entire sections of flesh had been removed, exposing muscle and fat beneath, like a grotesque parody of a medical illustration.

As a final indignity, his Para tattoo had been peeled off. The Chechens had stapled it to his forehead.

"Upside down," growled Gurney as they all stood there, eyes ranging over the torn body of Johnson. "They did it upside down."

"All right," said Bennett. "This means we're under attack." He reached for Drake. "Sir, we'd better get you in—"

But then came another sound. More engines. And they looked up to see a set of vehicles enter the approach road at the far end. Each man tensed, ready to make a run for it, back into the house, Shelley already thinking of the SIG Sauer that he kept hidden in the Saab and wondering if he could reach it in time, when he realized that the new arrivals were police vehicles.

"Oh Jesus," said Shelley. "Oh Jesus, I know what they're doing. Guy," he said to Drake. "Where was Susie going today?"

There were three cop vehicles, two vans and a car. One of

the vans had screeched to a halt, blocking the road at the far end. Shelley saw the words "Armed Response Unit."

The cops inside must have spotted them and seen the crashed car. On went the lights. A siren howled.

"What?" said Guy.

"Where's she going?" repeated Shelley, pulling out his phone.

"I don't know. A spa," said Drake, spiky, as if he couldn't believe Shelley needed to know shit like that at a time like this.

"Fuck's sake, don't you see? They'll be going after her. Which spa?"

Drake's face dropped. "I don't know!" he wailed. "Some spa . . ."

Speed-dialing Lucy. Turning to make his way back through the pedestrian gate. Trying to buy himself time. "Where, for fuck's sake?" he called back over his shoulder. "Which spa?"

"I don't know . . . someplace in Hampstead. She always goes. Bennett, you were there—what spa did she say?"

"I'm sorry, sir, I can't remember."

"Jesus," said Shelley. "Think, Guy, think."

Cop cars approaching as Lucy picked up, saying, "Hello, sweetheart, is everything all right?"

"Listen fast," said Shelley. "You've got to get to a Hampstead spa. Don't know the name." He threw a look at Drake just in case inspiration had struck, but no. "I'm sorry, Luce, you'll just have to find it yourself."

"Roger that. What's the situation?" said Lucy. And God bless her, God bless Lucy for being alert and on it.

"It's Susie Drake," explained Shelley. "You've got to reach her, Lucy."

"Before . . .?"

"Before a bunch of Russians do. Chechens, to be precise. The bleedin' Chechen Mafia."

Behind him the police cars had screeched to a halt. Armed cops burst out. He heard commands: "Freeze! Hands on your heads!" and then to him, "You with the phone! Drop the phone! Drop it now! Put your hands on your head!"

"Jesus, Shelley," said Lucy on the other end of the line, "what's going on?"

"Gotta go, sweetheart," Shelley told her. "Be lucky, won't you?"

He did as he was told and dropped the phone.

CHAPTER 36

OKAY, THOUGHT LUCY. *A spa in Hampstead.* She was driving and web-searching at the same time, snarled up in enough London traffic to do the two things simultaneously. *Spa in Hampstead, spa in Hampstead* . . . She didn't like the look of the first one produced by the search, decided to leave it to last.

Where, though? Where?

"Right," she said to herself, "imagine that you're the fabulously wealthy and gorgeous wife of a millionaire. But you're a down-to-earth, feet-on-the-ground type. Where do you go?"

They had them in the basements of hotels, didn't they? But Lucy knew that Susie had stayed overnight at the Connaught and she wasn't using whatever facilities they had there; she'd chosen Hampstead. So the chances were that it was a favorite haunt. Somewhere she'd been going for years.

Not this one, then—"Newly opened." Which left just two more that Lucy considered possibilities. "Right," she said, "we'll try this one first."

A short drive later and she was walking into number one on her list. "Hello, can you tell me if you have a customer by the name of Susie Drake here today?" she asked the over-tanned, perfectly primped, flawlessly made-up girl behind the counter.

"Um . . ." started the girl. She'd opened a book and put one exquisitely manicured fingernail to the page before she had second thoughts. "We don't usually give away those kind of details," she said.

Lucy smiled even more sweetly. "It's really very important that I speak to Susie Drake," she said. "It's a matter of life and death. Really very important indeed. If she's here, and I leave here without giving her the message, and she finds out that's happened, then . . ."

"Oh, she's not here," said the girl, just wanting the lecture to end.

Lucy was already out of the door.

Which left number two: Hampstead Health & Beauty. According to the internet this one had made the news a couple of years ago. A disabled customer had complained about the lack of facilities, and then posted the spa's dismissive response on Twitter. As a result, the spa had been the subject of a minor Twitterstorm and gained temporary notoriety as a result.

It was on the outskirts of Hampstead and a little bigger than the first. Lucy had left it until second because there was something new-looking about it, but now, reading the website in a little more depth, she saw that it was an established business that had relocated.

Yes, this could be the place. She dearly hoped it was. If not then she was perilously short on ideas.

She took a look around the small car park before realizing she hadn't the foggiest what she was supposed to be looking for anyway: BMWs, Mercedes, a Porsche. Normal rich-person's status symbols. None of them with a flashing sign on top saying "I belong to Susie Drake."

Right, she told herself. *Let's go.* Before leaving home she'd retrieved her SIG from the chimney breast where it lived, out of sight but available if needed, and holstered it inside the waistband of the jeans she was wearing, pulling a thick cable-knit turtleneck sweater over the top. She reached to the weapon now, feeling the butt against the palm of her hand and taking reassurance from it as she climbed out of her Mini and strode toward the spa building.

The entranceway was flanked by two perfectly trimmed potted conifers in brushed-metal vases. The kind of landscaping that said money. Lucy stepped in, wishing she'd spent a little more time on her appearance before she'd left the house; pleased, at the very least, that her jeans were cut right and the sweater she wore was expensive.

Sure enough, the reception area had the scent of luxury. Behind the desk stood—not sat, *stood*—a receptionist, while on a sofa nearby sat a woman wearing dark glasses and tailored clothes, a phone to her ear.

As Lucy approached the desk the receptionist looked up, and Lucy was about to speak when from the corner of her eye she saw that the sofa woman was looking at her. Not *at her*. Her face wasn't turned Lucy's way. But from the angle Lucy could just see behind the huge shades she wore and the woman's eyes were glued on Lucy.

It was probably nothing, but it was enough to make Lucy change her plan of action.

"Hi," smiled the receptionist, who in a place this swanky was probably called a "greeter." Lucy checked hard for signs the greeter thought she wasn't the right type to be hanging around the reception area of Hampstead Health & Beauty, but either she made the grade or the receptionist was a courtesy Jedi. "How can I help you?"

"I was hoping to have a look around," said Lucy.

The greeter's face fell. "Oh," she said, stitching on a sympathetic look and indicating the woman who was on her phone, hidden behind glasses, "this lady is also waiting for a tour. Did you want—"

"Well, I was hoping I might just have a quick look around by myself."

"Ah, it's not really our—"

"Look," said Lucy, "the truth is that a friend of mine has already had the grand tour and she was totally impressed, and I'm pretty sure that it's a done deal that we'll be joining, and—"

The greeter's smile froze just a little. "You *apply* for membership."

"Sorry, yes, that's what I meant," amended Lucy, who was amused to hear that her own voice had taken on posh tones. "Applying for membership is exactly what I meant. But prior to us doing that I need to check . . . Well, you see, my daughter is visually impaired and I need to make sure she'll be able to use the facilities."

Now the greeter's face really did freeze. Lucy could see that she was being assessed. Was this a joke? Some kind of test?

Lucy kept it innocent, played it cool. "It's really just the quickest look that I need to have."

Lucy saw the greeter's eyes travel over her shoulder. She

sneaked a look behind her to see that the sofa woman was no longer paying attention. Or, at least, none that she showed, continuing to listen and occasionally speak into her phone. She had a London accent, a bit cockney. Not Russian. That was good.

With no objection raised there, the greeter evidently thought it was safe to wave Lucy through, behaving as though the outcome were never in doubt. "Of course. Please do make sure, but I think you'll find everything is in order."

"I'm sure. I'm sure it is," said Lucy. She took a door, exiting the reception area and leaving the two women behind.

Back here was the same restful piped music that had been playing in the entrance area, but with added whale noises to boot. Lucy hurried along a corridor, past doors marked "Treatment Suite One" and "Treatment Suite Two," knowing that Susie Drake could well be in one of those but wanting to try a more communal area first. *A changing room, perhaps? Do they have a pool? They must have a pool.*

In fact, here it was at the end of the corridor: a square of shimmering light visible through the door.

She opened the door. The pool was empty. *Right, changing rooms. Where are the bloody changing rooms?* She took a left along the corridor, opaque glass to her right, swimming pool on the other side.

At the end was yet another door: "Changing Facilities." In she went.

And sitting in there, toweling her wet hair, was a woman Lucy thought she recognized . . .

"Susie Drake?"

CHAPTER 37

SUSIE DRAKE DID not stop toweling her hair, but inclined her head to regard Lucy.

"You're not a reporter, are you?" she said, scrunching the last of the damp from the ends of her hair.

"I'm not a reporter if you're Susie Drake."

"And if I'm Susie Drake then who are you?" She folded the towel quickly, laid it down beside her.

"I'm Lucy Shelley. Shelley's wife."

Susie Drake placed her hands on the bench on either side of her and looked long and hard at Lucy, as though assessing her. For a mad moment Lucy felt like a character in an old film, a nanny sent by the agency, coolly appraised by the lady of the house.

The feeling was quickly followed by the realization that Susie Drake knew Shelley well, or at least had known him well at one time, yet had never seen Lucy (unless she'd noticed her at Emma's funeral, which was unlikely), and had probably been curious about her, this mythical fiancée that Shelley had been saving up to marry.

"How do I know you are who you say you are?" asked Susie.

Lucy told Susie everything she knew.

"Okay, then," said Susie. "Years ago, Shelley and I used to have what he called a code phrase. Do you know the code phrase?"

"What if I don't know the code phrase?"

"Maybe I won't hold it against you."

"Okay, I'll try one. Be lucky."

"That'll do," said Susie. "So, you're Lucy. You were in the SAS, too."

Lucy nodded.

"I didn't know the SAS took women."

"They don't, officially. I came in the back door, via the SRR, the Special Reconnaissance Regiment. They put me and Shelley together, and that was it. Love among the black ops."

"You were in the same unit, weren't you?" said Susie.

"Well, the same 'patrol,' they call it: me, Shelley, and another guy."

"And you fell in love with Shelley?"

"Yes," said Lucy, "I guess I did."

"You're younger than he is."

Not sure how to take that, Lucy replied, "Yeah, but only by five years. Just that he's got the grumpy-old-man thing going on." There was a pause during which Lucy wondered if she'd just been disloyal. "The *sexy*-grumpy-old-man thing," she amended. And then she wondered if she'd put her foot in it, given that Susie was of course considerably younger than Guy Drake, who, by all accounts, was properly grumpy, not just Shelley-grumpy, and could not by any stretch of the imagination be described as sexy.

"Would you have fallen in love, do you think, if

you hadn't been thrown together in these high-pressure situations?"

Already slightly flustered, Lucy was taken aback afresh. Not just because the line of questioning was so personal but because she'd occasionally wondered the same herself, and what she told Susie Drake now was the same conclusion she'd previously come to. "I would have fallen in love with Shelley whatever the circumstances," she said. "He's straight up, full of truth. The most honorable person I've ever met. He's the kind of guy who changes your life without even meaning to. Doesn't know he's done it. Wouldn't even know *how* he's done it if you told him. That's who he is."

The way Susie Drake nodded, combined with a look of complete understanding, sent a shudder of momentary jealousy running through Lucy that she damped down quickly, changing the subject. "And lucky for you he's on your side. He's asked me to come here. He thinks that you might be a target."

Susie blanched. "Really? A target for what?"

"Would you believe me if I told you it was Chechen gangsters?"

Susie stared at her for a moment as her mouth tried to form words—words like "how?" and "what?" and "why?"

"Honestly, I don't have many more details than that. But when Shelley rings me up and tells me to find you—I didn't even know which spa you were at, by the way—I know it's got to be pretty serious, so here I am."

"This is Guy, isn't it? He's got us into trouble?"

"Again, this is stuff for later. We have to get going."

"Then step outside, let me get changed. I can see you in reception."

"Sure," said Lucy and turned to leave.

As she stepped through the door she almost bumped into the woman from reception, who stood with a spa representative. The rep stopped her tour mid-flow, excusing herself to speak to Lucy. "I gather you were ensuring that our disabled facilities are up to scratch?" she asked, with the same polite but mildly suspicious smile worn by her colleague.

"And they are," said Lucy, "I'm very impressed indeed. You can be sure that my friend and I will be submitting our applications soon."

"Well, I very much look forward to receiving them," smiled the rep.

Lucy turned to the sofa woman. "You're going to love it," she beamed. "The pool is absolutely to die for."

"Great, I love what I've seen so far, at least," said the woman. When she turned, Lucy noticed there was something odd about her right arm. It hung at a strange angle so that it looked as though she were carrying something underneath it, even though she wasn't. Lucy looked from the arm to the woman again. The sunglasses gave nothing away. The mouth was set. Her hair was well cut but the gold hoop earrings she wore were a little downmarket.

Their eyes met, and something unreadable passed between them, a moment that was broken when Lucy smiled and turned away. As she walked around the corner, she heard the rep start up again, like a recording that had been temporarily paused: "Excellent. Now, if you'd like to step this way, I shall show you our changing facilities . . . ."

Lucy returned to front of house and took a seat in reception, having repeated her glowing report to the greeter and told a story about bumping into a friend in the changing room. "We've arranged to go for a coffee together," she said. "Would it be okay if I wait here?"

"Of course," said the greeter and smiled. The woman's eyes flicked to the entranceway, and when Lucy turned her head she saw that a dark Range Rover had arrived and was backing into a car park space.

Nothing suspicious about that, she thought. *Just a Range Rover. Millions of them around.*

CHAPTER 38

HARDENED COPS HAD lost their lunch. Scene of crime units had been summoned. Uniformed officers looked pale and drawn as they busied themselves setting up a perimeter and trying not to look at the savaged corpse in the BMW.

In the meantime, Detective Inspector Phillips had arrived. He and Drake were acquainted; the two of them had talked during the Emma investigation, while Shelley, of course, had spoken to DI Phillips on the day of the aborted brainstorming session. That initial contact won them a little more courtesy than they otherwise might have expected, and so far Phillips had treated them all as though they were civilians in receipt of a terrible shock, their friend and colleague Adrian Johnson brutally murdered, and in turn they'd done their best to play up to it, but the pretense wouldn't last forever. Phillips was already beginning to lose patience.

"You had nothing to do with torching the unit last night. That's what you're telling me?" His question was aimed at all four men.

"I don't even know what you're talking about, mate," replied Shelley.

"If it's quite all right with you, lad, I'll wait until my lawyer arrives," said Drake, who as far as Shelley knew hadn't even called his lawyer.

They sat on stools at the center island in the kitchen. Gurney had made coffee. "Here's what I think, officer," offered Bennett, with a face commendably devoid of expression. "Whoever did this believes that Mr. Drake was somehow responsible for last night's fire, and they killed our friend in retribution."

Phillips shook his head at the insult to his intelligence, not even bothering to respond. "Wait there," he said. A uniform had appeared in the doorway and Phillips walked over to him, keeping an eye on the quartet at the kitchen island who in turn watched him as he bent to hear his officer's news and then returned and retook his place at the island. "Somebody claiming to be a neighbor reported men with guns, which is why we sent the armed response. Which of your neighbors has a Russian accent, Mr. Drake?"

"Well, I'm quite sure I don't know all my neighbors, lad," said Drake. "You'll have to do a door-to-door, would be my recommendation."

"Well, yes, we might well have to do that," said Phillips, leaning forward and putting his elbows on the countertop. "But you know what I think? I think that if we did do a door-to-door, then it would turn up the fact that none of your neighbors have Russian accents."

"Right, I'm getting sick of this. You." He pointed a finger at Shelley. "I want a word with you alone."

"Hey," said Drake, rising at the same time as Shelley, indignant. "This is my house."

"This is my crime scene," said DI Phillips, "and I want a word with a witness. You would have no vested interest in interfering with that, would you, sir? I mean, I'm not misjudging you, am I?"

Reluctantly, Drake sat down. Shelley followed Phillips out of the kitchen and into the entrance hall.

"Chechen Mafia," said Detective Inspector Phillips simply. "Wait." He held up a finger. "Don't give me any bullshit. Because I'm the one who tells Claridge what he tells you, do you understand?"

"You can ask Claridge," said Shelley. "He called me only an hour ago."

"That's the first you heard of Chechen Mafia."

"Yes," said Shelley.

"Doesn't mean to say you're in the clear for last night," said Phillips. "Perhaps you're just a bunch of fuckwits who decided to take on the Mafia by mistake. A bunch of fuckwits who hit the wrong building. Are you? Are you those fuckwits?"

Shelley looked past his shoulder and into the kitchen, where Bennett, Gurney, and Drake still sat, unable to hear what was going on but watching all the same.

Are we? thought Shelley. *Are we really that stupid?*

He looked at Gurney. Bennett. Drake.

Are we really that stupid?

He wondered how Lucy was getting on.

CHAPTER 39

SO, THAT WAS *Lucy Shelley*, thought Susie Drake, motionless on the changing room's polished-ash bench in the wake of the other woman's departure. The famous Lucy Shelley.

And then, with a shudder of something that was partly regret and partly desire, she remembered the kiss, a thank-you-for-your-help-today kiss that had become something greater—when, for the briefest moment, David almost hadn't pulled away.

"I'm sorry," he'd said at the same time as she was saying the same thing. They'd both reddened. Both surprised and yet not surprised that their sort-of flirtation had been allowed to flower despite the stable base of her rock-solid marriage and his forthcoming one.

And that had been it. One time only.

Still, though. She'd thought about it. She'd lain awake at night thinking about it, thanking God that neither Emma nor Guy, or anybody else for that matter, had blundered into the kitchen and seen them. Thanking God that it had not developed.

Thinking about it developing.

How did he feel? She'd never asked him. They had never discussed the kiss; they'd pretended it never happened. It didn't matter, though, because although nothing was said, the knowledge still existed between them. It was just . . . *there*.

Then had come the kidnapping attempt, and he'd announced he was leaving.

She'd been to see him. "I lost concentration," he told her. He held her gaze and they both knew what he meant, and why. They both knew that his position with the family had been compromised.

"You saved our lives," she told him, just as she knew Emma had.

"I was lucky," he replied. "But in my job, you don't rely on luck. It's about planning and forethought. Anticipation. That's what I lost. I've been distracted."

"What about if I don't want you to go?" she heard herself say.

"It's better that I go," he insisted. "It's better all round if I go."

She hated herself for what she said next: "Even if it means letting Emma down?"

"I've already let Emma down," he said. "Emma. You. Lucy."

And that was the only time he had, directly or indirectly, referred to what happened between them. The only time either of them had.

So to see—to actually *meet*—Lucy Shelley. No surprise, her heart was thudding heavily in her chest. Her palms were wet, nothing to do with the pool. Should she have felt anything? she wondered. Should she read any significance into the fact that David had sent Lucy here?

No, don't be ridiculous, Susie. The only thing to read into Lucy being here was that the situation was serious. That's all there was to it. Now was the time to stop daydreaming about a brief, stolen kiss that happened over a decade ago and time to start getting dressed and doing as Lucy said: getting the hell out of there.

Just then the door to the changing room opened and in came one of the smartly dressed spa staff, a really nice woman who Susie recognized as Judith—she gave great massages.

Behind Judith came a well-dressed woman who wore a pair of dark sunglasses—incongruous, even for Hampstead. Judith was telling her about the benefits of membership, nay, the *joys* of membership, and the woman was smiling and nodding as though hanging on every word. Even so, Susie got the distinct impression that the woman was less interested in Judith and more interested in her.

Susie stood up, smiling at the two women, and moved over to her locker. She wished she was wearing her contact lenses or spectacles; she always found it difficult to operate the combination locks in the dim light. That was the price you paid for luxury, she supposed. You got ambient lighting complemented by whale noises, but you couldn't see a thing.

She opened the locker, retrieved her clothes, and turned to where Judith was still rabbiting on about the spa's benefits, the woman continuing to nod appreciatively. Again, Susie felt that behind her shades, the woman's eyes were on her.

And now she started to wonder. Was it just coincidence? Was it her mind, or her eyesight, playing tricks? But she had the notion that she knew this woman from somewhere.

Yes, she did. It was like one of those moments when you saw somebody out of context. A waiter you associated with one restaurant suddenly turning up in another. A friendly shop assistant spotted in the street. Something so familiar about her.

But what?

Someone off the telly, perhaps? Or maybe it was just nothing, plain and simple.

Susie getting jumpy. Blame it on Lucy Shelley and her *we really have to go* business.

Yes, that's all it is, thought Susie as she let herself into a cubicle, acutely aware that Lucy would be waiting for her in reception.

In her bag was her phone. She fished it out and tried Guy, but there was no answer.

CHAPTER 40

A FEW MOMENTS later Susie had pulled on leggings, a top, and a zip-up hoodie, and laced up her sneakers. Judith and the sunglasses woman had disappeared to another area of the changing facilities, but now they returned, Judith still doing the sales pitch.

Susie smiled as she let herself out of the cubicle.

For the first time, she noticed there was something wrong with the woman's right arm, which hung in a slightly unusual way. She looked at the woman, trying to be discreet, but then again half hoping their eyes would meet and it would click, how they knew one another.

No such luck. The woman had turned—pointedly? Susie wasn't sure—and Susie was in danger of looking like a stalker if she hung around gawking for much longer. Then again, they were in a spa, all women together. What hurt could it do to ask?

"Excuse me," she said, butting in, "but do I know you?"

And then it was as though the woman had been playing a role, the part of "customer being shown around a health spa," and just for a second her mask slipped, like an actor who accidentally looks into the camera, and she faltered, she definitely faltered. "No, I don't think so," she said.

"Are you sure?" pressed Susie. "You're not from around Ascot way, are you?"

Judith stood by, hands clasped, no doubt delighted that the connection was being made.

"I'm sure," said the woman, but a steel had crept into her voice, a defensiveness that if anything made Susie even more determined to get to the bottom of this recognition thing that was going on, and so for a moment the two of them simply stared at one another with an intensity that caused Judith to clear her throat uncomfortably until, with a lurch of horror, Susie realized that she *did* know the woman. Oh yes, she knew her all right. They went way back.

Her mouth dropped open. And it must have been written all over her face, because the woman reached into her handbag.

"Oh my God," said Susie Drake.

CHAPTER 41

IN RECEPTION, LUCY wondered what was taking Susie so long. *Come on, come on*, she urged mentally, keeping up a game of polite-smile tennis with the greeter. At last she saw the light behind the door to the treatment suites change, the door open, and then Susie appeared.

Lucy was about to stand when she was stopped by the look on Susie's face. She was pensive, almost terrified. Behind her came the health spa rep. She, too, was ashen-faced.

And behind both of them came the sofa woman from reception. She still wore her sunglasses. Only this time she carried her handbag in front of her in a slightly awkward fashion. Like you might if you held a hidden gun.

In between bouts of smile-tennis with the greeter, Lucy had been leafing through a copy of *Vogue*—in Italian, of course—and now she pretended to be more interested in the magazine than the strange procession making its way through reception.

She threw a surreptitious glance at Susie, who narrowed her eyes almost imperceptibly, but enough to confirm Lucy's suspicions. The greeter watched quizzically, a half-smile drifting about her lips, not sure whether to say anything or not.

As the three women passed through reception with not a word exchanged, Lucy looked beyond them into the car park where two men had been lounging on the Range Rover. The men pulled themselves to their feet, ready, at the same time as the door swooshed expensively shut behind the three women.

Lucy stood. "Call the police," she said to the greeter.

"I'm sorry?" said the woman.

"Call the police, tell them that a kidnap attempt is in progress," repeated Lucy. She was no longer pretending to be posh. Instead she drew her gun, eliciting a gasp from the greeter, and placed it inside the copy of *Vogue*, out of sight. The door swooshed open, admitting her to the car park.

Oh God, she thought. *Oh, Christ.* So badly outnumbered it wasn't true.

She stitched on her widest, brightest, most innocent and happy-to-help smile as she crossed the car park, trotting up behind the three women. One of the Range Rover guys had seen her and was frowning but he must have assumed she was just a distraction, nothing to worry about, and he didn't reach for a gun or try to challenge her.

There were only two things she had in her favor, she realized grimly: surprise and the fact that they'd underestimate her.

"Excuse me," she called after the group. "Excuse me, I think you've forgotten your magazine."

Sofa woman told the other two, "Keep going," and then turned for the magazine. "Thank you, I'll take it."

And still she held her handbag in front of her, and Lucy

knew full well the handbag would contain her gun. What's more, there was something in this woman's eyes that told Lucy she'd know how to use that gun. This was it. There was no option now but attack.

Abruptly she sped up. At the same time, she discarded the magazine, showing her SIG.

The purpose was to surprise her opponent, and it worked, for in the space of a heartbeat the woman went from thinking of Lucy as a temporary irritant to knowing she was a real threat, but it was just the delay that Lucy needed.

She launched her offensive on the run, using all of her forward momentum, bending, feeling the torque in her body as she pulled back her right arm and swung, using the grip of the SIG like a knuckle duster and making contact with the sweet spot just below the woman's jaw. The kidnapper's sunglasses flew from her face as she staggered back and fell, releasing her bag and out of the fight for the time being at least.

Lucy heard a scream and from the corner of her eye saw the woman from the spa running back toward the safety of the building. Galvanized, the men beyond her went for their guns. One of them reached for Susie Drake and began to drag her to the car. The other, making his way over to where the sofa woman was trying to pull herself to her feet, produced a Russian Makarov, barrel swinging Lucy's way.

In the old days they'd called it "crack and thump." A round travels faster than sound so you'd hear the crack of the bullet followed by the thump of it leaving the barrel. Lucy heard it now, and the fact that she heard it meant that she hadn't been hit. She jinked across and out of the cone of fire just as she heard the thunderclap of another weapon. A third guy. He sat

in the driver's seat of the Range Rover and she saw a Glock
18 judder as he pumped three quick rounds across the seats
and out of the open passenger door. Glass behind shattered.
Bullets ricocheted off concrete. Susie's captor screamed in
Russian for his trigger-happy pal to hold fire but his comrade
had the light of murder in his eyes and he drew a fresh
bead on Lucy.

Susie, wrestling with her kidnapper against the bonnet of
the Range Rover, saw the driver level his Glock. Leaning into
her captor, she kicked the car door closed at the same time
as the guy inside opened fire again.

The vehicle shook from the impact as the driver shot up
the inside of his own car. Lucy dropped to a crouch and
raised the SIG two-handed to take aim at the man wrestling
with Susie, but she fudged the shot—too much movement,
too great a fear of hitting Susie, too fucking rusty—and the
bullet ricocheted off the side of the Range Rover harmlessly.
Over to the left the first guy reached the female kidnapper,
gun in hand, bringing it to bear on Lucy, just as the second
guy finished bundling Susie into the Range Rover and now
he turned, too, pistol in his fist, also bringing Lucy into
his sights.

Two guns against one. Lucy out of cover. The battle was
lost but she was going down swinging and she picked her
target: the guy by the Range Rover. Hoping her next shot
would be more effective than her first.

All three guns fired at the same time and Lucy saw the
bloody hole appear in her upper thigh before she felt a
thing. She'd been hit in combat before and she knew what
to expect—a few seconds of grace before the pain, and then
shock, and possibly unconsciousness. At the Range Rover

she saw the shooter clutch his shoulder and stagger back. She felt grimly pleased that she'd managed to hit one of the bad guys at least.

Nearby, the sound of sirens. The Range Rover door slammed shut, Susie inside. The guy Lucy had hit pulled himself to the vehicle, clambered in, and left a smear of blood on the paintwork. The woman reached the Range Rover, too. "Move!" she screamed at the final gunman, and dimly, Lucy realized that she, too, had been using a posh accent for her time in the Hampstead spa.

The woman threw a final baleful glare Lucy's way then climbed inside the car, followed by the last gunman.

Spooked by the sirens, thank God. Not stopping to finish off Lucy.

She raised a trembling gun hand and squeezed off a couple of shots at the tires, more in desperation than anything else, because of course they were reinforced.

And then it was gone, leaving her kneeling on the concrete, watching her own blood slowly spread on the ground beneath her, already beginning to lose focus. She scrabbled for her mobile to call Shelley, who picked up after only one ring.

"Babe," he said. "Have you got her?"

"No," managed Lucy. "I haven't got her. They've taken her. I've been hit, Shelley. I'm at the Hampstead Health & Beauty spa. I'm . . . I'm . . ."

"Babe!" he was yelling. "*Lucy!*"

She collapsed to the ground, and then passed out.

PART THREE

CHAPTER 42

"OH GOD," HE said, bursting into the hospital room, past the armed guard and into Lucy's arms.

She lay looking pale and weak, but not so weak that she couldn't gather Shelley to her. Her lower half was partly covered by the bedsheet, but he could see where the top of her thigh had been bandaged. The Chechen's bullet had passed straight through her leg, causing a huge loss of blood. The surgeons had told him that it had been touch and go, and that if the paramedics had arrived five minutes later she might have died.

The blood transfusion had been successful and she was recovering well, but she'd almost died. And that fact alone was enough to make Shelley want to clench his fists and cry out in fury. All those years spent in war zones when her life had been in danger every day—it went with the territory then. But now they'd decided to turn their backs on that life. She wasn't supposed to nearly bleed out in the car park of a spa in Hampstead.

*   *   *

Claridge arrived a short while later, laptop under his arm. He greeted the armed guard with a formal nod and handshake then approached Shelley, shaking his hand with a politician's grip. He turned his attention to Lucy, solemn and deferential. "You handled them like the old soldier I know you are," he said. "They can count themselves very lucky indeed that they have all escaped with their lives."

"Old soldier, eh?" said Lucy, consulting the heavens with her eyes. "Not quite sure how to take that."

"Take it any way you want. Just take it the right way," smiled Claridge.

Across Lucy's bed was a wheeled table on which Claridge placed the laptop. "I'd like you to take a look at some pictures," he told her. "Shelley, you need to look at these as well."

Up came mug shots. "These are our friends from the London arm of the Chechen Mafia," said Claridge. "Tell me when you'd like me to stop. We're looking for any of the men who attacked you and took Susie Drake." He began scrolling through the pictures.

"That's one of them." Lucy pulled herself up in bed with the excitement of seeing one of her attackers. "I'm pretty sure I winged that guy."

"Okay," said Claridge. He clicked to place a marker on the guy. "This is one of the soldiers, the kind of low-ranker that I'd expect to be mixed up in something like this. What about this guy?"

"Yes. I recognize him," confirmed Lucy.

"And this guy?"

"That was the driver. Mr. Glock 18."

"Makes sense. As far as we can tell, they operate as a kind of unit. Now, I'm particularly interested to know whether you recognize *this* gentleman."

A new face came up. Youngish. Handsome. Unfamiliar to either Lucy or Shelley. She shook her head.

"And this guy?" said Claridge. The next picture was of a slightly older but muscled man, wearing spectacles. Again Lucy shook her head.

"That last guy was Sergei Vinitsky. High up in the organization. This guy is Dmitry Kraviz. As far as we know he is the head of the London branch."

He navigated back to the shot of Sergei Vinitsky. "As you know, the Chechens are based in Moscow and Grozny. Now, in Moscow this chap's brother, Ivan Vinitsky, may or may not have attempted to organize some kind of takeover. Intelligence is patchy but a short time after, he disappeared for good, never to be seen or heard of again."

"Well, I don't think he was part of the kidnapping," said Lucy. "Neither of those guys. There were just the gunmen, a driver, and the woman." Lucy's eyes shifted. "Do you have any details on the woman?"

"Right, yes," said Claridge, "I'll come to that . . ."

Just then, Shelley's phone rang in his pocket.

CHAPTER 43

SHELLEY STOOD. "CALL of nature," he said, and although Claridge barely turned a hair, Lucy shot him a searching look, knowing him too well, as he stepped out of the room and into the corridor.

He pulled the phone from his pocket. "Hello," he said as he hurried away from Lucy's room, casting a look up and down the corridor. It was deserted.

"Is that Captain David Shelley of the Special Air Service?" said the voice. It was Dmitry Kraviz; he recognized the voice from Drake's phone earlier. The weirdness of it struck Shelley. Seconds ago he'd been looking at a picture of Kraviz. Now he was talking to him.

Shelley moved quickly down the hall, thinking that you're not supposed to use your mobile in a hospital. It's forbidden; phones interfere with the machines. Or at least that's what they used to say.

"It's tough to speak right now. How about you ring back in five minutes?"

Dmitry Kraviz chortled. "Negative, my friend," he said, "we need to speak now."

Here. A restroom. Shelley ducked inside, relieved to find it empty. "All right," he said, "you win. Proceed."

"Well, I ask again: is this Captain Shelley?"

"You got my name and number from Johnson, did you?"

"He's been a very valuable source of information," said Dmitry. "But that woman at the spa today . . . who was she?"

"He didn't tell you about her, then?"

"No, I'm afraid not."

"One of our operators," said Shelley. *Need to keep Lucy out of this*, he thought. *At all costs.* "And when she's recovered from her injuries she'll be an ex-operator."

"Oh, is that so? I was told she fought like a lion."

Shelley felt himself glow with pride, hating himself for what he said next: "She's a silly bitch who had one job, to provide close protection for Susie Drake."

"An 'operator,' you said. Isn't that what you call your troops in the SAS, Captain Shelley?"

"It's a figure of speech. Now listen, what are you doing calling me, and not Drake or Bennett?"

"Because you are a level head," said Dmitry. "Because I know that you are experienced in kidnap situations, and for that reason you will know better than to involve the police."

"I think it's a bit too late for that."

"Well, yes, your incompetent operator saw to that. But there are ways and ways, are there not? Ways that police involvement can be minimized—circumvented."

He was right, of course. Shelley knew full well the dangers of getting the authorities involved in a kidnap situation. He was familiar with cases in South America where the intervention of the cops meant things had gone badly wrong, ending in a bloodbath. Body parts. Broken-hearted parents. Nobody wanted that.

"Now *you* tell *me* something. Is Susie Drake unharmed?"

"Not only unharmed but well cared for. My darling wife is seeing to that. Now, listen carefully, Captain. I'm going to ring this number later today, and I expect to speak to Mr. Drake at that point. I think that if you really are experienced in kidnap situations then you will know better than to involve the police in this."

"I agree with you, but first I need proof of life as well as certain assurances from you."

Dmitry sighed. "So impatient. Wait until later, and if all is well then you shall have your proof of life. That shall be your assurance, Captain. And if you involve the police then I'll supply proof of death, one piece at a time."

"You'd do that, would you? You'd kill his wife as well as his daughter?" Shelley was fishing, wondering how Dmitry would react, still trying to answer those questions.

In response Dmitry sounded affronted. "Daughter? I had nothing to do with his daughter's death. I didn't give his daughter the drugs. I didn't put a gun in her mouth. I didn't even recruit the girl to work in my studio. All of these are Emma Drake's own actions, with a little help from her friends and her drug dealers and maybe, yes, with a little help from her parents. Because we need to ask ourselves, do we not, Captain Shelley, why such a nice girl was mixed up in such a terrible business."

"That's true, is it?" said Shelley. "You give me your word, do you? Emma Drake killed herself."

"How else do you think she died?" Dmitry sounded

genuinely puzzled. "Perhaps you were hoping that she was murdered, is that it? Is that the most desirable outcome for her friends and family?

"No, I had nothing to do with Emma Drake's death. You know what is funny? I would never have known that she was this millionaire's daughter were it not for the fact that he employed men—men like you, Captain Shelley—to try to do harm to my business. Why am I saying 'try to'? You have *significantly* harmed my business. And you have insulted me, which is perhaps the worst offense of all, something that I'm afraid cannot be tolerated.

"Now, for that insult I make a charge and to ensure that charge is paid I have Susie Drake in a safe place, ready to be exchanged for the money. Now, please, you must excuse me, Captain. This business is really little more than a diversion, and there are plenty of other things I have to attend to."

"The godfather's work is never done, eh?"

Dmitry gave a theatrical sigh. "Something like that, yes. Just make sure that Mr. Drake takes the call later, and we can get all of this over and done with as soon as possible."

"Oh yes, that's her," Lucy was saying as Shelley reentered the room. This, presumably, was the woman in sunglasses from the spa.

Lucy glanced at Shelley as he stepped toward the bed. They knew better than to try to pull the wool over Claridge's eyes. He'd spot any meaningful looks. Instead Shelley turned his attention to the laptop screen, where Claridge scrolled through a series of pictures, each showing the same woman: dark-haired and slightly hard-faced, though not unattractive, usually clad in black.

"Who is she?" he asked, the question drawn out and thoughtful. As with the photographs of Sergei Vinitsky, Dmitry Kraviz and Co., these had been taken with a long-range lens or were screen grabs from CCTV footage, but there was something about this particular woman . . .

"Her name is Karen," said Claridge. The pictures showed her getting in and out of a BMW. Going about her business, a handbag in the crook of her arm. "As far as we know she is married to Dmitry Kraviz."

"Another Russian?" asked Shelley.

"No," said Claridge slowly, aware of Shelley's interest, "she's British."

"Shelley?" asked Lucy. "Something you need to share with the group?"

"Just that she seems familiar," said Shelley.

"Could you have been briefed about her on a previous operation?" asked Claridge.

"Possibly," said Shelley. "Wait, can you loop the pictures? Can I just see them again?"

Claridge did as he was asked, the pictures going round and round, a carousel.

"I know her," said Shelley. He was racking his brains.

And then it hit him. "Christ," he said. "I think I know who she is."

CHAPTER 44

SUSIE DRAKE HAD often wondered what it would be like to be a prisoner. Now she knew.

Driving away from the spa, a state of shock had descended over the Range Rover's occupants. One of the men had been hit and was bleeding, his breathing shallow. The car interior reeked of sweat and blood and what she took to be either gunpowder or cordite, and everywhere she looked was bullet damage.

As for her kidnappers, their sullen attitude was testament to the fact that the operation hadn't been a total success. On the other hand, she was their prisoner, so nor had it been a failure. All that dissonance they handled in the time-honored manner of staying silent and sulking—apart from the injured man, who sat by her side with his eyes half closed, breathing hard through his nose, grunting occasionally and gripping his shoulder.

Outside, through smoked glass, the streets of London sped by. Inside was sealed off, silent and hermetic. She gathered herself, needing to speak, praying her voice wouldn't shake. She didn't want them to know she was afraid.

"It *is* you, then?" she said.

The woman in the front had been massaging her jaw, having flipped down the vanity mirror to inspect the damage done by Lucy Shelley, but when Susie spoke she glanced at the driver and then in her mirror at the two heavies on either side of Susie. The injured guy lay slumped against the door, pale but conserving his energy; the other one returned her gaze impassively, perhaps knowing better than to show undue interest. There was no doubt in Susie's mind who the boss was.

The woman turned in her seat. The side of her face was red and swollen where Lucy had hit her. "Who are you talking to?" she said, in what Susie realized was her real voice, brassy and peevish-sounding, like a permanently indignant woman in a soap opera. Quite different from the measured, polite tones she'd been affecting in the spa.

"I'm talking to you," said Susie.

"Well, address me then," the woman hit back.

"I don't know your name."

"It's Karen," said the woman, twisting around in her seat to face front once more, turning her attention to her phone, adding over her shoulder, "And if you want to talk to me, you say, 'Excuse me, Karen.'"

Silence descended. Susie let the build-up of tension subside before she spoke again. "Excuse me, Karen?" she began.

A pause.

"Yes," said Karen.

"Is it you?"

"Don't know what you're on about. Next question."

Susie was about to say, *You know exactly what I'm talking about*, but bit her tongue, saying instead, "All right, then. Are you going to kill me?"

Karen sighed. "If we were going to kill you we would have done it just now, back there. Fuck's sake. Is that it? Is that all you want to know?"

"Then what are you going to do with me?"

Karen gave a short snorting laugh, like a horse sneezing. "Your husband's one of the richest men in the country, what the bloody hell do you think we're going to do with you?" She turned to regard Susie. "He'd better love you. Does he love you? Would you say you've got a strong marriage, you and the microchip man?"

There was an edge of bitterness to Karen's voice that made Susie wonder if she had issues of her own in that department. Still, this wasn't the time or place for a girlish heart-to-heart. Instead Susie simply said, "We do."

Karen faced front again. "Good. In that case, he'll want to pay up, and you get to go home alive and . . . well, maybe not with every single one of your fingers and toes, because people usually need a little bit of convincing, however much they love you."

"Why me?" asked Susie, even though, of course, the answer was glaringly obvious. From up front was silence. "It's because of Emma, isn't it?" said Susie.

"It ain't because of Emma. Well, not directly. It's more to do with your husband and his mates taking a sledgehammer to our business. You think he could just walk away from that? Not in our world. Your husband can count himself lucky that he's so minted or he'd find himself having an appointment with the Skinsman. Who knows, when all this is done, maybe he still will. He's pissed a lot of people off, has your old man."

"The Skinsman? Who's that?"

Once more Karen twisted around in her seat. When she smiled, Susie saw that one of her top teeth was crooked, giving her a predatory look. "A bloke in your operation called Johnson, you know him?"

Susie nodded slowly.

"He met the Skinsman. The Skinsman took several hours making his acquaintance. Trust me, you don't wanna know any more about that."

She turned back, started fiddling with her phone. Texting, probably. For a moment or so silence reigned, and the streets blurred past, life viewed as if from the inside of a goldfish bowl.

Susie swallowed. "Did Emma meet the Skinsman?"

Karen's fingers had been moving on the phone with all the speed of the most addicted teenager, but now they stopped. "Your daughter killed herself. Her killing herself is the reason for all this shit."

"She really did, did she? We—"

"Hoped it was the other way?" finished Karen with a nasty chortle.

Susie looked away. "No, not hoped—of course not. I couldn't hope she was murdered. But I can't bear thinking of her being so unhappy . . . so unhappy that she'd want to kill herself. I just wanted to know the truth."

Karen sniggered. "Well, the truth is that she was a junkie who was in over her head. A fat cat's daughter reduced to getting her kit off for pervy old men online. She couldn't take it anymore so she topped herself. How does that feel, Mom?"

Feels like you're a bitch. "As long as it's the truth."

"Oh yes, it's the truth," said Karen.

But Susie noticed something. She noticed that Karen

looked around the car at the faces of her men as she said it. As if saying it for their benefit, too.

Shortly after, they arrived at what Susie thought was some kind of car service center. She was dragged inside. The injured man slumped into a seat in reception.

"Sofia, ring the doctor," commanded Karen, and then Susie was taken through the office area, through the workshop, and to a room at the back barred with a chain, with a sign on the door saying "Machine Shop."

She was imprisoned in that room. Along one wall was a camp bed, beside it an old cabinet that had seen better days, topped with a bedside lamp. A portable DVD and TV combo had been set up on a child's school desk and chair, and beside it a DVD: *Dirty Dancing*. Lastly, and most incongruously, a deck chair had been set up against the far wall.

"What do you think?" said one of the men who had been detailed to take her to her new quarters. "A home from home, yes?"

"How long will I be here?" she asked.

"Who knows?" shrugged the guy. He told her that somebody would visit her soon with something to eat and drink and in the meantime to make herself comfortable. He retired, leaving her alone.

Something caught her eye. In a corner of the room was a scrap of brown packing tape and a little strip of clear plastic, about the size of an envelope.

It was splattered with blood.

CHAPTER 45

"KAREN?" SAID SHELLEY, staring hard at the screen. "That's her name? Karen?"

"Yes," replied Claridge. "That's Karen."

And now Lucy was looking at the MI5 man with great interest. "Okay, so why do I get the impression that there's something about this Karen that you're dying to tell us?"

"Ah, well," said Claridge, "she's a bit of a one is our Karen . . ."

" 'Our Karen,' " parroted Lucy.

"We tend to think of her as one of ours, yes. Something of a throwback really. She's the granddaughter of Dexter Regan. Do you know the name?"

"It rings a bell," said Shelley.

"Well, Dexter Regan was reputed to be one of the masterminds of the Great Train Robbery, died in Strangeways in 1997, where he was serving out a sentence for aggravated assault.

"While he was inside his son Malcolm Regan had taken over running the family business. Dexter was what you might call old school, he kept his house in order. Liked to do things the Kray twins way; Malcolm, on the other hand, not so much. In the 1990s he tried his hand at property development. To all intents and purposes he aimed to take the family business and make it legitimate, so he went into business with a consortium of bankers in order to develop in Docklands. What went wrong? Who can say, but the development never happened, the business didn't go legitimate, and lots of bankers and developers turned up dead.

"After that, Malcolm Regan pretty much abandoned any plans he had of going straight and instead concentrated on building a reputation as ruthless and sadistic. All those activities that overseas gangs were apparently monopolizing—drugs, prostitution, human trafficking—that the English families had been reluctant to touch, because they were still clinging to those old-school values of family and community, Malcolm Regan embraced them fully.

"And he did a very good job. So good, in fact, that it brought him to the attention of the Chechen Mafia, who wanted to make inroads in this country. Regan joined forces with the Chechens in order to rid themselves of an Irish problem they had. I don't know which union came first, but it was around then that Regan's daughter, Karen, married the head of the Chechens' London operation."

"Hold on a minute." Claridge tapped on the laptop and scrolled through a new selection of photos until he chose one of an older man whose face resembled the images of

Karen they'd just been looking at. "This is Malcolm Regan," he said.

Claridge flicked the screen back a couple of images. "The guy I just showed you. Dmitry Kraviz."

"So Karen was pimped out?" asked Lucy. "An arranged marriage of convenience?"

"Oh no," said Claridge, "there's a reason we call her 'our Karen.' She has a lot more agency than you give her credit for."

"She served her apprenticeship," said Shelley.

Lucy and Claridge both looked at him. "Okay," said Lucy, "so now I feel like *you're* the one with something to tell us." She glanced at Claridge.

Shelley nodded. "This is the woman." He turned his attention to Lucy. "The woman who was part of the attempt to kidnap Emma fourteen years ago."

"Okay," said Claridge, "I think you're going to have to clue me in."

Shelley told him all about the kidnapping attempt. The trip to Waitrose. The Peugeot, the VW Passat —

"Wait a second," said Claridge. "You broke her arm? Was it a nasty break?"

"It wasn't under surgical conditions," said Shelley. "I snapped it across the door. It was practically hanging off. So yeah, it was a bad break."

"Because Karen has an injured right arm. She has the use of it, but not full functionality, as I understand."

"That's definitely her then. I saw it," confirmed Lucy. "So she was into the crime racket years before she got with the Chechens."

"Oh yes," said Claridge. "And as far as we know she's as active as she ever was in the organization."

"And part of the organization involves the cams," said Shelley.

"Exactly."

"They met again," said Shelley. Things were making sense to him now. His voice was low. "Karen and Emma. Fourteen years later, they were reunited."

CHAPTER 46

THREE NIGHTS BEFORE her death, Emma Drake had arrived for work and gone to the office to make herself known and say hello to Jason. After that, she planned to get a hit and then go live.

She liked Jason. The other guy who sat in the office, whatever his name was, Dan, was a bit of a sleazeball. The kind whose eyes were always roaming. Christ knows why; he got to sit in the office where he could look at each of the five rooms, see the girls fully naked and performing to the punters' hearts' desires whenever he wanted, and yet he still did that thing with his eyes.

Emma knew why. A power trip. A mind fuck. A way of saying *I'm in charge*, a way of being a bit of a dickhead, basically.

Jason wasn't like that. Any sexual interest that Jason had was obscured by a cloud of pungent weed smoke. His eyes didn't go traveling the way Dan's did.

Funny, though, Jason had been slightly different with her that night. There had been an edge to him.

"Are you all right, Faye?" he'd asked, except it didn't feel like a genuine inquiry after her well-being. And there was something about the way he stressed the word "Faye."

Had she imagined it? After all, she'd never really relaxed about using her assumed name. She guessed that pop stars and actors and people in the witness protection program just got on with it and their false name became their real name, but she'd never quite managed that trick herself.

"How are things?" he'd asked.

Things. How were *things*? Emma wasn't stupid. She was mixed up, lost and lonely, and a good many other undesirable characteristics besides, but she certainly wasn't stupid, and she knew that her recent graduation from smoking to inject-ing was proof that *things* weren't good, and were getting worse. But even so, she tried to rationalize the situation. She told herself that an addiction to heroin was not dissimilar to needing coffee, cigarettes, or alcohol.

After all, people often talked of "high-functioning alcohol-ics," those people who, despite their addiction, managed to lead fulfilling home and work lives. Their addiction didn't hold them back. It didn't result in them engaging in criminal behavior. No doubt it was occasionally problematic in the way that consumption of any mind-altering substance can be, but generally, on the whole, not a *big* problem.

So it was with her own addiction. Yes, the huge difference was that alcohol was legal and heroin was not. But so long as you had dealers, which she did, and a job, which she did, there was no reason not to maintain that habit. No reason she couldn't be a "high-functioning heroin addict."

That was what she thought if she was feeling upbeat and positive. A lot of the time, though, she wasn't feeling at all upbeat or positive. She saw in stark detail and in color—that color being gray—the reality of the life she had chosen for herself.

And in those dark moments she would remember exactly what her "job" entailed, and why she was forced to do it; she would remember that she experienced periods of crippling sickness unknown to all but the most chronic alcoholics, and that she regularly indulged periods of bingeing, rather than just maintaining. And it was because of those binges that she'd built up debt with her dealers which they forced her to pay off by working at the cam house.

She knew that while all this hung over her head, she could never go home. Despite the fact that every day she longed to be back there. She could never face her mom and dad.

And so when Jason asked, "How are things?" she'd known better than to try and pull the wool over his eyes. "Oh, you know, Jason, could be better I suppose."

"Well, you never know, you might be about to go up in the world. Our lord and master has been showing quite an interest in you."

She looked sharply at him, liking absolutely nothing about that sentence. "'Lord and master'?"

As far as she knew—and this was according to Jason—Foxy Kittenz was owned by some Russian types. He called them the Russian Mafia and of course she'd always assumed that it was just him being flippant. But whatever they were, Mafia or not, she certainly wasn't keen on anybody showing her undue interest.

She tried not to let her unease show. "What do you mean—the Russians?"

"No, the Russians never come round here. It's one of

the wives who occasionally shows her face, a woman called Karen. You'll see her eventually, no doubt. Always dressed up to the nines. Bit of a clotheshorse if you ask me. Can't for a second think why she's interested in you."

It was a joke, a bit of banter, and yet Emma detected the hint of a question to it as well. Jason was digging. And Emma wondered whether she was right to suspect that he knew a little more about Karen's interest than he was letting on. Jason, for all that he was a nice guy, also knew on which side his bread was buttered. "I love my job, me" was one of his favorite sayings, and she had no doubt that for a guy like him, being paid to sit around watching women undress while he smoked weed all day had to be high up the list of dream occupations.

And then, later that day, she saw the mythical Karen for the first time. She had been making one of her apparently rare visits and Emma caught sight of her in the corridor.

"You're Faye," she had said, smiling.

Emma had just taken a little hit in the restroom, so her mind was a bit floaty and scrambled. The woman's voice was different, her hair was much longer, but Emma recognized her. And it was all she could do to keep the recognition from being obvious. "Yes, hello," she'd said.

"Jason says you're settling in well."

The woman had looked hard at her, Emma thinking it must be written all over her face: that mixture of shock and surprise, hatred, and rank, outright fear. Like seeing a ghost.

Afterward, she had tried to tell herself that she might simply have been wrong. Maybe she was projecting. After all, it was so many years ago. They were both different then, the context so different.

Yet she found herself worrying, wanting to know, and her thoughts went to Shelley, her special forces. She wondered about getting a picture of the woman and texting it to him, realizing that she could still recall his number. (Would he have the same number?) She could remember him making her recite it every morning. He'd made it into a game.

They were the good times, she had thought wistfully. Happy times. But then there had been the kidnap attempt, and Shelley had left, and the man who replaced him was never the same. Oh, he'd tried, bless him. He'd done his best to be jolly, friendly, and warm, but he was like an embarrassing uncle, and Emma had seen right through him. She had wanted Shelley back. She had pined for him like other girls pined for boyfriends.

Well, anyway.

Emma spent twenty-four hours too scared to get in touch with Shelley. And of course if she had managed to screw up the courage and call then it might have saved her life, because she was at work one night and about to go to her room, when she saw the door at the end open and in came a Russian-looking man.

Behind him, Karen.

They had both seen her, and Karen smiled. "Hello, love," she'd said, and right then Emma knew that she knew. And she knew that Karen knew that she knew.

She let herself into her room, heart hammering. She took out her phone and tried him at last, but there was no answer. It went to voice mail. Not even his voice.

She had opened her mouth, about to leave him a message, when there came a knock at the door.

CHAPTER 47

SUSIE SAT ON the deck chair in her new prison cell, also known as the machine shop, wondering what happened now and knowing that in reality the answer was nothing—nothing happened now apart from waiting.

All those years ago, David had sat her and Emma down and told them that if the unthinkable happened and they were taken and found themselves captive then they should do their best to be as amenable and open as possible with their captors.

The idea was that their captors should see them as human beings rather than just negotiating tools. Doing that would make them more difficult to hurt and ultimately more difficult to kill.

At the same time Susie tried to recall films she'd seen involving kidnap situations. Then again, maybe not; they never seemed to end well. So in the meantime she just took a seat and let her mind wander, waiting but not really waiting.

The door rattled. She sat up straight as it began to open, had second thoughts, and stood up to greet her visitor instead.

It was Karen. She wore the same clothes she had earlier, and Susie guessed it was her usual attire: black boots that stopped just below the knee, expensive and showy, black jeans, and a knitted turtleneck in the same color. The only thing missing from the ensemble was the belted woolen overcoat she'd had on, and Susie, dressed in her gym outfit of leggings, tight white base layer, and zip-up hooded top, was in the rare position of feeling underdressed in the other woman's presence.

Karen stood by the door, motioning for Susie to step back against the far wall. When Susie was in place, Karen turned and was handed a small tray.

She caught Susie looking at her arm. "It's never repaired. Permanent nerve damage. I have restricted movement, limited mobility, no grip, numbness, and tingling. Most days I wish that they could have just taken the whole fucking thing off."

She placed the tray down on the school desk. Next she winced as though something was bothering her, and then reached to her waist and took out a gun that she placed on the tabletop, doing the whole thing quite casually, almost absentmindedly.

Karen indicated for Susie to take a seat.

"Some food for you," she said, and Susie nodded in thanks, looking across. Close to the food was the gun, placed about halfway between the two women.

Karen pulled the school chair across, its legs scraping on the concrete floor of the cell with a sound like dinosaurs yawning. She sat and crossed her legs, staring at Susie with a strange, unreadable expression. "'It is you'—that's what you said in the car."

"Yes."

"Well, it is me, yeah."

But you didn't want to reveal that in front of your men, thought Susie, but decided it was wiser to keep that observation to herself. "And your arm?" she said instead. "The injury to your arm, I mean. That happened on the day of . . ." She tailed off, not sure how Karen would have chosen to describe her attempted kidnapping.

But Karen grinned, her snaggletooth making an appearance. "Oh yes. I get to think about that moment a lot. Like, every five minutes or so. On cold days, when the arm really plays up, maybe even more often than that."

Good. You deserve it. "I'm sorry."

Karen sneered.

"No, I am," insisted Susie. "You probably think that I'm just saying that—"

"Oh, you reckon?"

"But I'm not. You were just doing your job."

Karen was rolling her eyes and Susie knew the tactic was a bust. "You're not sorry," she said, "and if you really are then you're a bigger pussy than I take you for, and believe me, I take you for a pretty big pussy as it is."

"So . . . what is it?" sighed Susie. "You've been biding your time ever since? A fourteen-year wait to get even?"

Karen scoffed. "Get over yourself, Lady Muck. Just because I'm pissed off about my arm doesn't mean I based my entire life around it. There have been other bits of business to attend to, you know. I got married, helped build up the business. All with only one and a half arms. Not bad for a cripple, eh?"

She paused and Susie thought that she was probably supposed to wince at the use of the word *cripple* and lower her eyes apologetically, so that's what she did, thinking, *Fuck you*.

"But, yeah," continued Karen, "now you come to mention it, I did often think about one day meeting the people responsible for doing this to me." She lifted her arm. "I wondered how I'd feel."

"And then you got to find out," prompted Susie.

Karen grinned, that snaggletooth making a reappearance. "Yes, then I got to find out."

Susie leaned forward. Emotions began to shift inside her. She and Guy had reacted so differently to Emma's death. Susie had resolved to remain stoic; more than anything she wanted not to fall victim to thoughts of anger and revenge the way Guy had done. Not through some misplaced sense of that being The Right Thing to Do, but because she saw the damage it did. Like David, she knew no good could ever come of feeling so wrathful, so driven by a need for revenge.

But she felt it every now and then, of course she did. It rose up like noxious bubbles of swamp gas, and although most of the time she dealt with it, and made sure it stayed submerged, there were times, like now, when she let it sit there, because now she knew one thing for certain: one way or another, she was sitting opposite the woman responsible for her daughter's death.

She tried not to look at the gun, not wanting to draw Karen's attention to it. Instead she simply asked, "Are you going to tell me about it?"

"Oh yeah," beamed Karen. "I'm going to tell you *all* about it."

CHAPTER 48

THE TROUBLE WITH Jason was that he thought he was best mate to all the girls, Karen had thought. And what with him thinking that, it was only a matter of time before he let on that Karen was unusually interested in Emma.

When they bumped into one another, while Karen hadn't been 100 percent certain, she'd thought she saw that spark of recognition, and she had known that something had to be done. Why? Because she was worried? Because she was concerned about being brought to book for something that had happened a lifetime ago?

No. Because she was Karen Regan, daughter of Malcolm Regan, granddaughter of Dexter, and she had another, much more personal reason for wanting to deal with Emma Drake.

She rang her father.

Later, she would wonder whether she had rung him in the sure knowledge that she'd get the answer she wanted. After all, he'd been in the backup vehicle during their aborted kidnap attempt. He had been driving the Peugeot, and so he'd seen at first hand what had been done to her.

But for the time being she just wanted to hear his voice, wanted to say the words "Emma Drake" and hear his reaction.

"What is it, sweetheart?" he'd growled on the phone. It struck her that she missed him. Being among the Chechens was good, treated like a queen the way she was, schmoozed like a foreign ambassador, but there was no substitute for genuine affection.

"It's Emma Drake," she told him.

From the other end of the line came a sharp intake of breath. "Wait a second there," he said, and she heard him light a cigarette, exhaling loudly. She thought of him with his Benson & Hedges and his gold Zippo and knew that he'd be regarding the world through a cloud of blue-tinged smoke, thinking of Emma Drake, casting his mind back to the whole sorry episode.

"Not one of our finest hours, was it, sweetheart?" he said at last.

You can fucking say that again, she thought sarcastically, but didn't say. She was in poor-little-girl mode for this call. "I think about her all the time, Dad," she said, pouring all that pent-up hurt into her voice.

"I don't doubt it, sweetheart, after what they did to you."

It wasn't just the nerves in her arm. Emma Drake's bite marks were another permanent reminder. A large patch of scarred and mushed-up skin on her hand. Little cow had bitten her hard.

"She's working for us, Dad. She's got a new name and she's a junkie, but it's her."

There was another sharp intake of breath at the other end. "And have you told Dmitry? Or Sergei?"

"You know what would happen if I did."

"Yes, of course."

There was a pause. He'd be thinking of her, she knew, taking her hurt feelings into account, but there was also the relationship with the Chechens to consider. He had worked hard to broker the union. Merging had created a single, untouchable consortium. Nobody wanted to do anything that might undermine all they had worked toward.

After a while he said, "You know, don't you, that you could have got to her any time over the last—how many years has it been?"

"Fourteen."

"Fourteen years you've had, Kaz. We could have taken her out if we really wanted to, but we didn't."

She sniffed, hoping she wasn't overplaying the poor-little-princess bit. "It was your wishes, Dad. You wanted to leave it. You said the whole thing was a stain on the family name."

"Which it was."

"I did what you wanted." She was being merciless, she knew, preying on his guilt for what happened. On the other hand, what was the bloody point of having feminine wiles if you never got to use them?

"I never realized you felt that strongly about it, sweetheart," he said with an almost crestfallen tone in his voice.

"The thing is, Dad, neither did I. Not until I saw her again. Having her right under my nose has brought it all back. I don't want to make a big fuss about it. I don't want to dig up bad memories of our failure that day. I just want . . . I just want . . ."

There was another pause. When her dad next spoke it was

in the comforting fatherly tones she knew so well: "What do you want, sweetheart?"

"I just want to kill the fucking bitch who crippled *me*, Dad. I just want to fucking kill her and watch her bleed."

"And God has brought her to you," said her dad. He wasn't especially religious but would occasionally invoke a higher power in order to justify a certain course of action. That was a good sign, she knew.

"That's right—that's right, Dad, it feels like that. God has brought her to us."

"All right," he said, and she let out a silent sigh of relief. "The Chechens can't find out. It wouldn't be good for business. It would be bad news for the union if they discover that we passed up the chance to earn so much easy dosh. Wait— you don't think you could ransom her and *then* kill her?"

"I thought of that. I don't think so, because of Dmitry. Besides, it's not what I want, Dad. I want this just between me and her. I want it so that right at the end she knows that her money couldn't save her. She can't hire a bodyguard and buy her way out of this one."

"I gotcha, babe," he said. "I've got your back, I understand. Just as long as you know that anything you do, you need to do without them lot knowing. Is there any way I can help you? Do you need a couple of men?"

"It's all right, thanks, Dad. I've got men here that are loyal to me."

"Oh yeah?" he said, suddenly suspicious. "Not up to anything, are you, Kaz? I mean, anything *else*?"

She'd avoided answering that question, asking after his health instead. He had a new girlfriend, a woman called Sheridan who Karen had only met once and loathed on sight, so she asked him about her, and forced him to say that no-body could ever replace her mother, God rest her soul, and they'd finished the call.

Then, ten minutes later, he'd rung back. "You want them all to suffer, though, don't you?" he said. "The whole of them Drakes."

"I don't care, Dad. I just want to watch her die."

"But wouldn't it be good, princess?"

"I don't see how, without the Chechens getting suspicious."

He chuckled. "Well, sweetheart, there are ways and there are ways . . ."

CHAPTER 49

SUSIE FELT STRANGE, surreal, as though her mind and spirit had lifted outside of her body and she was looking down on events with an almost dispassionate air, as though what was being discussed was nothing to do with her. How else was it possible to process the fact that this woman was sitting there calmly, smiling almost sweetly, presentable and reasonable, talking about the time she made plans to kill Emma?

On the table lay the gun. Watching over them was the CCTV camera. Susie had dredged up those lessons Shelley had given her. Safety catch. Cocking the weapon. Don't snatch the shot.

At school she had been a gymnast and a good sprinter. She knew she was fast—or used to be, at least—and maybe she could be fast again, now, when it counted. Could she make it to the gun before Karen? Would she be able to use the gun if she got there? How long would it be before more men came rushing to the bitch's aid?

"You're telling me," she heard herself say—again, there

was that detached part of her that registered the disbelief in her own voice—"you're telling me how you killed my daughter?"

"From one mother to another," said Karen. She pronounced "mother" like "muvva." *From one muvva to anuvva.* "I think it's only right that you know the truth. I know I'd want to if I were in your shoes. I'd want to know everything.

"It's out of respect that I'm telling you this, Susie. Because we're women, aren't we? We know that we're stronger than the other lot. We suffer." She patted her stomach. "We know suffering that they'll never know, and we know that we can take it, because we're tough, ain't we? That's why you're not sitting there shitting yourself, blubbing like a baby. That's what your husband would be doing in your position, ain't it? How did he react when darling daughter died?"

Darling daughter. Susie felt her hatred increase by a couple of notches.

"I bet he started ranting and raving, didn't he? The checkbook came out. Because they're all like that, aren't they? Worst combination is a bloke and a bit of money—it turns them into big babies. Is that how your hubby was, Susie? Did he throw a tantrum while you watched calmly on? Now I bet that's right, ain't it? I bet he did. Come on, answer me."

Susie found herself nodding despite herself. Why not? It was true. Guy had not been there for her; he had nurtured his hatred instead. The way she felt now. Was that what it was like inside Guy's head all the time?

"You see? And is it him who has been taken? Is it him sitting in some grotty cell in a garage with only *Dirty Dancing* on DVD to watch? No, of course it ain't. It's you who has to carry the can. You who has to suffer. Always you, Susie."

"And Emma," Susie heard herself say.

"Oh yes, and Emma," said Karen. "You see? I knew you were strong enough to carry on."

It was as if the whole world was in this cell. As though the planet had shrunk to consist of just Susie and Karen, facing each other across a grubby room, with a glass of water, a sandwich, and a gun on the table between them.

"Then carry on," said Susie.

Karen nodded, satisfied her little speech had done the trick. When she looked away, Susie found her eyes going to the gun once more. She had attended a course once, the sort of thing that bored housewives like her did when the kids left home, "mindfulness" or something like that, and one of the techniques they'd taught was visualization. You had to picture yourself doing what you wanted to do. You had to imagine yourself succeeding at it.

"So we went in to see her that day."

The day she died. "How did she look?" Susie found herself saying.

"Did you not see the video?" said Karen, surprised. "You must be about the only person who hasn't."

Susie shook her head. "In any case, I want to know how she looked when she arrived for work, not how she was when she was all dolled up to do a job."

Karen threw her head back, snorting with laughter. Her earrings danced. "It's not fucking Hollywood, you know. She just came in with the same slut clothes she normally wore. She was a gorgeous girl, no doubt about it. They all are at Foxy Kittenz, it's our stock-in-trade. But between you, me, and the gatepost, she looked zonked out. She looked like somebody who did too many drugs, you know, too much heroin." Karen stopped, looking sharply at Susie. "Did you know that about her, Susie? Did you know that little Emma was using the spike?"

Susie shook her head slowly. "Not at the time."

Karen smiled her strange grin again, making her look almost vampiric. "Of course not. Of course you didn't. There's a song, ain't there? About a posh girl with a rich daddy who decides to slum it just for the hell of it, to see how the other half lives. 'Common People.' You know the one?"

Susie didn't bother to answer, just stared at Karen as though observing an alien life form, aware now that there was nothing remotely truth-telling about this session; it was simply an exercise in mental torture.

"'Common People' by Pulp, that's the one. That's what I think of when I think of Emma. She started to mix with the likes of us, then it all got a bit too much for her, didn't it? In the song, the girl can ring Daddy and Daddy can stop it all, but your Emma didn't do that, or couldn't do that. Why was that, Susie?"

"We're not posh," said Susie, dimly wondering why she even bothered making that point. "Guy was an engineer. Up north. He was made redundant. He used his redundancy pay to—"

"I googled him," spat Karen. "I googled him fourteen years ago. Fuck, it was so long ago, I probably didn't even use Google. It was probably Ask Jeeves or some shit like that. It's not him I'm accusing of being posh, Lady Muck, it's you."

Karen's color was rising and Susie wondered if she should be afraid, but with a dim sense of triumph she realized that she wasn't.

"Because you certainly didn't live in the north or

get made redundant from any engineering job, did you? Privately educated, that's you. Met Guy Drake at a charity function.

"Poor old Emma, she probably didn't know where the roots lay. On the one hand she's got all this wealth, public-school friends of her own, privileged money; on the other hand, there's Daddy, giving it the big 'when I were a lad' speech. Working-class hero, all that malarkey. Am I right? No wonder she ended up so fucking confused.

"Here, I wonder if she ever thought that Daddy might secretly approve of what she was doing. What do you think? What do you think a psychiatrist might have to say about that? Like, was there something deep inside? Was she trying to win her daddy's favor? They say that's what all little girls do."

"Like you, you mean," said Susie.

"Very good, missus."

"You wanted to win your father's love by murdering my daughter."

Karen sneered. "I didn't need to win my dad's love by murdering your daughter. This is the whole fucking trouble with you, you have such a high opinion of yourself, you think the whole world revolves around the Drake surname. I already had my dad's approval, I gained it years and years ago and I gained it by not being a pussy. And I gained it by being clever, which is why I offered Emma a choice."

A damp stillness seemed to settle in the room. Susie knew that they'd arrived at the part of the story where Emma dies, and she wasn't sure she was ready. Just as she'd never wanted to watch the film, she didn't want to hear it from her killer's lips.

"But you didn't kill her," she said weakly, "she killed herself."

Karen nodded sagely, as though expecting credit for her wisdom. "I gave her a choice. I laid it out for her. I introduced myself, I told her who I was and what she'd done to me. I told her that if she'd just come along with me that day and we'd have got our money, she would have been returned safely and then maybe none of this would ever have happened. Her whole life might have taken a different course.

"I told her that she was going to die because some body-guard told her to bite me and then broke my arm. That this was the reason she had to die; that honor had to be satisfied. I told her that my need to satisfy that honor was as real to me as the need for heroin was to her. A good comparison, don't you think?

"And then I told her that she had a choice: either she come with me, and I would take her somewhere, to one of my dad's lock-ups, and I'd let the lads have their fun with her before I'd kill her. Or she could take her own life, there and then, on camera."

Susie swallowed. All she could find to say was "It wasn't much of a choice."

"I wanted to do it myself," said Karen. Her voice was bright, but her eyes were dead. "I really wanted to do it myself. I would have had fun in the lock-up. But it was better the way it happened. It put me in the clear. Plus I got to put it all online.

"I told her that I'd be uploading the footage, you know. I told her that her death would stand as a warning to others. Like, look what happens when pretty little rich girls mess with drugs. I told her that she might even prevent another girl from getting into the same predicament. And if she did that, then wasn't that a good thing?"

"You bitch," said Susie. The words escaped her like air from a balloon.

Karen nodded, smiling. "Yeah, I was very convincing. And she was so zonked out that she bought into it, without really thinking what it might do to Mommy and Daddy. Or maybe . . . maybe she *did* actually stop to consider the effect it would have on you. What about that? What if she thought that with her death she could land one final blow to her mommy and daddy? Or what if she thought that with her death she could make you *proud*? Christ, that's an even more twisted thought, isn't it?

"I could have done it another way that might have been more satisfying in the moment, pulling the trigger, slipping the blade in. But I liked this way too. It had the feel of a plan, and if it came out who she was, and anyone put me together with her, then there was no way Dmitry could turn round and accuse me of being behind her death. It was all up there on the screen.

"It would have worked like a dream but for the fact that men will always behave like men, and your husband had to have his tantrum." She lapsed into silence, seeming to think.

Susie prompted her: "So that's what happened? She did it herself?"

Karen nodded. "She used the gun I gave her. Dad would make sure there were people who could say she bought the gun herself.

"And then, when the deed was done and all the girls had stopped screaming and Jason had stopped puking, I got Jason to ring Sergei, who came down, and that was it. Think I told Jason not to breathe a word to anyone that I'd even been there, and good old Jason, he didn't. He didn't ask any questions. Just did as he was asked: rang Sergei, calmed the girls down. I rewarded him for his help by slitting his throat."

"You can add that to your tally," said Susie through clenched teeth.

"Oh, Mrs. Drake," said Karen, cocking her head. "It makes you angry to hear about this, doesn't it? How angry does it make you?"

And suddenly it struck Susie. She realized Karen had been clever, but not nearly so clever as she thought. She had overplayed her hand. The gun had been left there to tempt Susie. That's exactly what Karen wanted. Under the gaze of the CCTV camera, she *wanted* Susie to make a move.

Susie had been sitting forward in the deck chair, perhaps unconsciously readying herself to leap for the gun. She saw now that Karen was adapting her own body language to seem as relaxed and as casual as possible, practically inviting Susie to make her move.

She would have a knife hidden in those sleeves. Maybe the gun wasn't even loaded.

"And what about me?" said Susie. Very deliberately, she sat back in the deck chair, almost reclining, noticing a vexed look pass across Karen's face. They had both known that Susie was about to go for the gun. They both knew that Susie had changed her mind.

"What *about* you?" said Karen, her mouth set, knowing how close she'd come to executing her plan.

"Well, I was in the car, too," said Susie. "Don't you look at me and wish me dead?"

"You didn't bite me," said Karen unconvincingly.

"I don't believe you," said Susie. "I think that if you had your way you'd kill me just as you killed Emma, and maybe"—her eyes went to the gun so that Karen could see—"just as cleverly."

Karen was practically snarling.

"And of course, your husband . . . Dmitry, is it?" continued Susie. "He'll want to go through with the ransom demand and deliver me safely back in return for the money. Depriving you of the opportunity for further retribution."

And now Susie knew that she had to be careful not to antagonize the other woman too much. There was every possibility that Karen might simply lose her temper and attack. *Be careful now. Tread carefully.* "Perhaps you've made a mistake," she said softly, trying to be assertive but not overtly threatening. Thinking, *If I can just play this right . . .* "Because now I know, don't I? I mean, you've told me everything. And I in turn could tell Dmitry, perhaps? Or one of my guards."

Breathing heavily, nostrils flared, Karen said, "They'd never believe you."

"Oh really? Wouldn't they? Maybe not straightaway, but I'd be sowing the seeds of doubt, wouldn't I? They might be wondering what was said back there in the car. Why things didn't go according to plan at the spa. Maybe I'll tell them that things went south because I recognized you. And *why* I recognized you."

"You say a word and I'll slit your fucking throat."

Susie smiled. "But you can't do that, remember? You can't give yourself away." She raised her chin, indicating the CCTV camera that watched over them, and for a moment or so the two women simply stared at one another. God knows what Karen was thinking, but she'd played her hand and now her cards lay on the table.

As for Susie? Well, she was hardly in a position of strength. But maybe, just maybe . . .

"I've got a proposal for you," she said.

Karen looked at her carefully. "Go on."

"I won't say anything—"

"Like I say, you better fucking not."

"I won't say anything if you let me go," Susie finished.

"I let you go and I'm dead."

"Oh come on, you're clever. You can do this. You can work something out." She paused. "Look, just think about it. Decide what do you want to do. I won't say anything just yet."

Karen looked at her, breathing hard. "You think you've got the upper hand here, do you?" she said at last.

"Karen, you and I are about as different as two people could be. I'm talking to the woman who killed my daughter. Believe me when I say that I have *nothing* but hatred and contempt for you. I'd rather make a pact with the Devil himself than with you.

"But what I'm suggesting is for our mutual benefit. Believe me, I wouldn't be suggesting it otherwise. Let me go, and you can deal with your demons here, I'll deal with mine, and we'll both go to our graves knowing that with all this shit going on, at least we did one thing right."

Karen stood. Smiled. She reached for the gun on the table and for a moment Susie thought she might simply put a bullet in her there and then. Instead she tucked it into the waistband of her trousers.

"There is no deal," said Karen. "You tell Dmitry all you want. I'll take my chances. And you and your daughter can both burn in hell."

She spat on the sandwich, turned on the heel of her black boot, and left.

CHAPTER 50

SHELLEY HAD FOLLOWED Claridge back to the Drakes' home, Shelley in his Saab, Claridge in an agency Lexus.

"What if the media get hold of all this?" Shelley had asked before they left the hospital. "Back in the day Drake was what you'd call a celebrity."

"I wouldn't worry about it too much," Claridge had said.

"Really? Some inquisitive journalist—"

"'Inquisitive journalist'?" Claridge had scoffed. "They don't exist anymore. Journalists get all their news from Twitter and Facebook, and people like us telling them things we want them to hear. Fortunately, like you say, Guy Drake's day was before the advent of social media. He might as well not exist as far as the new world is concerned. A few lines about his daughter's death is pretty much where the interest in the Drakes starts and stops. The media are far more interested in Kim Kardashian unveiling her new bottom."

As for the crash at the Drakes' gates and the ongoing investigation, the police had managed to impose a media blackout. The road was closed off, supposedly with works, although Shelley knew that the men in hi-vis jackets were in fact cops.

Driving up to the gates Shelley saw that Johnson's BMW had been removed, though there were a couple of scene of crime officers still in attendance. Wearing white Tyvek suits, they were gathering the last of the evidence. The SOCOs looked up briefly but without much interest as Claridge and then Shelley passed through the twisted gates and onto the driveway, where their two cars joined what was a veritable fleet of police cars and other vehicles.

Inside the house was a hive of industry. Guy's home was in the unique position of being the center of two major crimes: the gruesome mutilation and murder of ex-Para Johnson as well as the kidnap of Susie Drake. There were so many cops there, all getting under each other's feet, that as officer in charge DI Phillips was ordering men to leave.

Also unique: the cops knew—or at least were 99 percent certain—exactly who were the perpetrators of both crimes. They even thought they knew why, despite the fact that Drake, Bennett, Gurney, and Shelley were all staying tight-lipped about the raid on Foxy Kittenz.

Needless to say, all of this was business that would need attending to in due course, when the dust had settled and it was time to make a forensic analysis of how the situation had advanced from point A, the suicide of Emma Drake, to point Z, the kidnap of her mother, Susie. But for the time being all such considerations were prioritized down. The cops, despite their suspicions, prejudices, and in some cases outright hostility toward Drake's crew, had one priority and that was to see Susie Drake returned safely.

Back in London they'd knocked on doors, of course.

Detectives had been laughed at by Chechens who provided them with cast-iron alibis.

In one corner of Drake's vast lounge were Drake, Shelley, Bennett, DI Phillips, and Claridge. In other parts of the room were the members of the Met's tech support team, ready to intercept and triangulate any call, even though, as they were constantly reminding the others in the room, there were ways for the bad guys to work around it.

Claridge had opened up his laptop to show Drake pictures of the perpetrators. Which was where the cracks that had already begun to appear developed into much more severe fissures.

Drake shook slightly, Shelley noticed. And his breath stank of Scotch. He was a man at the mercy of his demons, internal and external. Shelley found his heart going out to him. He wished he'd done more, been more emphatic, put his foot down. He wished he'd picked up the phone to Emma. He wished that he hadn't left in such a hurry all those years ago. He wished that he and Susie Drake had never shared that kiss.

"So these are the Russians, are they?" said Drake. And it wasn't just his hands that shook.

Claridge peered over the top of his glasses at Drake with concern. They could all smell the booze. "They're Chechens, Mr. Drake. They don't like being called Russians."

"Then I'll call them Russians if it's all the same to you," snapped Drake, and Claridge nodded, the way you do when a man at the end of his tether says something patently ridiculous.

Shelley tried to catch Drake's eye, telepathically tell him to calm the fuck down, but failed. The bigwig smiling on page four of the *Daily Mirror*—that geezer was unrecognizable now.

The MI5 man continued flicking through the pictures until they got to Karen. Here, Shelley took over.

"You remember the kidnap attempt, of course," he said to Drake. Once more he tried to bring him to a place where they could have a reasonable conversation, one untainted by anger and resentment and all the shitty emotions bobbling around them like escaped party balloons.

Drake nodded.

"There was a woman, remember?" pressed Shelley. "I broke her arm."

"I've not lost my marbles. I remember, Shelley," barked the older man defensively.

"Right, well. This is her. This is that woman." He told Drake about her involvement with the Chechens, the union of the two families, adding, "Now, it's possible . . . well, look, what I'm thinking is that she crossed paths with Emma somehow. Say the two of them recognized one another. Maybe that's why Emma killed herself, out of fear. Or maybe she was compelled to do it somehow, I don't know. I can't speculate about that right now. Just that there's this connection. Just as she—"

"She killed Emma?"

All eyes were on Drake. He was breathing heavily through his nose.

"I'm saying it's possible, yes," replied Shelley carefully.

"Now she's kidnapped Susie," stated Drake.

"That much is beyond doubt," said Claridge. "Positive IDs from Lucy, and from the women at the spa. Unfortunately, we also have thirty Chechen women who will say that she was at a charity function the exact moment the kidnap was taking place, meaning that right now, we haven't got a thing on her."

Drake turned a scornful gaze on Claridge. "So you're just sitting on your arse waiting for her to call the shots?"

Claridge met Drake's fierce stare. Perhaps he was thinking that Drake only had himself to blame for his current predicament. But ever the diplomat, the good civil servant, he held his tongue on that score and said, "It's the only avenue open to us, Mr. Drake."

Shelley jumped in, thinking this would be a good time to speak to Drake alone. "Listen, let's call a break, shall we? I want to have a word with Guy, if that's all right with you."

Judging by the relief written all over the faces of the men around the table, it was a popular decision.

CHAPTER 51

"GUY, YOU HAVE to calm down, mate. You're losing control. And you've been drinking. Why the fuck did you think your wife being kidnapped was a good time to start knocking back the booze in the middle of the day?" He spoke loudly and in a way that he doubted Drake had been spoken to in a long, long time. If Shelley didn't need him to stay calm and focused for Dmitry's impending phone call, he would have been happy to keep him out of the game altogether—send him to bed with a big glass of Scotch and a couple of happy pills. Perfect. "I need you to stay strong," he told Drake.

Drake spluttered, "What the fuck do you mean, *you* need *me*? Why are you even here? Your fucking wife didn't help Susie—"

In the next second Shelley had Drake's shirt bunched in his fist and was shoving him backward, the older man's heels skidding on the kitchen floor before he thumped heavily into the refrigerator, the kind with huge double doors in brushed steel, one of which was now dented.

"Don't you dare," hissed Shelley, "don't you *fucking* dare.

Lucy—*my fucking wife*—almost died trying to keep Susie out of their hands. She winged one of them. Got descriptions of the rest. It's because of her that we know exactly who we're dealing with here. And you can count yourself lucky that I need you in one piece to keep Susie alive, or God help me I'd knock your block off right now."

"The problem being that I wouldn't let you do that, Shelley," came a voice from behind.

It was Bennett, voice calm with the kind of authority you get when you're holding a gun on someone.

Shelley relaxed his hands on Drake's shirt. "Did you hear what he said?"

"It wouldn't make any difference, my friend. I'm paid to provide security, and I'm pretty sure that not allowing my boss to get beaten up falls within my remit. Are you all right, sir?" he added, directing his question to Drake.

Drake pulled himself out of the dent in his fridge, shrugging off Shelley, who stepped away. "I'm all right."

"Would you like me to ask Mr. Shelley to leave?"

"No, Mr. Shelley can stay for the time being," said Drake, glaring at Shelley.

"Then perhaps we should all relax," said Bennett.

Shelley turned as Bennett holstered his weapon. "The kidnapper's been in touch," he told Bennett, which was what he'd planned to tell Drake in the first place.

"*What?*" blasted Drake. "You never told me that—"

"You never gave me the chance," Shelley clapped back. "But that's why I need you calm. He's ringing back with his demands later."

Bennett nodded thoughtfully. He pushed his glasses up his nose. "And I take it you want to keep this between us?"

"There's no way they could have bugged this place, is there?" asked Shelley.

"They haven't had the chance," Bennett assured him.

"Well, look, ultimately the decision about whether or not we tell the cops lies with Guy. It's his wife whose life is in danger; it's his money the kidnappers will be asking for. Guy, do you think you're in any fit state to make that decision?"

"Oh, go fuck yourself, Shelley."

"Grow up, Guy," Shelley shot back.

They glowered at one another. For a second, Shelley thought Drake might blow, but perhaps there was a semblance of the old Guy beneath all that scar tissue, for he seemed to take stock for a second. And perhaps he realized how childish he'd sounded.

"I am," he said, chastened. "Of course I am."

Shelley breathed an inner sigh of relief. "Well, in that case it's a decision you need to make sooner rather than later," he explained. "I've been involved in hostage situations, and so has Bennett here," he looked across and received an affirmative nod in return, "and I expect he's going to agree with me that things very quickly go tits up when the police get involved. You get the cops on board and they'll tell you that their main priority is to keep the victim safe, and it is—kind of—but only if it doesn't conflict with their next priority, which is to capture the kidnappers.

"On the other hand, if you decide not to tell the cops, then you're also agreeing to giving in to the ransom demands. And it may well be that they choose not to play by the book."

Drake nodded as he processed the information. "What are your impressions of this guy Kraviz?" he asked.

"First of all, he's a Chechen, not a Russian. You need to

get your head around that. Second, he's pissed off with us. He thinks that we've damaged his business and insulted him, and we've got every right to expect him to want some pretty brutal payback. If you were ordinary Joe Public then that's what you'd get.

"The advantage you've got is that you're rich, so he's got the chance to make a lot of money quickly. He's tasted blood, thanks to poor old Johnson. But from the way he's conducted himself after that, I'd say he's going down the route of wanting the cash in lieu of any more reprisals."

"So what now?" asked Drake.

"Now? Now we wait."

"Sir," said Bennett, "not long ago you were telling us about your kidnapper money. Is that still available?"

Shelley gave a start. "Wait a second. What's this? What 'kidnapper money'?"

Bennett deferred to Drake to explain, and Drake shot Shelley a look of distaste, still harboring a grudge, before he said, "A year or so ago, when I suspected Emma was in trouble, I put some money aside in case something like this happened. Money in an offshore account, that can be transferred quickly and without alerting my bank or the authorities."

"The rich-man equivalent of mugger money?"

"Something like that."

"How much?"

"Twenty million," said Drake.

Shelley looked from Bennett to Drake. "That's why he asked for twenty million earlier. This conversation, when you told Bennett about it. Was Johnson involved?"

Drake nodded.

"Figures."

CHAPTER 52

CLARIDGE HAD LEFT. In charge was DI Phillips, who still didn't seem to know how to handle Guy Drake and his men. Were they suspects or victims?

In the end, Phillips decided to hedge his bets and treat them like a mixture of both, which meant he was stuck playing good cop one minute, bad cop the next, so every now and then he'd ask them politely whether they'd heard from the kidnappers. No, they'd say, each man playing his part to perfection. Of course not. After which he'd accuse them of hiding something. And they'd say no we're not.

By now Gurney had been clued in, but he stayed on the sidelines, and thank God for that, as far as Shelley was concerned. A couple of hours passed. Shelley and Bennett kept themselves away from the cops on the pretext of making tea or checking on Drake. All four of them were shooting each other anxious glances, waiting, waiting.

And then suddenly Drake sped past and flashed Shelley a significant look, Bennett not far behind. Shelley checked the cops were oblivious to the exodus and then followed them into the kitchen, gently closing the door and moving to stand with the others.

For a moment or so Drake merely held the vibrating phone, and Shelley wondered if he was even going to answer it, when abruptly he raised the handset to his ear. "Hello," he said simply, and Shelley was relieved at the lack of needle in his voice. Thankfully he'd remembered that a kidnapping situation was all about negotiation. Then, "Yes, this is Guy Drake speaking. Is this Dmitry?" He held the phone away from his ear, putting it on speaker.

"Yes, it is I, Dmitry," they heard. "The last time we spoke you were discourteous and disrespectful, but I think you will not make that mistake again, am I right?"

Drake reddened but remembered himself, cleared his throat, swallowed his pride, and spoke: "No, I won't make that mistake again."

"Good, and I trust your colleague Captain Shelley has kept you abreast of all the latest developments?"

"He has."

"Good. A go-between is very useful, I think."

"I would like to talk to my wife," said Drake, and once again Shelley found himself breathing a sigh of relief. Drake was getting past Dmitry's jibes, moving on to deal with the important matter impressed on him by Shelley: demanding proof of life.

"Of course," said Dmitry. His voice went slightly distant. "Mrs. Drake, please tell your husband how well you're being treated."

The next voice belonged to Susie: "Guy, I'm all right, they're being good to me—" She was cut short, as though the phone had been snatched away.

"Sweetheart, honey, I love you," Drake was saying quickly. The words tumbled out of him. His eyes gleamed with tears. And for a moment, the space of a heartbeat, he looked like a lost child.

"No, no, Mrs. Drake," they heard as Dmitry returned to the call. "You can have this conversation another time, later tonight, maybe, when you are back home safe and sound, drinking tea and telling of your exciting day with those lovely Chechens, yes?"

"What do you mean, *tonight*?" asked Drake. His jaw clenched, chewing.

Shelley and Bennett exchanged a look. They wanted to do the exchange right away. *Good news*, thought Shelley. They could have got more, but were prepared to settle for £20 million in return for a quick and painless trade.

"I am about to give you the details of an account," said Dmitry. "Transfer the money from your secret offshore account into that and, when it is done, I will deposit Mrs. Drake at . . ."

Shelley was shaking his head. Drake looked at him, confused, in need of more detail.

"Ah, you're being coached," they heard Dmitry say. "It is Captain Shelley again, is it? Put him on, Mr. Drake, so that he can tell me himself what he wants to say."

Shelley took the phone. "There'll be no money transfer until we see Susie. When she's standing there in front of us, unharmed, and when we're confident that you plan to honor the agreement. Only then are we pushing buttons, got it?"

There was a pause. "We are the ones with the hostage, Captain Shelley," said Dmitry, firmly but agreeably.

"I'm not disputing that. And believe me, I've no intention

of trying to double-cross you on this. Just that it makes no sense for us to pay up ahead of time. Don't take us for fools, Dmitry, because if you do we might be tempted to act like fools. Be straight with us and you'll get the same in return."

Dmitry gave a short chortle. "Oh, he drives a hard bargain, and yet I find I have to agree. Let us all meet together and do our business."

"Tell me what I have to do," said Drake.

"You do, of course, remember my studio. Not the studio in which your daughter Emma died, but the other one. The one that you burned to the ground. That one. We meet there at midnight tonight. Mr. Drake, do you understand me so far? We will bring your wife, unharmed, to the meeting point, and you will bring the means of transferring the twenty million that you have in your ransom fund to me. When the transfer is made you may have your wife back in one piece. It really is that simple.

"Now, I hardly need to tell you that this negotiation operates on trust. You trust me to bring your wife unharmed. I trust you to provide the money. Because I know that there are police there with you now, I have to insist that the person in charge of the handover comes alone."

Shelley shook his head and did the slit-throat motion with his finger. *Absolutely not.* In response, Drake nodded that he'd got the point. "I want to bring one of my men," he told Dmitry.

Dmitry chuckled. "Mr. Drake, I haven't finished outlining my terms. And I'm afraid to say that one of these is that you, personally, will not be present at the handover."

"No, no," protested Drake, "Susie's my wife. All this is down to me. I'm coming."

"No, Mr. Drake," replied Dmitry almost wistfully, "for you it is all too personal. As you say yourself, it is your temper, your pride that has brought us to this unfortunate crossroads. Besides, your house is crawling with police, is it not? You have to remain where you are. This is the beauty of the plan. This whole transaction will take place under their noses."

Yes. Shelley could see it. There were police at the house; no doubt there were cops keeping watch on the Chechens, too. Having handed over the money and collected Susie, she would have to be left somewhere and from there contact the police with a story about being dropped off. The cops might suspect collusion; they might think that an exchange had taken place. But with the Chechens and Guy Drake both under surveillance and no evidence of any withdrawal from Drake's bank account they'd come to the conclusion that the Chechens had got cold feet and released Susie. Providing she was unharmed they were unlikely to continue the investigation with a great deal more enthusiasm. It was virtually end of story.

It was a good, maybe even great, plan. And of course it meant that the Chechens were less likely to feel the heat. Any heat at all.

Mostly, though, it was encouraging for what it suggested to Shelley, which was that the Chechens intended to keep up their end of the bargain. It was in their interests to make sure everything went smoothly.

For that reason Shelley allowed himself to believe this whole shitstorm could have a positive outcome, and instantly reversed his previous reluctance, indicating to Drake that he should accept the plan.

"Good," said Dmitry, and Shelley thought he detected a

note of genuine relief below all the bonhomie. "Then we shall see Mr. Shelley tonight. Shortly after, you will be reunited with your wife, Mr. Drake. We will consider your debt to us paid, and I myself will disregard the insult you have given to me.

"But let that be an end to it, do you hear me, Mr. Drake? You have watched me demonstrate my power. Believe me, you do not want a second example. Good night, sweet dreams."

CHAPTER 53

THEY HAD POSTED a round-the-clock guard in Lucy's room, which was a good thing, of course. But it did mean that talking to her was difficult. In the end she and Shelley had a truncated and very one-sided telephone conversation during which he told her the plan for later.

He told her the ins and outs, the way he thought the plan would work and why it was engineered in such a way that he doubted the Chechens planned a double-cross. And when he'd finished she said "Okay," but in a long-drawn-out fashion that suggested she might have her doubts—doubts they weren't in any position to discuss. Maybe he was even somewhat grateful that the guard was present, because it meant she wasn't able to quiz him on all that other stuff bubbling just below the surface: the loyalty, misplaced or not. The sense of duty. The guilt.

"Just be careful," she told him, which he supposed was about as much as she could say without arousing the suspicions of her guard.

*　　*　　*

Drake did what Shelley had wanted him to do earlier, he took himself off to bed. A couple of hours after that, Shelley announced he was leaving.

"Really? I thought you were on Mr. Drake's security team?" said DI Phillips, who himself was preparing to depart for the night.

"You thought wrong. I'm a consultant," said Shelley, "and I've got a wife in the hospital. Bennett will keep me informed of any developments regarding Susie Drake. Otherwise I'm needed in London."

For a moment he wondered if Phillips was simply going to forbid him from leaving. He could picture the thoughts flashing through the other man's head. Did he have any legal right to stop Shelley leaving? Was there any investigative justification for making him stay? Phillips, of course, knew that Shelley was friendly with Claridge and had the MI5 man's trust, his seal of approval. No doubt all of this played a part in his decision. "All right, leave if you must. But don't think about going too far, will you?"

Shelley briefly considered pressing the point—*So what if I do?*—then decided against. He made a show of saying good-bye to Bennett and Gurney and that was it. He put Guy Drake's mansion, with its twisted metal gates and so many memories, to his back, and headed for home.

He had a job to do.

CHAPTER 54

ALTHOUGH GRANDFATHER LIKED to watch his films from the machine shop every now and then, in the afternoon he mostly preferred to watch soap operas, especially the Australian ones: *Neighbours* and *Home and Away* were his favorites.

Around him that afternoon there had been a great deal of activity. He'd heard talk of a snatch, some woman apparently. And dimly, amidst a general irritation at the constant noise that interrupted his viewing, he had wondered if his skills might be called upon.

It had been a long time since he'd worked on a woman. It would be good to get the chance. Still, he had no intention of broaching the subject with his idiot grandson Dmitry. That boy had no idea of the old ways. To him the camps and Gulag were something ripped from the history books, as distant and remote to him as Jack the Ripper was to the East Enders of London. Dmitry's idea of the relationship between fear and power was vague and received. He could have no concept of terror's potent hold because he had never experienced it for himself. Dmitry believed that his old grandfather and even his father were men out of time; to him their means of keeping order were an anachronism, embarrassing like coarse manners.

Neither did he know of the sheer pleasure one could experience by inflicting such intense pain. That in itself was a form of power. Grandfather saw how Dmitry and his ilk would react. Men who carried guns and used their fists with impunity, men of violence, would wince and pale when he produced his instruments. His art was too much even for them. He took them to places they'd rather not go, and doing that conferred upon him an even greater authority.

And of course they thought he was stupid because that's what the young think. They couldn't see past the trembling hands, defective hearing, and battered eyesight. They interpreted a slowing of thought as a decline in intelligence. They paid lip service to the idea of experience, but that's all it was because secretly they believed all their bright ideas were new ones.

Think of me as a dinosaur all you want, Dmitry, but this organization was built upon the rusted blade of my saw. Relic I might be, totem I definitely am.

Later on, things began to calm down. There was less noise. Fewer folk coming and going. Once more Grandfather was able to concentrate on the television. He had increased the volume to a near-ear-splitting level as a form of protest, but now he reached for the control and returned it to its normal setting.

Still, he thought. It would have been interesting to make this woman's acquaintance. What fun he might have had.

And so his spirits rose when one of the men came to him

shortly after dark, entering the front room tentatively, as they all did, bowing and showing his respect, as they all did, and said, "I have been asked if you would like to accompany me to the machine shop, *Ded*."

Grandfather enjoyed the effect his smile had on these underlings. "Dmitry?" he asked.

"No, *Ded*. It is Mrs. Kraviz who asks if you would come to the machine shop. She has a task she thinks you might enjoy. She has asked me to inform you that it is her gift to you, as a sign of respect."

Now, this was a lot better, thought Grandfather. Dmitry's wife Karen was a Londoner and spoke like *cor blimey, guv'nor*, but she had a toughness Grandfather admired.

Like most of them in the organization, he detested the Regans and longed for the day the merger would become a takeover. But unlike his grandson he knew there were things they could learn from the old-fashioned gangsters. The Regans knew how to keep their house in order. The Regans had gone down the path that Dmitry wanted to take. They had seen the error of their ways. They had corrected their route.

"Get my coat," he said, already looking forward to the task ahead. "Oh, and I will also need my instruments, I take it?"

"Mrs. Kraviz has asked me to tell you that your instruments are waiting for you," said the visitor.

"Excellent," drawled Grandfather. "Excellent."

CHAPTER 55

SHELLEY PUSHED THE curtain aside, looked out of his window, and saw the car in the road. He pulled on a coat, went out, and tapped on the car window. It slid down.

"Hello, mate," he said.

The guy inside, a plainclothes if ever Shelley had seen one, said, "All right, mate."

"What are you doing here, then?" he asked. "In a quiet cul-de-sac like this."

"Waiting," said the cop defensively. "No law against it, is there?"

"Well, *you* should know," jibed Shelley.

The guy blinked but said nothing.

"It's someone who lives on this street, is it, that you're waiting for?" pressed Shelley.

The guy nodded.

"I see. Well, you need a residents' parking permit to stop here," Shelley told him primly. "If you don't get one, I'm afraid I'm going to have to call the police."

For a moment, he wondered if the guy was simply going

to drop the charade. But, "Well, you'd best do that then," the driver replied.

"Tell you what," said Shelley. "I'm just going to be in my room watching a box set on my laptop. There's my car"—he pointed at his Saab. "I won't call the cops if you keep an eye on it for me."

The surveillance guy clenched his jaw, looking even more severely pissed off than he had before. Satisfied that he'd done a good job of winding him up, Shelley disappeared back inside.

In the house, he moved quickly into the kitchen, minuscule compared to the Drakes' snooker-hall-sized version, but home. There were lots of drawers in the kitchen, but only one that he and Lucy called "the kitchen drawer," and he went to it now, yanking it open and raking through the contents until he found what he wanted: a timer, the type you plug into a wall to control appliances.

Moving to the bedroom, he set the timer and switched on the light. It was the oldest trick in the book, the kind of thing used to deter burglars in 1982, but he was hoping it would satisfy Philip Marlowe outside.

Then, on the off-chance that his friend outside had the means of hacking into his internet, he started something streaming on the iPlayer.

Now then. 10 p.m. That gave him two hours until the exchange. He dressed: jeans, T-shirt, sweatshirt, bomber jacket. Into the waistband of his jeans he clipped the holster carrying his SIG then grabbed his phone and, lastly, the spare keys to Lucy's Mini.

Next he returned downstairs, checked out the window, and then, very quietly, let himself out the back door.

He stopped to listen, savoring the quiet—a low, humming, thrumming city kind of quiet—and then climbed the wall that separated their yard from the cemetery behind. He dropped onto the soft ground and made his way through gravestones silhouetted against the night like rotting teeth, until he reached the entrance gate, locked and chained.

The climb was short work. A second later he was in the street, satisfied nobody had seen him. He pulled his cap out of his pocket and fixed it on his head, feeling human again. He found a minicab, "Hampstead, please," and about forty minutes later he was dropped off at the health spa. There he saw the aftermath of Lucy's gun battle: boarded-up windows, bullet holes in the car park surface pinpointed by forensic marker spray—and Lucy's car.

He checked there was no one around, and that he hadn't been followed, then opened up and climbed inside.

The scent of her stopped him for a moment. Lucy smell. And for a second he longed to be with her, sitting by her bedside or preferably at home with her, eating dinner or in front of the TV, even bloody "brainstorming" to find new work if that was what she wanted.

This was where his need to know the truth and his sense of duty had brought him: her in the hospital, him off to meet Chechens. *Jesus.*

He started the car.

CHAPTER 56

GRANDFATHER'S CAR PULLED into the car park of the MOT & Service Center, where his driver knew better than to attempt to offer a hand, waiting patiently for Grandfather to climb out.

The driver unlocked the service center door. Lights inside the reception area flicked on as Grandfather led the way through reception, through the office area and then into the workshop. Here the lights were already on, the place empty of its usual clinking-clanking industry, the machine shop door at the end closed with its chain and padlock fastening hanging loose.

Grandfather stood slightly to one side in order to allow his chaperone to open the door, and then together they entered the room.

His face fell. He had rather hoped the woman would already be in place, but although the chair was in situ there was no sign of a subject. At least his instruments were there, laid out on the table: scalpel, surgical saw, pliers.

He was about to make his way over to the table and

take a seat when he felt arms grasp him roughly from behind. "Hey—" he started to say as the first man was joined by a second and he was lifted bodily, dragged to the chair, and shoved down. In a routine that he himself had witnessed many times before, the men fastened him to the chair.

"What are you doing?" he said with no hint of fear or surprise in his voice, because he had always half expected that something like this might happen. "Who is behind this?"

His answer came as one of the men dragged across a second chair and set it up in front of him. A silver laptop was placed on the chair and opened. The man fiddled for a while before an image resolved.

"Full screen, make it full screen," said another. Now Grandfather could see who was behind this role reversal.

It was Sergei. At the other end of the link he sat and dispassionately surveyed a scene that he had presumably masterminded. More than ever now, Grandfather was pleased that he had made Ivan Vinitsky suffer. Now he understood it was Sergei's intention to make him suffer in return, to avenge his brother, but—and here Grandfather smiled—they would not have the stomach to inflict the kind of pain that was his specialty. They were too weak for that.

"Hello, *Ded*," said his grandson's second in command over the link. "All has gone according to my plan, I see."

"Your brother begged," snarled Grandfather. A grin split his lips despite himself, despite his situation.

"As will you, *Ded*, as will you," Sergei assured him. "Now, where shall we start? Is everything ready?"

"Yes, boss," said one of the men.

"Tell us, *Ded*, where should we begin?" asked Sergei politely.

"The nipples," croaked Grandfather. "I always start with the nipples."

He looked into the eyes of the man who had betrayed him as they cut off his sweater and then sliced his nipples away. And when that was over, he told them, "Next . . . next, the ears."

Sergei shook his head in disgust and closed his laptop, leaving a black screen to watch the rest of the old man's torture.

CHAPTER 57

RIGHT, THOUGHT SHELLEY. He had just enough time to get to Millharbour across the river, a journey he had to make quickly, but without attracting attention from the cops. In his favor: he had an hour. Points against? This was London and you never went anywhere fast.

As he drove he watched Canary Wharf Tower grow in his windshield, steam rising from its pyramid roof, the aircraft-warning light blinking on and off hypnotically. Soon enough he had passed it, and he knew he was close to Millharbour. Now it was as though he were in its shadow.

Funny, he thought as he traveled, he had been brought up not far from here, in Limehouse, but it might as well have been another country for all he recognized it. In his time it was abandoned dockyards. There were no towers, just neglected cranes. He'd gone away, joined the army at seventeen, and when he returned the London he knew had gone.

As he left Canary Wharf behind, the elevated tracks of the railway line—the Docklands Light Railway—rose to his left, tracing his journey as the gleaming office blocks eventually gave way to the more modest units at the far end of Millharbour, all of which backed onto a less picturesque and therefore less expensive section of the River Thames.

Here there was little to no traffic. The main reason anybody had to be in this area was to work at one of the office blocks or factory units, and most of those were shut for the night, workers tucked up in bed.

And then he came to it, the road he needed. He hadn't realized the last time he'd come — something to do with being cooped up in the back of a van — but it was a cul-de-sac. On one side was a row of office units, on the other a patch of land fenced off, signs promising more office units to come.

Further down the road he saw that three of the units were burned-out shells, and parked close to them, in the middle of the road facing toward him, was a black Jeep Cherokee, headlights on half beam. Shelley stopped. A stretch of road lay between his Mini and the Cherokee.

Taking a look around, it struck him that with the undeveloped site on one side and the cover of the burned-out buildings on the other, they were shielded from view. Anybody coming down here would be doing so by accident. The other units were vacant, so with Foxy Kittenz and the building next door out of commission, there was literally no reason for anyone to use this road.

He switched off the engine and then reached into his trousers to drag out his phone, about to dial Dmitry when it rang in his hand.

"Hello?" he said, raising it to his ear.

"Hello? Is that Captain Shelley?"

"It is."

Pause. "I mean to say, is that Captain Shelley whose car I am looking at?"

Shelley flashed his lights twice.

"One, two, three in a row, please, just to satisfy me."

Shelley did as he was asked.

"And you have come alone?"

"It's in our interests to keep up our end of the bargain, Dmitry. I only hope you feel the same."

In the rearview mirror he saw the shape of a black Transit van about a hundred yards at his six. They were boxing him in.

"Who's that behind?" he said sharply. "Is that your men?"

"Why, yes, of course. There is a need to prevent anybody accidentally using the road, no? We do not want to be disturbed."

Okay, thought Shelley. *Stay frosty. He's making sense.*

On the other hand, they could be blocking the road to stop Shelley and Susie leaving.

But no. Everything so far pointed to Dmitry wanting a smooth exchange. Shelley had to go with his gut on this one.

"Well then, Captain, would I be right in assuming you have brought the necessary details you need to make the transfer?"

"I need to know something first," said Shelley.

Dmitry sighed. "Really?"

"Just humor me."

"Go on."

"Emma's death," said Shelley. "You said you weren't involved . . ."

"And I wasn't."

". . . but what about someone else in your organization?"

"You see," said Dmitry, "this is what I am trying to tell you, Captain Shelley. This is what you don't understand. There are two types of people in this world. There are the bosses, and there are those who *have* bosses.

"The bosses, there are very few of them, and they're people like Mr. Drake, who answer to no one and nothing, not even the law. And it is their attacks of pride, their whims, to which we must attend. They are the reason we find ourselves in positions such as this one.

"Then there are the second type of people. That is people like us, Captain, you and I, who must do the bidding of our masters. Carry out their orders. Now, in most instances, people like you and I have only one aim. And that is to not displease bosses, and we do that by doing what is good for business. And what is good for business is making money.

"Bodies, on the other hand, are bad for business. Because as soon as you have a body you have emotion. You have angry rich fathers, you have policemen becoming interested, ex-SAS men trying to make a quick buck. All of it is bad for business.

"I would have had nothing to do with the killing of Emma Drake simply because it was bad for business and that would displease my bosses. My own employees would have nothing to do with the death of Emma Drake because that would displease me. Do you understand?"

Now Shelley got to the point: "Okay, so not you. Not your men. What about your wife?"

"Karen?" said Dmitry with a mixture of surprise and affrontedness. "What on earth do you mean?"

"What I say. Did Karen have anything to do with Emma Drake's death?"

"Karen works for me," laughed Dmitry loudly, "I am her boss. She also understands the need for good business. No. The answer to your question is no. Now," he sounded irritated, "shall we proceed? You have a smartphone, I take it, or did Mr. Drake furnish you with a laptop?"

"I'm using my own smartphone. I've memorized the information I need . . ."

"Of course you have. I would expect nothing less."

"But here's the deal," said Shelley. "I'll transfer half to you now. I get Susie to the car, drive to the end of the road where your men are stationed, and only then do I transfer the other half."

He could hear Dmitry suck on his teeth. "And if you fail to do it?"

"You tell your guys 'fetch.'"

He seemed to consider. "I'm not sure how this benefits you."

"I like those odds better."

"Very well," said Dmitry. "Just don't forget, Captain, that I intend to abide by this arrangement. If, however, I think even for a second that you do not, then my retribution will be swift and ruthless. Do we understand each other?"

"All that's important to me is making sure that Susie Drake is safe," said Shelley.

"And all that is important to me," said Dmitry, "is my twenty million."

"Then yes," said Shelley, "we do understand each other."

"At last. Now, step out of your car, please, Captain Shelley."

Shelley found himself reaching to the grip of his SIG for

comfort. "You'll need to do the same your end," he said. "I want to see you, whoever is with you, and Susie."

The Cherokee sat, keeping its secrets, the lights on low beam but still xenon-white and bright.

"Captain Shelley," began Dmitry, "please stop trying to play the hand as though you hold all the cards. I find it a little annoying. I will show you Susie Drake. After all, she is the reason we are all here. Now, step out of the car, please. I enjoy our little chats, but maybe not as much as I will enjoy getting home at the end of the night."

"Okay," said Shelley. "I'm getting out of the car."

Heart hammering, he picked up his hat and fitted it to his head. Then he reached for the door handle and stepped out.

CHAPTER 58

OUT OF THE car he was in the open. A sniper could take him out. But then again, no, what would be the point?

This was what he told himself. To take a shot at him before the cash transfer would be crackers, the behavior of a fool. And one thing he was pretty sure of when it came to Dmitry: he wasn't a fool.

But on the other hand, maybe it all felt too easy. Thanks to Johnson the kidnappers had the whole process sewn up. After all, the snatch had happened that morning, and here he was ready to do the exchange. This was a procedure that Shelley had known take months to complete, being wrapped up in just a matter of hours. They'd used the word *negotiation*, but there hadn't been one: just two sets of people who couldn't wait to get it over and done with.

Was that it? Was it all going *too well*?

The Cherokee was about a hundred yards away. He turned his head. About the same distance in the opposite direction was the Transit. There were already men standing close by. Their breath billowed and he saw the outline of the handguns they held, but otherwise they were silhouettes, like targets at a shooting range.

Facing front again he watched as the Cherokee decanted its passengers. First came a woman, and for a disorienting second Shelley assumed it was Susie, but no, of course not, it must be Karen Regan. She wore a dark, belted coat and from this far away it was too difficult to make out features, no way of recognizing her as the same woman who had put a gun to the back of his head fourteen years ago.

Now came a second woman, this one with rounded shoulders, wearing gym gear. No doubt about it, this was Susie. Again, it was impossible to say from this distance but she looked unharmed. As he watched she seemed to straighten, as though remembering herself, wanting to present a proud face to the world. "Well done, Susie," he said under his breath. "Give 'em hell."

Next to Susie stood a man with dark hair and a pronounced widow's peak, who Shelley recognized from the photos. This was Sergei Vinitsky.

Beside him came Dmitry Kraviz, slightly taller, wearing a T-shirt with some kind of logo, an unzipped top worn over it, and a pair of spectacles, the kind that hung on a chain around his neck like schoolteachers used to wear.

Now they faced each other, like gunslingers, which he supposed at least three of them were. Dmitry raised a hand, beckoning Shelley forward, calling at the same time, "Come, Captain Shelley. Let us finish this thing, yes?"

Shelley walked forward, seeing his own breath cloud in front of him, dragon's breath that billowed then evaporated, billowed then evaporated. He felt in his chest the rhythmic but reassuring thump of his heart, calmed by the fact that he had long ago learned not only to control but to harness his fear, and feeling a little bit of that old buzz back at the same time.

Opposite, the four of them began to walk forward. Behind them, the two front doors of the Cherokee opened again and a couple more guys made their presence known, standing close by the vehicle, ready if needed.

Jesus, how many guys have they brought? Shelley was relying on Dmitry's integrity, telling himself that it didn't matter who was along for the ride because what they didn't have was the money, and they wouldn't get that until Susie was in the Mini and they were home and dry.

Just a few yards apart now, and the Dmitry quartet drew to a halt. Nighttime mist, lit by the headlights of the Cherokee, swirled around their feet. He could see their features now: Dmitry, relaxed and cool, Sergei and Karen unreadable, Susie proud but unable to completely hide her fear.

"Susie, are you all right?" he asked her.

She looked at him, staring hard at him, and he thought she was trying to tell him something, trying to warn him of something, maybe. But what?

Dmitry said something in Russian to Sergei, who nodded in response, before Dmitry took a few more steps forward.

And then, behaving as though he had just caught sight of Shelley across a crowded pub, his face split into a broad grin. "Captain Shelley," he exclaimed, spreading his hands. For a crazy second Shelley thought they were going to embrace but instead Dmitry continued, "I am very reassured by the sight of the phone you have in your hand, Captain. Less reassured, I must say, by the bulge at your waistband."

Shelley tipped his head behind and then at the Cherokee

beyond. "By the looks of things you've brought an entire army."

"I had to," said Dmitry, as though such things were not beyond dispute. "I had to make sure that we had the place to ourselves." He gestured at the burned-out buildings to Shelley's left. Through their blackened skeletal ruins Shelley could see the silvery gleam of the river, and beyond that a distant mosaic of lights from blocks of luxury flats on the far bank. In those flats people lay in bed or sat watching TV. Or perhaps they sat by their windows, enjoying their moderately expensive view of the Thames, oblivious to what was taking place on the other side of the water.

"Can't tell a lie, Dmitry, it doesn't half make me nervous seeing all these guns," said Shelley.

Dmitry pulled a mock-doubtful face. "Oh, I doubt that very much. You are Captain Shelley of the SAS. A few guns shouldn't worry you."

"Tell you what, then," said Shelley, "how about you holster those sidearms, just as a show of good faith?"

"Sounds fair," said Dmitry, pushing his Makarov into the front of his jeans. He tilted his head backward and Sergei did the same. Karen, however, did not. Her black-gloved hands remained crossed, the gun held in front of her.

"Your wife doesn't seem to want to cooperate," said Shelley, speaking to Dmitry but directing himself to Karen.

"Awright, hero?" she said. "You know who I am, then?"

"I know exactly who you are," said Shelley.

"Good. That's nice of you to remember," she said. She moved her right arm away from her body so that Shelley could see for himself that it had never fully healed.

"You had to learn to shoot with your left," he said, saw

the look of fury that passed across her face and immediately regretted his words, knowing that to antagonize her was a bad move.

Meanwhile, Dmitry was looking from one to the other, Shelley to Karen and back again, like a man who had just made a delightful discovery, and who knows? Maybe he had. "You know each other, it seems," he said. Shelley caught the glint of a gold tooth.

"Yeah, you could say that," replied Shelley.

"We had a bit of business years back, love," said Karen without taking her eye off Shelley.

"Oh," said Dmitry, rearing back. "You weren't . . . you know . . . were you?"

She gave a dry laugh. "Not likely. It was all business."

"Unfinished business, I think, by the looks of things," roared Dmitry, enjoying his own joke. "Don't you think, Sergei?"

"Yes, boss," said Sergei.

"Well, I shall look forward to hearing all about this business later, Karen. Now, Captain, shall we begin with the part where you show me the color of Mr. Drake's money."

"First Susie comes by my side," said Shelley.

"Suit yourself. Mrs. Drake? Please do as our friend asks."

Susie shook herself free of Sergei's restraining arm then stepped forward without a backward glance. Gratefully she took a place by Shelley's side and they greeted one another with their eyes.

Next Shelley loaded the banking app he'd been given by Drake, a strange, unfamiliar icon on his handset. It was already primed for the first phase of the transfer. "Here," he said to Dmitry, handing him the phone, "input your details."

"Tsk," said Dmitry, smiling, as he took the phone and began to tap away. "It's like living in the future, where everybody has jet packs and water comes in pills. Now we just press a button and his millions become our millions."

Shelley looked up to see Karen and Sergei watching him. Every nerve ending, every cell felt alive. It was as though electrical currents ran through his arms and to his fingertips, ready to draw his weapon if anything untoward took place. There was something about this situation that was wrong, something just slightly off-key. But he couldn't put his finger on what it was.

"There," said Dmitry, handing back the smartphone. "I have taken the liberty of entering the amounts. Perhaps you would like to enter the password."

Shelley looked at the phone's readout and then raised his eyes to meet an impish grin from Dmitry, who had entered the full £20 million.

"Forgive me," said Dmitry, "my idea of a little joke. By all means stick to the agreement."

You had to admire him, unfortunately, Shelley thought. The guy had balls and a sense of humor. But you didn't get to head up the London section of the Chechen Mafia by being a likable bloke.

Shelley put through the transfer and prayed Dmitry would continue to play nice.

CHAPTER 59

"THE TRANSFER IS made," said Shelley.

Dmitry looked over to Sergei, who had produced his own phone. Sergei nodded to confirm that the money had arrived. "Ten million, boss," he said.

"Then we are halfway there," said Dmitry delightedly.

"Good," said Shelley. "Susie, start walking back to the car." Susie moved off and Shelley began walking backward, holding the phone aloft as though it were a detonator.

Dmitry, looking supremely unconcerned, called to him, "So you don't need my bank details again, then?"

"No, mate, I don't need your bank details again. I'll do the transfer when we reach your barrier at the other end. You can let the guys know and they'll let me through. You might want to check that none of them have itchy trigger fingers while you're at it."

"And what if I have changed my mind?" asked Dmitry innocently.

"Then there will be bodies," said Shelley, "and you know what you said about bodies being bad for business."

"True," agreed Dmitry, his eyes up and to the left, as if the thought was occurring to him for the very first time. "Yes, true. But only if the body in question is that of a millionaire's wife. But the body of an ex-soldier? Maybe not so much."

What is he getting at?

Behind him, he heard Susie say, "Shelley . . ."

"I think perhaps the police might ask fewer questions about that," continued Dmitry. "Don't you think, Captain?"

"Shelley," repeated Susie. There was a note of distress in her voice that he couldn't ignore, and he turned to find out what she wanted, only to see that the men at the far end of the road, the three guys who were supposed to be waiting for the second phase of the transfer, had left the Transit behind and were advancing toward them.

Shelley turned back. "Stay with me," he whispered to Susie.

"Why? What's going to happen?" she replied in the same whisper.

Shelley shifted his hand to the grip of his SIG. He did it slowly, deliberately, not to get anyone overexcited, but at the same time wanting to show his discomfort at the turn of events. "What's going on, Dmitry? I thought you were keeping up your end of the bargain."

"I am. The bargain was that I would exchange Mrs. Drake for twenty million. These men are going to escort Mrs. Drake to a place of safety, and I in return will get my twenty million. I am definitely upholding my end of the bargain."

"But you *won't* get your twenty million," said Shelley, holding up the phone to make his point.

"Oh," smiled Dmitry. "But I will."

Shelley was aware of everything. He felt the cold snap in the air. He felt his own nerve endings, every single one of them raw and on high alert. He felt Susie at his side, the men behind advancing, Karen's eyes on him, a look on her face that he dared not decipher for all the imminent triumph he saw there. He felt his SIG and saw the light from the Cherokee headlights and the mist that bubbled around the Chechens' feet. He saw death, treachery, and deception.

He saw a double cross.

"Shall I tell you how it all began?" asked Dmitry. "This whole thing?"

"By all means," answered Shelley. He glanced behind. The three men were closer but appeared to have drawn to a halt.

"It was your friend Corporal Johnson," continued Dmitry. "He came to us, did you know?"

"I thought as much."

"Oh yes, he had learned of our involvement in the Foxy Kittenz enterprise and so he came to us with a plan— a suggestion, you might say. It was a rather short-sighted suggestion but nonetheless, he wanted to know if we were interested in, what's the word, 'bagging' an SAS man. Johnson knew, of course, that your regiment has interrupted the activities of our organization many times in many different countries over the years, and especially with regards to our supply lines in Afghanistan. And he was right to ask if I was interested in a little prize to show my bosses in Grozny, because as I was saying, we all want to please our bosses, don't we? We want to do the best we can to earn their praise and avoid their displeasure. There was bad blood between you and Johnson, I hear."

"You might say that."

"This was his mistake, you see," continued Dmitry. "He let

it all get so personal. Perhaps he might not have missed the bigger picture were he not so intent on revenge. A lesson for all in your camp, you might say.

"So anyway, I spoke to my superiors about this SAS man that Johnson said I could bag. 'Who is this SAS man?' they wanted to know, because one SAS man is pretty much like any other SAS man.

"Except later, when your friend and mine Guy Drake decided that a sensible course of action was to have his old and out-of-shape ex-soldiers attack me, and Corporal Johnson emerged as nothing more significant than an irritating man chancing his arm and meddling in affairs he really did not understand, I gave your name to Grozny and we looked harder at this Captain David Shelley. We looked at him and we realized that Captain David Shelley wasn't just your average run-of-the-mill SAS man. Oh no. We learned that you served with something called Special Projects.

"You weren't just any old dog, were you, Captain? You were top dog."

CHAPTER 60

THERE WERE EIGHT of them. Eight of them, one of him. And he was out in the open with no cover. He was dead. He had no chance. But if he could save Susie . . .

Sergei pocketed his phone and moved his hands to rest on the butt of his pistol; Karen's fingers fidgeted at her Beretta. Shelley stayed in position with his hand on the grip of his SIG. Every one of them, it seemed, was ready to draw apart from Dmitry, who was lost in the enjoyment of his reminiscences. "Bagging the most wanted man of all the wanted men! The leader."

Shelley's mind was racing. So they had his name as leader, but not the other two. And that was why Dmitry was clapping like a seal and talking about the most wanted "men," when in fact, one of these "most wanted men" had been at the mercy of his guys just a few hours earlier.

"You are what they call a person of interest, Captain," continued Dmitry. "You worry about my men coming up behind you, and of course, being so gallant, you worry for the safety of Mrs. Drake. But your concern is misplaced. You have been right to assume that I will hand over Mrs. Drake in return for the provision of the money, because that is exactly what I intend to do. However, I do intend to take a prize. And that prize is you, Captain David Shelley of the SAS. That prize is you."

"Okay, Susie, this is what we call a double cross," said Shelley calmly, knowing there would be combat, and ready for it.

"I'm sorry," said Dmitry. "If it makes you feel any better, Mrs. Drake, it is only the captain that we are double-crossing. You may be on your way escorted by my men and with my blessing."

Susie was looking from one player to another, trying to understand a nonsensical situation.

"But you only have half the money," said Shelley. "You can't seriously tell me that some SAS grunt is worth ten million."

"Quite right, you're not, Captain, but don't you worry, we will get the rest of our money."

"You'd need the passcode."

"We shall get the passcode from you," said Dmitry.

"You won't."

"You leave that problem to us."

Shelley was about to draw—a heartbeat away from doing so—when something happened.

That something was Karen making her move.

CHAPTER 61

KAREN RAISED HER Beretta. For perhaps half a second Shelley considered reaching for his SIG at the same time, but there was no point in making these guys feel even more jumpy than they already were. One raised gun was enough. He needed to see how this played out. His hand stayed on the grip of his SIG.

"Shelley ain't going anywhere. Nor is Susie Drake," said Karen.

Dmitry looked at her. Her gun was pointed not at Susie or Shelley but at him. "Karen," he said, managing to make the word sound like neither a question nor an exclamation of surprise, "what are you doing?"

"What do you think I'm doing, *dear*?"

"Well," said Dmitry without apparent concern, "it seems to me that you are holding a gun on me. Holding a gun on me in front of my men. And, it seems to me, you are insinuating that you intend to stage some kind of coup? Is that right? Could that possibly be right?"

Suddenly Shelley felt like a bystander, somebody who had

blundered into an unfortunate family dispute. He inched closer to Susie, adjusting his elbow so that their arms met.

"Karen," continued Dmitry politely. "I'm afraid I don't hold out much hope for your coup. Not only are you hopelessly outnumbered, but these are my people." He waved an arm to encompass his men. "We are Chechens, Karen. I can assure you that counts for a lot more than your Regan family."

Shelley shifted in order to look in both directions. What he saw was the men looking around at one another, each eyeing up their neighbor. None of them seemed to know where their loyalties lay. All was confusion, and he could capitalize on that.

"I have support," Karen told Dmitry, "don't you worry about that."

"Oh, really?" Dmitry was looking around at his men. "Which of my men is loyal to you?"

"Men," she called, countermanding his order, "don't reveal yourselves."

Could be clever, thought Shelley. On the other hand, it could be that she didn't have the support she needed. Either way, nobody spoke, which Dmitry chose to interpret his way.

"We are Chechens, Karen," Dmitry repeated. "We stick together."

"Oh yes, I know that, Dmitry," smiled Karen. "Family. It's very important to you, isn't it? You tend to get very worked up, don't you, when family comes into things?"

"What are you trying to say now?" he said, but the look he wore was no more serious than polite puzzlement.

Credit to Karen, if Dmitry's lack of concern bothered her she wasn't showing it.

Why?

Because she had an ace, of course. An ally.

"Sergei," she said, indicating with the gun.

Dmitry wheeled around to see that his lieutenant had also drawn his gun and was pointing it at him. His face fell. "Sergei," he said, suddenly disconsolate, "my friend."

If there was something of the pantomime to his performance, then it was lost on Karen. "Why don't you tell Dmitry what we mean when we talk about family, Sergei?" she said.

His sidearm still trained on Dmitry, Sergei said, "The Skinsman. He killed my brother Ivan."

"Yes." Dmitry cast his eyes downward in apology. "Yes, I know this to be the case."

Yet there was something about the way Sergei had delivered the news, and something about Dmitry's subsequent reaction, that struck Shelley as even more odd. His eyes went to Karen, instinctively knowing that things had taken an unexpected turn where she was concerned.

Indeed, when she next spoke she sounded uncertain. "I'm sorry to tell you, my dear, that one of the men loyal to me has killed *Dedushka* this very evening. I gave the order with Sergei's blessing."

Once more Dmitry's response took her by surprise.

He smiled.

And then laughed, throwing back his head and guffawing into the night as everybody looked on.

At last his mirth died. "No," he said. "No, I'm sorry, Karen, but you don't understand. It is I who gives the orders around here." He raised his hand. In response, the two men at the Cherokee moved to the boot, opened it, and reached inside, struggling with something that took two of them to remove.

Shelley knew it was a body. He knew it was a body as soon as the boot was open. Out it came, covered in black plastic and badly applied packing tape. The two men brought it close to where Dmitry, Karen, and Sergei stood and then dropped it with a thump to the ground.

Karen looked sharply at one of them. "I said nothing about bringing the body here."

"Again, no, Karen," said Dmitry with a kind of patient sympathy you reserve for a child who can't grasp a simple math problem. "It is not what you think it is. This, my dear, is my present to you. The order to kill *Dedushka*—you may think you gave it, Karen. But I did. I hated my grandfather."

Karen had been looking at the man she considered one of her own, her assassin, with wide disbelieving eyes, the eyes of somebody watching their plan unravel. The man returned her gaze impassively. His expression remained unchanged even when Dmitry strolled over and threw an arm around his shoulders, beaming with pride.

At that, Karen looked as though she wanted to be sick. Her gun hand began to shake, and her gaze flicked to Sergei, who until mere moments ago she'd considered her ally, her co-conspirator.

All Sergei said to her was "And I hated my brother."

One of Dmitry's men—because of course they were all Dmitry's men—stepped forward. A Stanley knife clicked. He slashed open the plastic, slicing too hard, so that as the black fell away, they saw that he had slashed the face of the fresh corpse beneath.

Even so, judging by Karen's reaction, there was no doubt who it was.

Malcolm Regan.

CHAPTER 62

IN THE DISTANCE a DLR train trundled past on its elevated rail. Canary Wharf's aircraft warning light blinked implacably. And Karen Regan looked down at the body of her late father, at the line of freshly parted skin on his face. No blood, almost as though his flesh had been unzipped.

"Sergei told me everything, Karen," said Dmitry. "How you tried to enlist him in a plot against me, thinking he might want to avenge his brother. But of course you hadn't told him the whole truth, had you? And so for that I needed to listen in on your conversation with Mrs. Drake. Very interesting. What planning. What cunning.

"Ladies and gentlemen," he continued, raising his voice, "when we look back and wonder how all this began, we need only look at my wife, Karen, for it is she who killed Emma Drake and brought the wrath of her father upon us. Should I be thanking her or should I be cursing her? Do you know, I really cannot decide."

But if Karen was even listening to her husband she made

no sign. Instead she stared in horror and disbelief at the corpse on the tarmac. "Daddy," she said, and the harsh head-lights seemed to accentuate her pallor as the blood drained from her face.

A ripple ran through those present. Shelley could have sworn he heard one of the men giggle. Even Susie Drake seemed to be watching with an ugly fascination.

And for perhaps ten seconds that was how Karen stood. Statue-like. Absolutely stock-still. Almost as though she was gathering the strength for a primal howl of grief.

Maybe Dmitry and the Chechens thought so, too, and had been hoping to savor this moment. Perhaps they'd expected a more visceral and therefore less decisive reaction from Karen.

But, if so, they'd underestimated her. Because Karen was a killer, a survivor—she was her father's daughter—and in the instant that she had seen his body on the ground she'd realized she only had one option.

To switch sides.

Shelley was her ally now.

She caught his eye, and he was the only one not taken by surprise by what she did next.

"*Run!*" she called, and then she jinked to the side and twisted, her coat billowing and her bad right arm raised for balance as she put two well-grouped shots into a man who stood behind her, who jerked as though punched, spitting blood as he fell.

Men bellowed in Russian. Guns were raised. And it should have been a shooting gallery but for the fact that the Chechens flanked their enemy on both sides and risked hitting each other. For a precious second confusion and hesitancy reigned, enough time for Shelley to pull Susie out of the line of fire an eyeblink before the shooting began.

And then it did begin.

Rounds whistled past. There was the familiar thump of bullet hitting body. Karen screamed, and in the half-light Shelley saw that half her face was torn away as she dropped to her knees, Beretta held two-handed, still firing off shots.

Shelley's own gun was drawn, and in the next instant they were plunged into near darkness as his first two shots took out the Cherokee's headlights. Using the sudden darkness and Karen's gunfire as cover, he manhandled Susie to the side of the road, away from the bullets.

Karen was screaming—"Fuck you!"—and blasting indiscriminately. The Chechens were trying to return fire but still worried about hitting each other, trying not to get killed in the process.

And then, as Shelley and Susie reached the edge of the road, Karen's mag emptied and she was firing dry.

A flashlight came on, highlighting Karen, who knelt with most of her face gone, snarling and pulling the trigger uselessly. Regrouping, the Chechens picked her out, pouring rounds into her.

Karen knelt in a mist of blood, her jerking body held upright by the bullets that tore into her, until at last she fell.

CHAPTER 63

SHELLEY AND SUSIE dashed into the car park of the burned-out Foxy Kittenz, using the blackened shell of the building as cover and heading toward the rear, past the charcoal-colored brickwork to a walkway with the river ahead of them.

For a second Shelley dithered over which direction to take. They'd expect him to make for the car. *Sorry, Lucy.* Her beloved Mini was going to have to be sacrificed. "This way," he whispered harshly, pulling Susie in the opposite direction.

As they set off, he thought about the options open to the enemy. The Cherokee was no good to them, not without headlights. Unless they fancied piling into Lucy's Mini, their only transportation was the black Transit. Plus they were in disarray. With no transport of his own, he had to hope that would be enough.

"When was the last time you did any running?" said Susie, sprinting at his side. He hadn't done any for months. He'd taken it up after Frankie died, but it had never really been his thing and he was feeling it now. A burning in his chest.

"Okay, then," she said, "slow down, take it easy, set a steady pace, and keep to it. Come on."

They slowed, Susie setting the pace. Then about fifty yards ahead he saw the station. Docklands Light Railway. Crossharbour. The line would take them back into town.

Moments later they'd climbed the stairs and stood getting their breath back. The platform towered over the road beneath, as though on a steel gantry, and Shelley peered through rain-streaked Perspex to keep an eye out for a vehicle below.

According to an information display, the next train, the last of the night, was just two minutes away.

Come on, he willed it. *Come on.*

Then—there it was. The black Transit below, approaching the station.

At the same time so was the train. It was rounding a final bend toward the end of the straight track, slowing before it entered the station. The only other passengers on the platform, two young men in suits, moved forward to greet it.

On the road below, the Transit stopped.

"Here," said Shelley. He beckoned Susie to stay out of sight on the other side of a passenger lift and did the same himself, peeking around the edge to check on the vehicle below. Its doors opened. Men appeared. Shelley saw Dmitry gesticulating, sending two men up the stairs to the platform, where they stood, the train just seconds away from coming to a stop.

"This way," he said. The two of them raced up the platform to get as far away from the steps as possible. Meanwhile the train stopped at last, humming and modern, doors gliding open, automated announcements, and bright lights promising sanctuary.

They plunged inside, the sound of the Chechens pounding up the stairs ringing in their ears, and then right away crouched beneath the windows, ignoring the stares of the only two other people in the carriage.

In the reflection of a window opposite Shelley could see the Chechens on the platform. They wouldn't board the train unless they were sure Shelley and Susie were on it, so they began to make their way along the platform, peering inside the carriages, shouting to one another in Russian.

Still crouched, Shelley threw a glance to his left and saw the two other passengers wearing puzzled expressions, their eyes going from Shelley and Susie to the approaching Chechens on the platform. He put a finger to his lips, willing them not to give away their position. In the reflection of the window, he saw one of the gangsters arrive, watched him peer inside, and then, apparently satisfied, move away down toward the end.

The doors closed. There was no way they could board now, but even so, Shelley still didn't want to be seen.

No such luck. "Hey!" he heard, and looked up to see the Chechen towering over where he squatted, drumming at the window as the train began to move. The Chechen moved along with them for a few steps then relented as they gathered speed.

CHAPTER 64

SHELLEY AND SUSIE stood from their hiding place and took seats as far away from the other two passengers as possible.

"What do we do now?" said Susie, still breathing hard. They were the first words she'd spoken since the running tutorial back at Millharbour. She seemed cool, but her eyes were a little wild.

"We ride the train," he said. "Try and get you to safety. They've still got ten million. Maybe they'll leave it there." He didn't believe it for a second.

"By the sounds of things, they wanted *you*," she said.

He shook his head. "I'm just the cherry on top, a way of Dmitry being able to impress his bosses. He's big on bosses is Dmitry. Besides, you saw them back there. That's an organization with a lot of housekeeping to do. Chances are they'll just cut their losses."

Who are you trying to kid?

"Or maybe they'll come after you *and* the other half of the money," said Susie, cutting right through his bullshit.

"Something tells me that we'll know soon enough," said Shelley. He stood as the train slowed to pull into the next station, South Quay, another smaller, gantry-type affair, not much more than a glorified bus stop.

"They'll be here, they'll be waiting for us," he said. He dipped to check the platform as the train glided into the station with a descending whirr of electrics. They stood by the door, ready to make a move, but the platform was deserted. No sign of anyone, let alone their Mafia pals.

Susie went to disembark but Shelley stopped her. "No point in getting out if they're not here," he said. He scanned up and down the empty platform, prepared for their pursuers to spring a surprise.

But none came. The doors closed. A soothing voice informed them that the next station was Heron Quays and that this service would terminate at Bank, which was central London. If they could reach Bank then surely they were home and dry.

The train was pulling away as Shelley and Susie resumed their seats. "You think they should have been here?" she asked.

"Yup," said Shelley thoughtfully. "They could have made it from Crossharbour to here in time. By my reckoning, there should have been a welcome party. I don't know why—maybe something held them up."

But what? What?

He tried Drake's number. No reply. Maybe zonked from the booze and pills. He tried Bennett. Again no reply. Which was a bit more puzzling.

And then his phone went. He raised it to his ear. "Hello, Dmitry," he said.

"Shelley, my old friend," replied Dmitry, breezy as ever.

"You double-cross and then plan to torture all your old friends, do you?"

Dmitry chuckled. "Well, you saw what I did to my wife and my father-in-law."

"True." Shelley paused. "Look, mate, you can stop this, you know. You've got your ten million. Your bosses are gonna love you for that. Ten million and no heat from the cops. Come on, that's a good day's work."

"Oh, Captain," said Dmitry regretfully, "the problem is that I promised them twenty million, plus you, and the annihilation of the Regan family. One and a half of those promises is not enough. I'd like to be able to deliver them all."

"Really? At the risk of more bodies?"

"Even at the risk of more bodies, Captain."

"Because it's not going to come easily," said Shelley, "you know that, don't you? You know who I am and what I'm capable of. You know there's no way in the world I'll let you take me alive, and when I go I'll take as many of you lot with me as I can. Maybe even you, Dmitry. And I promise you this, you're not going to get the rest of the money."

"Oh, I'll get it, Captain," purred Dmitry.

"Don't be an arse."

"By the way, I've been meaning to say, I'm most disappointed in you."

"Why is that?"

"You lied to me."

"Go on," said Shelley.

"The woman at the health spa. She was not an incompetent

buffoon, was she? She was not working close protection for Mrs. Drake."

"I don't know what you mean."

"Oh, I think you do, Captain."

The line went dead.

CHAPTER 65

SHELLEY LOWERED HIS phone, wondering just how much Dmitry knew about Lucy—if anything. Could be a bluff. On the other hand, the Chechen had sounded distinctly unfazed.

"I wish I could have done it myself," said Susie beside him, dragging him from his thoughts.

"I'm sorry?"

"Karen. I wish I could have killed her myself."

Shelley sighed, pulled off his cap, and ran a hand through damp hair. "No you don't," he said, feeling very tired all of a sudden.

"She killed Emma. Or maybe I should say that she forced Emma to kill herself. She did that and then she uploaded film of it to the internet. And then, you know what she did, Shelley? She sat there gloating about it. Taunting me about it. 'From one muvva to anuvva.'"

As the train wound its way through Canary Wharf she opened up, telling Shelley everything Karen had told her in her cell. And when she'd finished they were both silent for a long time.

That was it, he thought, his suspicions confirmed. When Emma had rung him that night it was to tell him about Karen. Everything else: the means of suicide, the single bullet, the body being moved. It all made sense now.

"Say something, David," she prompted, her voice soft.

"I dunno," he started, "I dunno what to say."

"She was going to get to you next."

"That's why she called me."

"I beg your pardon?"

"Guy said that you were gutted that Emma had called me and not you. But that was why, wasn't it? Not because she turned to me for support, a final cry for help. Just because she needed to tell me about Karen."

"Yes, I suppose so."

Maybe Susie would feel better knowing that, but he doubted it. He wanted to tell her that he'd started off needing to know the truth himself, but it was no consolation now that he did. It didn't bring Emma back. If anything it made it worse, knowing that she might have found her way out of the hole she was in, given the time that Karen took from her.

They fell back into silence. Eventually she said, "I'm sorry, Shelley."

"You've got no reason to be sorry."

"I do. For what happened all those years ago."

He knew exactly what she meant. "It wasn't just you. It was me too."

"Was it?"

"You know it was."

"Could anything have happened between us?" she asked.

"No, Susie," said Shelley. "I love Lucy."

"It broke Emma's heart that you left."

"But I did have to go," he told her.

"I know," she said, adding, "I met Lucy."

"Of course."

"She's beautiful," Susie said. "Beautiful and tough and clever. What on earth do you see in her?"

He chuckled, but the laughter died in his throat as it hit him why the Chechens hadn't met them at the DLR station at South Quay. Why Dmitry was so fucking calm.

They were going after Lucy.

CHAPTER 66

LYING IN HER bed at the Chelsea and Westminster Hospital, Lucy Shelley awoke with a start, instantly needing to use the toilet.

"Oh, bollocks," she muttered. Even on a good day, the last thing she wanted to do was get up at three in the morning for a pee.

She lay there for a while, thinking that the urge might just disappear. Why did she always do that? It wasn't going to.

Okay, she decided, there was no point in denying it. She had to get out of bed, whether she liked it or not.

Christ, it was hard enough at the best of times. Like at home, where it was relatively warm and she hadn't just been shot—well, most days at least—but here, this was going to hurt. She braced herself for the pain and the cold and then moved one leg out of bed. She'd always had the impression that hospitals were supposed to be warm places, overheated almost, but this one certainly wasn't, and she was very glad now that she wore a pair of pajama bottoms over her bandages. She thought fondly of Shelley, who'd gone home and made up a bag for her before he came hurtling round to the hospital. She wondered what he was up to. Whether the exchange had gone well. Hoped he was okay.

Her bare feet touched the cold floor of her hospital room. "Ouch, ouch," she gasped. All those years in hostile environments and here she was, defeated by a cold floor. She tiptoed across the room to the toilet. "En suite bathroom," she'd scoffed earlier.

"We do that for all our gunshot wound cases who have their own private guard," a doctor had told her drily.

"Remind me to get shot more often," Lucy had replied, unsure if she was flirting or not. Probably not, on balance.

Close to her "en suite bathroom" was the door to her room, beneath it a sliver of light from the corridor outside. Her guard was a guy called Trevor. She'd struck up quite a relationship with him in the few hours she had been there and saw no reason not to peek outside and say hello now. She was, after all, wearing pajamas.

When she did manage to hobble over to look, however, his seat was empty. Just a copy of that day's *Daily Mirror*, but no sign of Trevor. Opposite was the men's room. *Must be in there*, she decided. She cast a glance up and down the corridor. The lights were slightly dimmed and there wasn't a soul to be seen, the only sound a far-off moaning of some poor soul needing attention.

She stood there for a moment, maybe half hoping Trevor might reappear. But he didn't, and it was cold, and she needed a pee, so *Later, Trevor*.

She hobbled back into her room and closed the door gently. Then she turned to the bathroom, letting herself in. The light flickered on.

Still bleary, it took her a second or so to work out what was obscuring her view of the white porcelain of the loo that she really rather desperately needed to use.

It was a man. He wore leather gloves and a black denim jacket. He held a pistol fitted with a suppressor, and it was pointed at her.

CHAPTER 67

SHELLEY HAD TAKEN the opportunity to try Lucy's mobile before the DLR train went underground, but it was off. Of course it was off, she was in the bloody hospital; there was no other way of contacting her unless he intended to ring the switchboard, who would want to know why he planned to wake his wife in the middle of the night, and might not like it when he told them that armed Chechens were on their way to kidnap her.

If, of course, they even were.

Because why would Dmitry even consider Lucy a target? He didn't know she was Shelley's wife. Johnson was dead when all that kicked off. When Shelley spoke to Dmitry in the hospital, the Chechen was none the wiser.

Which meant that he had learned something in the meantime. In other words, from somebody other than Johnson.

And that was when it struck him, the thing that had been bugging him. The smoothness of the operation. The fact that Dmitry had always seemed to be one step ahead of him.

They had an inside man.

Not Johnson. They had *another* inside man.

"Come on." Susie's voice yanked him from his thoughts. By now they were at Bank, which was surprisingly busy for the hour. Late-night drinkers and clubbers gave it a boisterous, raucous air.

Shelley and Susie hustled onward, taking the tunnels toward the Central line where they boarded another train. This one was busier, full of even more exuberant youngsters: drunk and shouting and laughing way too loudly. Shelley and Susie kept their heads down and were delivered to Holborn, where they disembarked.

And then Shelley saw him: a tall guy with that look of Chechen danger that made it 100 percent certain he wasn't a clubber. How long had he been on their tail? Shelley wasn't sure. Neither could he be certain if he was one of the same men present at the exchange in Millharbour.

They were closer to the center of the city now, and there were more revelers on the trains, so that when Shelley looked back he could no longer see the guy following. For a moment he wondered if it was just his imagination, or perhaps they had lost him.

But when he next checked he saw another face—and this one he recognized.

It was the inside man. The traitor. It was Gurney. He was the one who knew enough to feed the Chechens with information. And of course he must have informed them about Lucy.

Gurney, you fucking rat, thought Shelley. The ex-Para was some way back, using as cover a throng of partygoers haphazardly making their way along the tunnel. He had risked a look just as Shelley glanced back and the two men had seen one another. The game was up. The mole was out in the open. For a second it looked as though Gurney would try to hide his face, but he knew he'd been seen. Instead, as their eyes met across the noisy crowd of people, a grin appeared, and it was as though the mask that Gurney wore, which had only occasionally slipped before, was finally discarded for good.

"We're being followed," he told Susie urgently. "You have to speed up. Use the crowd, thread in and out, shove a few of this lot if necessary. We need to build up a lead."

"Right," she said. "Where are we going?" Her voice trembled despite the attempt at calm.

"Piccadilly line for the hospital," he replied, thinking, *Stay with me, Susie. Stay with me.*

They barged and bustled. Shelley threw a couple of "don't mess" stares at anybody who objected. The whole time he kept an eye out behind, pleased to see that they seemed to have lost their shadow. No. *Shadows,* plural.

They made it to the Piccadilly line platform, where they were greeted by a blast of air and the howl of a train arriving as it burst from within the tunnel, like a bullet from a gun. A cheer went up some way down the platform and Shelley decided they should make their way toward the crowds, hoping to use them as cover.

They boarded, and the last thing Shelley saw before he ducked inside the closing doors was an empty platform, no sign of either of their two pursuers. Should he take comfort from that? He wasn't in the mood.

They took seats. The stations ticked past. Covent Garden then Leicester Square and Piccadilly Circus, the carriages filling up.

Green Park. Hyde Park Corner. Knightsbridge. Next would be South Kensington.

And then, with a sinking feeling, Shelley caught sight of the Chechen guy. *Shit.* They saw each other at the same time, locked eyes, and something that might have passed for a smile crossed the gangster's face. As Shelley watched, the guy reached for his phone. *No signal down here, pal.* But when he slid the phone back into an inside pocket, and his hand withdrew, Shelley saw the dull glint of a sidearm. Now he began to make his way down the carriage toward where Shelley and Susie sat.

"Come on, let's go," urged Shelley. "We've got company."

They got to their feet as the train pulled into South Kensington and took up position at the door. Down the carriage the Chechen guy checked his progress. He, too, moved toward a door, ready to jump off if Shelley and Susie did the same.

The doors bleeped, then shivered open. Passengers jostled, getting on and off, throwing Susie and Shelley dirty looks as they stood by the doors doing neither, just getting in the way. Susie looked at him, waiting for him to make his move.

"Wait," he said out of the side of his mouth.

They watched the Chechen guy. He watched them. All three playing a game of brinksmanship.

The doors bleeped to close.

CHAPTER 68

"WAIT, DON'T MOVE, it's a feint," hissed Shelley to Susie, and then he stepped off the train, flicking a glance to his right and seeing the Chechen guy do the same.

They hit the platform together, except Shelley reversed instantly and he squeezed in between the closing doors at the last second, back on the train with the Chechen guy stranded on the platform.

"Yes," he hissed, triumphantly. But then, just as he thought he'd outfoxed his pursuer, there came another raucous cheer, latecomers crowded onto the platform, and the doors reopened.

The Chechen had been on his way off the platform but turned and managed to scramble back onto the train, sideways through the closing doors—and once more they were back to where they were.

"We'll have to get off at Gloucester Road," Shelley told Susie.

The gangster seemed to consider resuming his progress toward them, a crowd of passengers between him and Shelley and Susie, but he held his position, all three of them watching each other warily. The journey between South Kensington and Gloucester Road seemed to last a century, but at last they arrived and Susie and Shelley jumped off, ignoring abuse and complaints as they barged past other passengers and—hopefully—left their pursuer in their wake.

Lifts, lifts. Shelley shot a look back, saw the Chechen some way behind and decided against, making for the stairs instead: eighty-seven steps according to the warning sign, a long spiral staircase up to street level. The gangster checked his progress. He was temporarily blocked from following but there was no doubt he intended to take the same route.

Another thing: they were the only passengers taking the stairs.

"You go on," he told Susie.

She stopped and swiveled on the stone steps, face full of worry. "Why? What will you be doing?"

"Me? I'll be having a meeting with our friend here." He looked around meaningfully. "There's nobody about, Susie. I won't get another chance. Just go."

"What are you going to do to him?" she asked.

"Christ. Just run, Susie," he urged. "I'm going to do whatever it takes to stop him. Now go."

That was it. She needed no further invitation, taking off up the stairs, sneakers slapping on stone.

Meantime, Shelley climbed ten or so steps and then stopped, flattened himself to the inside of the spiral, listening for the approaching feet of the gangster. He heard footsteps as the man came onto the stairwell, helpfully cursing in Russian, and he tensed, ready—ready to take a life.

A second later, there he was. Taller and meaner up close,

he reared back in surprise as Shelley sprang from around the central column and struck with the heel of his left hand.

It was a clean blow, and it was met with a sickening crunch as the gangster's jaw shattered and his head snapped back, mouth spurting blood that Shelley felt like warm rain on his face.

The guy staggered. Punch-drunk boxer. Tough guy: he reached into the overcoat he was wearing, presumably for his gun. But Shelley wasn't finished and he used the same heel-of-the-hand strike, only this time just below the Chechen's nose.

Which shattered. Shards of bone driven into the brain killed the guy instantly. His eyes rolled back in his head and he slumped to the handrail, still gripping it, his hand wedged, which was the only thing that prevented him from sliding back down the steps. He let out a final death rattle and then was silent, thick rivulets of dark red blood and cerebrospinal fluid leaking from his nose and mouth, coating his chin.

Shelley looked at him. He was just a guy trying to do his job—like Dmitry said, trying to please his boss. Shelley stepped over the body and continued bounding up the steps to catch up with Susie.

He was close to the top, able to see the opening that led into the street-level section of the station, when he was brought up short.

Susie was there all right. And holding a gun to her head, using her as a shield, was Gurney.

CHAPTER 69

SHELLEY STOPPED ON the stairs. He gauged the distance between himself and Gurney and knew there was no way he could cover it and still keep Susie safe.

"You," he said to Gurney, who grinned in response, the kind of grin Shelley had heard described as "shit-eating."

"Yeah, me," said Gurney. His left hand moved quickly and Shelley was about to throw himself to one side when he saw a flash of silver steel. Now Gurney held a knife to Susie's throat in addition to the gun at her temple, and in the next second the gun was pointing at Shelley. "Now, let's not waste any more time." Gurney's voice had an echoing quality in the stairwell. "Use forefinger and thumb to lift your gun from its holster; drop it to the steps."

Shelley did as he was told.

"SIG Sauer," sneered Gurney. "Truly old school, aren't you, mate? Right, now take out your phone. Do it nice and slow, and don't make me nervous, because you know how that's likely to end." His eyes flicked meaningfully to Susie. "And then start making the transaction. I'll give you the details."

"Oh, really?" said Shelley. "You're not putting it into Dmitry's account, then?"

"Fuck that, mate. Just start the transfer."

Susie was held in place by the knife. Shelley saw blood make its way from beneath the blade and run down her neck. "You're hurting her," he warned.

"Better hurry up then, hadn't you? Let's get this over and done with."

Shelley saw what was going to happen next half a second before it did. He recognized the blue of the jacket sleeves that appeared behind Gurney, two hands, one either side of his head, one poised ready to grab Gurney's knife hand, the other holding what looked like a brushed-metal ballpoint pen.

Too late, Gurney sensed that somebody was behind him. Perhaps he saw the hovering hands in his peripheral vision. Either way, his mouth dropped open just as Bennett jammed the ballpoint pen into his ear, the other hand snaking around to take the knife at the same time.

Bennett had rammed the pen into Gurney's ear overhand, and then, with the pen still protruding from the side of Gurney's head, he used the heel of his hand to ram it into his brain.

The only sound from Gurney's mouth was a strangulated mixture of surprise and pain. His eyes widened and bulged and blood sluiced suddenly from his nose. His gun fell and Bennett supported the body as it dropped to the steps.

Gurney's legs kicked feebly as his brain closed for business. Perhaps the last thing he saw was his former commander standing over him, staring at him with a combination of pity, sadness, and genuine grief.

"How could you?" was all Bennett said, then he turned his

face to Shelley. "I'm sorry, Shelley, I had no idea. Johnson I can understand. But James . . ."

"I'm sorry, mate," said Shelley, who knew what it meant to be betrayed by an old comrade in arms. The pain. He turned his attention to Susie, and what he saw concerned him. Perhaps the sight of Bennett shoving an expensive ballpoint pen into Gurney's brain had been the final straw, for she gazed down at the dead man with a blank, nobody-home look on her face, and there was no light in her eyes.

But Shelley didn't have time to worry about Susie. He didn't have time to sympathize with Bennett and he only barely had time to thank him for saving their bacon.

He needed to reach Lucy, before it was too late.

CHAPTER 70

THEY'D GIVEN LUCY a walking stick but she hadn't brought it into the loo with her. If only she'd brought the walking stick, at least she'd have a weapon.

That was her first thought. Her second thought was that if they'd wanted her dead they would have done it by now. And it wasn't a dart gun pointing at her, it was a plain old Makarov fitted with a suppressor, used in a way that its bearer hoped would be enough to intimidate her. In fact, what it told her was that the guy in the restroom had brought the wrong tool for the job.

"Put your hands behind your back and turn around," he said, accent as expected. His other hand dipped into the pocket of his denim jacket and emerged gripping a cable tie.

"You woke me up," she said. She'd been glad of pajamas before—now she was *really* glad. "I was dreaming about Hugh Jackman. Not P. T. Barnum Hugh Jackman, either. Wolverine Hugh Jackman."

"Turn around and put your hands behind your back," he repeated, stony-faced.

He'd have a backup, of course. Perhaps another guy stationed out of sight at the end of the corridor, just to make sure they weren't disturbed. There were back stairs, she knew. If they managed to get the cable tie on her, they could take her down to the parking lot below. She didn't want that.

"I'm a bitch when I'm woken up in the middle of the night," she told him. "Really, honestly, like a bear with a sore head. You don't want to mess. Especially if it's in the middle of a Jackman dream."

"You think I won't use this," he said, "but I have my orders and I can put a bullet in you without killing you."

"How about you let me use the loo first?"

He shook his head. "Negative. Turn around now."

She turned slowly, keeping her hands by her sides.

"Put your hands behind your back and keep your wrists together," ordered her bathroom stalker.

She now had her back to the bathroom, facing the open door into her room. One bad guy and a lot of porcelain behind her, sanctuary in front. What's more, the bathroom door opened outward, standard hospital design in case a patient had a fall behind the door, and she was pretty sure she could make that work in her favor. Mainly what she thought was *I can't let him cuff my hands.*

They had seen her in action at the spa. But the fact that they were coming after her now suggested some fresh intel. Something to do with Shelley, perhaps? Either way, they knew exactly what she was capable of. The guy would be careful. He'd be expecting her to try her luck and expecting it now.

That couldn't be helped; it was now or never. She cast

her eyes down to between her feet, watching his shadow on the tiles.

"You will do what I say," he insisted. "I do not ask a second time."

Slowly she moved her hands back, at the same time almost imperceptibly bending at the knee (and yes, *really*, thank Christ she was wearing not just pajamas but loose-fitting pajamas). All the while she watched the shifting light patterns on the floor as he moved closer behind her, gauging his distance, timing her move, knowing that if she did it right she could pull it off, because this was a guy who needed more than one pair of hands to do what he intended to do: wield the Makarov, gather her wrists, tighten the cable tie.

All she had to do was time it right.

She wrenched one of her arms forward, jabbed her other elbow back, and at the same time used the side of her foot on his knee.

It worked. He grunted and stumbled, opening a window of opportunity she could exploit.

But when she sprang forward it all went wrong. Pain from the gunshot wound lanced along her thigh, making her scream out in shock, her pained leg almost buckling beneath her. Yelling with the agony, she twisted, slammed the bathroom door behind her just as the Chechen regained his composure, ready to give chase, and then wrenched open the door to her room and hobbled out into the corridor.

Trevor. If only Trevor had returned. But there was no Trevor, just another Chechen blocking her path, even bigger and more lumbering than the last one.

"Jesus," she panted, backing away as she said it, trying to

buy time. "No wonder they didn't send *you* to hide in my bathroom."

Her leg was aflame. From behind she heard the door open and knew that the first man was about to appear. She dimly realized she couldn't take them both on and win. But it didn't matter, because in the next moment, before she'd had a chance to overcome her agony, regain her balance, and adopt any kind of defensive stance, the new guy's fist was lashing out, big as a joint of beef, and knocking her unconscious.

CHAPTER 71

BENNETT HAD TAKEN advantage of the antisocial hour, and his Mercedes was parked right outside the tube station, inconceivable during the daytime. Together they helped put Susie in the back seat. She was trying, and she was in good shape, in the sense that she was physically unharmed, but she was wiped out: exhausted and severely traumatized. Shell shock, they used to call it. Nowadays, PTSD.

"Susie," said Shelley gently but urgently, desperately aware of the need to move fast. "Stay with me. You're going to be all right. We'll get you home soon."

"It's good to see you, ma'am," said Bennett. Twisted around in the driving seat, he found her eyes with his. "I'm sorry for what you had to see back there."

"That's quite all right, Mr. Bennett," she said. Her arms were folded across her chest, hugging herself. "Oh, and Mr. Bennett?"

"Yes, ma'am?" said Bennett.

"How is Guy?"

Shelley and Bennett shared a look—Susie inquiring about Drake, after all she'd been through.

"He's fine, ma'am, as far as I know," Bennett said gently. "He's at home, resting."

She nodded as if that was all she needed to know. "Good," she said, a little too dreamily for Shelley's liking, and resumed staring out of the window.

"Right, where are we going?" said Bennett.

He twisted back to face front, pulled his seat belt across him, and was already moving off as Shelley directed him to the hospital. His driving was assured and fast, a sense of purpose to it that gave Shelley hope as he ran through the events of the evening, ending with a question of his own. "So how did you come to be ramming a pen into Gurney?"

Bennett gave a dry laugh. "There's a first time for everything. Not bad for a bit of on-the-spot improvisation, I thought."

"But you knew, did you? You'd worked out that Gurney was working with them?"

Bennett nodded sadly. "Johnson—I don't suppose we'll ever know whether he went to the Chechens of his own accord or not. But the more I thought about it, the more I realized Dmitry seemed to have so much info that Johnson couldn't possibly have told him. Where Susie Drake would be that morning, for instance. Christ, even mobile numbers. They had to be getting it from someone other than Johnson."

"I came to the same conclusion myself," said Shelley.

"And so when Gurney let himself out just after midnight, I decided to follow," explained Bennett.

Shelley chuckled. "Pool room window?"

"That's the one."

Bennett drew up to traffic lights. Shelley found himself

unconsciously putting his own foot down, wanting to urge them forward; it was night, there were no cops around. But then again, he supposed Bennett was doing the right thing. No point in risking drawing unwanted attention.

"And now you think they're going for Lucy to get at you?" asked Bennett, looking across at him. "A bit of collateral."

"Looks that way. To be honest, I'm not sure what they know about Lucy. Whether they know she was in the Regiment or not, I couldn't say."

"They know she's important to you, though?"

"Looks like it. And they could have got that from Gurney."

"So you're about to put yourself back in the firing line?" said Bennett.

"We'll see."

They drew away from the lights, Bennett cruising through the gears, the hospital just moments away now. "Okay, so let me get this straight. Dmitry said something that made you think he was going to snatch Lucy? In other words, he *revealed* his intel? Why would he do that, do you think, Shelley? Why let you know his game plan?"

"He didn't . . ."

"Not directly, but he dropped a massive fuck-off hint, didn't he? He led you to believe it, and you drew exactly the conclusion he wanted you to draw. Which means that by racing over there right now, we're doing precisely what he wants us to do, Shelley. I say 'we.' I mean you, my friend. You're playing right into his hands. Just remind me, if you would: is that what we recommend in the forces, playing right into the enemy's hands?"

Shelley knew it, always had done. He took a deep breath. "I know, but look, this morning, after the crash at the gates, when you thought Johnson might still be alive, you approached the car even though there was a greater-than-average possibility that the car might be booby-trapped. You remember that?"

"Of course," conceded Bennett.

"At the time I thought it was a dick move. Stupid and reckless. But the thing is, even though I didn't approve of it, I understood it. I knew why you had to go out there, even though tactically it was the wrong thing to do." *And besides, this is Lucy we're talking about.*

"Even so, Shelley," sighed Bennett, "I'm not sure I can stand by and watch you do this."

"Put it this way: you don't have any choice."

"Why did I have a feeling you were going to say that?" said Bennett ruefully. He shifted down and floored it, a statement of intent that gave Shelley hope as the city streets flashed past.

CHAPTER 72

SERGEI DROVE THE black Transit, Dmitry at his side with the phone clamped to his ear. His man Bogdan, dispatched to follow Shelley on the trains, had gone offline, much to his irritation. But Albert and Boris, sent to the hospital? Ah, now that was a very different situation indeed.

He came off the phone. "Albert and Boris have the girl," he told Sergei.

"It is fortunate that they were able to mobilize so quickly, Dmitry," replied Sergei.

Dmitry glanced into the rear of the van, where just one of their men, the Ukrainian, Wladimir, sat silently. He was big and blond and—though known to be a little squeamish when it came to the sight of blood—a man you would want by your side in a fight.

This night had taken its toll on them as an organization. Dmitry looked across at Sergei. "An interesting evening for us, Sergei," he said, part statement, part question.

"Indeed, Dmitry."

"We have at least managed to sort a few things out."

"Indeed, Dmitry," said Sergei. He checked the satnav suction-cupped to the windshield. The Chelsea and Westminster Hospital was just a short distance away now.

Dmitry reached into the front of his jeans, drew his pistol, and exhaled as though it had been digging into him. He held it in his lap. "Sergei," he said with a mildly quizzical tone, "tell me, were you ever tempted to join with Karen?"

Sergei gave a small chuckle. "Certainly not, Dmitry. As you are aware, I came to you the second that her treachery became apparent."

"You did, Sergei," nodded Dmitry, "you did. And for that, you know that you have my eternal gratitude. Who knows? With a less conscientious and loyal lieutenant, perhaps her plan for takeover might even have succeeded."

"Perhaps," said Sergei.

"But of course you knew what she could not have known, which is that our friends in Grozny have been tiring of our association with the Regan family. You above all knew that forming an alliance with Karen Regan was suicide."

Sergei's jaw tightened. "Are you suggesting to me that I exposed the traitor merely out of self-preservation and nothing else, Dmitry?" He sounded genuinely hurt. "Does our friendship mean nothing?"

Dmitry threw back his head and laughed. "You made the right decision, Sergei, that is the important thing," he said. "You may be sure that you will be well rewarded for your loyalty tonight. We all will be. Twenty million in the bank. And not just one, but two of the British Army's most celebrated SAS operators as a prize. If Alexander is unhappy about the loss—the temporary loss, mind you—of the studios then he will not be for long."

Sergei was slowing, trying to make sense of a forest of sign-age at the entrance to the hospital complex, just as Dmitry's phone rang. It was Boris. He had details of where to come in order to collect the girl.

Yes, it has been an interesting night, thought Dmitry as he relayed directions to Sergei and instructed Wladimir to be ready. However, although everything had gone to plan so far, he had a distinct feeling that the night still had a surprise or two in store.

CHAPTER 73

THE MERCEDES CAME into the entrance road of the hospital and then drew almost to a standstill. "Where to now?" said Bennett, peering in evident confusion at the signs. Shelley, too, leaned forward to gaze through the windshield. He was about to direct Bennett to the main entrance when he saw it: over to their right, a black Transit van headed across the front of the main building just below them.

Of course. Some kind of rear entrance.

"Down there," he pointed. "The van. Do you see it?"

"Got it," said Bennett.

They slipped smoothly down a ramp in pursuit. Shelley drew his SIG, checked the mag, chambered a round. He unclipped his seat belt, ready. Did they already have Lucy? He didn't know. Was he running right into the trap they had laid for him? He didn't know that either.

Some way ahead the Transit rounded a corner, taking the service road to the back of the building, just as Shelley had thought.

No, thought Shelley, there was absolutely no point in

running right into a trap. He remembered Lucy and the guard in Iraq. They saved lives that day precisely because they didn't go in all guns blazing.

"Stop," he said.

"Really?" But Bennett was already hitting the brakes, ABS bringing them to a fast but steady and, more importantly, quiet stop.

The Transit was out of sight now. "What are you—" started Bennett, but Shelley had already opened the door and stepped out, keeping his SIG low and his target area small as he scuttled along the service road until he reached the corner of the building. He could just about hear Bennett's harsh, stranded whisper behind him: "Shelley, what the fuck are you doing? Shelley? Get your arse back here . . ."

At the corner he risked a quick look and saw a large, locked roller door, possibly for deliveries—laundry, something like that. Further back was what looked like a fire escape. Near that, the Transit, backed up so that the rear was close to the fire escape. The driver and passenger doors were opening and he pulled back sharply as Sergei and Dmitry both got out at the same time, carrying handguns and checking the coast was clear.

Shelley glanced behind at the Mercedes, where the driver's door had opened and Bennett was climbing out. Shelley didn't want Susie left alone but right now he was running out of options. Lucy was the priority. *God, I'm sorry, sweetheart*, he told her silently, and risked another peek around the wall.

A tall blond guy had clambered out of the back of the Transit. Dmitry ordered him to take up position and watch their rear, while he and Sergei approached the fire escape. At that moment the door opened with a chunky sound, loud in what was otherwise a still night. Framed in the doorway were two men who grumbled and bitched in low voices as they manhandled a body.

Lucy.

Shelley's breath caught in his chest. Her blond hair hung over her face. The wound in her thigh was bleeding, blood spreading across the front of her pajamas. But he was almost certain she wasn't dead, just stunned. *And yes. There.* Her eyelids fluttered. Her head lolled as though she was trying to raise it.

Dmitry had his phone to his ear. Shelley wondered what he was doing. Summoning more men perhaps? Demanding some kind of status update?

It occurred to him that if Bennett was right about it being a trap, then the trap required Shelley's presence, which meant . . .

Too late, he realized. The call Dmitry was making.

It was to him.

CHAPTER 74

SHELLEY'S HAND SLAPPED at his pocket just as his phone rang and his position was revealed.

He thought fast and decided his only option was to claw back the element of surprise. So as the Chechens reacted, Shelley broke cover.

Bursting forward, he took out the blond guy on the run, his SIG bucking but controlled in his grip as he pumped two shots into the guy's chest, an instructor-perfect double tap.

The guy staggered, swaying. Beyond him, Sergei and Dmitry both dived for cover behind the Transit, Sergei snatching off a shot that went wide, Dmitry screaming something at him in Russian.

The blond guy's body was still dropping as Shelley passed it. By the fire escape door, the two heavies had finished bundling Lucy into the back of the van, drawn their guns and joined the fight, firing recklessly, seemingly ignoring whatever Dmitry was shrieking at them.

Crack. Thump. Night split by gunfire.

Shelley dropped to one knee. Death was just a blink away

but he felt a strange calm, that same mastery of his fear he'd felt at Millharbor kicking in afresh. He squeezed off a shot that took out one of the kidnappers, who dropped with crimson spraying from his throat. Shelley twisted his torso and found the second kidnapper in his sights. This guy had leveled a pistol fitted with a suppressor and was pointing it at him but Shelley stayed calm, found time in the moment, and his aim was true. Another double tap and the Chechen fell.

And then Sergei did what Shelley had feared might happen since the beginning of the firefight. He emerged from the rear of the Transit holding Lucy, who was slumped in his arms, her head swaying gently from side to side as though she were gradually recovering consciousness.

Next Dmitry stepped around from the other side of the van, the third point of the triangle, positioned about halfway between Shelley and Sergei. No doubt Dmitry thought he'd gained the upper hand, but Shelley had two things in his favor. One, he knew the Chechen wanted him alive. Two, Bennett had yet to make his play.

Shelley's gun was aimed at Sergei, and at this range he knew he could take him out and save Lucy. Not a case of if. Just a case of when.

But then Shelley felt the barrel of a gun at the back of his head.

"Game's up, I'm afraid, Shelley," said Bennett.

CHAPTER 75

"DROP YOUR WEAPON," said Bennett.

Shelley's gun was still trained on Sergei, who held Lucy, slumped, her knees bent. "I'm not going to do that," he replied evenly.

"I'll put a hole in your head if you don't."

"Will you indeed? Did you hear that, Dmitry? The ten-million-quid bullet."

"Be careful, please, Mr. Bennett," warned Dmitry.

"Tell you what, we'll put a bullet in Lucy instead," Bennett called across. "Sergei, could you do the honors, please?"

Shelley kept his cool. "Do that and the next person to die is you, Sergei. No, I'm sorry, lads, but from where I am it looks like your only option is to put a bullet in me and kiss goodbye to the ten mil. You ready to do that?"

"Dmitry?" asked Bennett.

"*Wait*," said Dmitry.

"Dmitry," urged Bennett, "shots have been fired. The cops will be here soon."

"You're ready to do it, are you, Bennett?" said Shelley. "You'd put a round in me, just like that."

"It's nothing personal, Shelley. Never was."

"Oh yeah? And you behind it all along, were you, being not-personal all this time?"

"Not quite," said Bennett. "Not quite 'all along.' I'm afraid I can't claim credit for the original idea. Would you believe that honor goes to—"

"Johnson?" said Shelley.

"Exactly," replied Bennett. "He had the right idea."

"And Gurney?"

"Yup. Cooked up a little plan with Gurney and then cooked him out of it. They both had the right idea. Just needed a little finesse, that was all."

"Finesse you were able to provide."

"Cooked up with my good friends here, yes. I look forward to enjoying preferred fundraiser status with the most powerful criminal organization in the world. I intend to have a good time with it, Shelley. I'm only sorry that you can't join me." He addressed Dmitry and Sergei: "Now, gentlemen, it really won't be long before the police arrive. Might I suggest we speed things up just a tad?"

"Then how will I get my money, Mr. Bennett?" said Dmitry. There was a note in his voice that Shelley found intriguing. Did he imagine it, or was Dmitry suspicious of Bennett?

"Oh, very simple," Bennett responded. "I have Mrs. Drake in the car. Which means that we have no use for Shelley at all. Nor his wife. Put a bullet in her now, Sergei. I'll do the same over here. Guy Drake will pay up for the return of Susie, and nobody will miss a couple of ex-SAS grunts. Plus you get to impress your friends in Grozny. Oh," he said suddenly, as if the thought had just occurred to him, "don't forget to film it, Dmitry."

Shelley knew they were a hair's breadth from it ending. Bennett was making a lot of sense. Opposite he could see that Lucy was still out for the count, though perhaps beginning to regain consciousness.

And then it came to him. The truth. The truth that had been staring him in the face all the time. "That's what you told Dmitry, is it?" he said to Bennett.

"I beg your pardon?"

"You told him that you were taking over as inside man, is that it? That you could add the finesse, give him everything Johnson was promising and more, right?"

Perhaps Bennett suspected where Shelley was going with this. "Shut up, Shelley," he ordered. But a note of disquiet in his voice was enough to alert the Chechen boss.

"Let him speak," said Dmitry.

"Because you know what I think, Bennett?" continued Shelley.

"I'm not interested in what you think," snapped Bennett. "Sergei, we really need to get on with this."

"I think that you were always the inside man," said Shelley. "Just that you offered Johnson up as a patsy to grease the wheels and give everyone a fall guy. But you were always there."

"You're reaching now, my friend. Straws, meet drowning man."

"Drake going crazy at the cam house—was that part of the plan?"

"I had no idea he was going to do that."

"Didn't hurt the cause, though, did it? Tell me, when did

the idea first come to you? When you were investigating Emma's death? You made the connection with the Chechen Mafia way before the cops, right? You knew there was gold in those hills."

"Time to stop talking," said Bennett.

"No," ordered Dmitry.

"You just needed an ally. Dmitry, did Bennett come to you, or did he go through Sergei? Think back now . . ."

"He came through Sergei," said Dmitry slowly. His gaze went to his second in command.

"And Sergei, you saw your chance, did you?" said Shelley. "What, to avenge your brother Ivan? To do what he had failed to do and stage a takeover? Karen was on the right lines back there, wasn't she? Just that you weren't in the market for a partner."

"Dmitry, let's finish this," called Sergei from across the way. He was struggling with Lucy, a deadweight.

"You see, Dmitry, all that housekeeping back in Mill-harbour? There's a bit more to come. And you're it."

"Sergei?" said Dmitry. And while the hint of suspicion in his voice encouraged Shelley, it terrified Sergei.

"No, Dmitry," he said, sounding hurt and slightly panicked at the same time, "this is bullshit. We interrogated Johnson, remember? He said nothing about working with others."

"Exactly. Don't listen to him, Dmitry," chimed in Bennett. "He's just trying to sow the seeds."

But Bennett hadn't witnessed the near coup at Millharbour. Bennett hadn't heard that note of suspicion in Dmitry's voice. He didn't know those seeds had already been sown.

What's more, Shelley was speaking the truth.

Now he directed himself to Dmitry. "This interrogation of

Johnson. Did you ask him about his collaborators when you were torturing him?"

"No, I do not recall that we did," replied Dmitry slowly, thoughtfully.

"That means nothing," yelped Sergei indignantly. He was struggling to hold Lucy now. Shelley saw her eyes flicker.

"Come on, this is all smoke and mirrors, you must see what he's doing, for fuck's sake," urged Bennett. "Let's finish this."

"*No*," commanded Dmitry.

"That's because they wanted you to think he was working alone," pressed Shelley, "so that Bennett could swoop in with the kidnap idea. That's how it happened, am I right? Through Sergei again, yes?"

Dmitry nodded.

"Dmitry, this is lies," pleaded Sergei. The most beautiful sight in the world was the sweat that glistened on his forehead.

"Come on, Dmitry, you can't seriously believe Bennett just breezed in after Johnson. What did you think was happening? Musical conspirators? You said yourself that Johnson's plan was short-sighted. He wasn't the sharpest tool in the box, but do you really think he was so stupid that he'd come to you with some half-arsed plan to bag an SAS guy? He was a pathfinder put up to it by Bennett. He did the same thing to his other man, Gurney. They were nothing more than a pair of firewalls thrown up to protect himself and avoid suspicion. Worked a bloody treat as well."

"This is fiction," called Bennett, but he sounded unnerved.

"Easy for you to be the hero and go to Johnson when you knew the car wasn't booby-trapped, wasn't it?" said Shelley, and then returned his attention to the man on his right. "You've been played, Dmitry. We all have. How does it feel? Betrayed by your wife and now by your second in command?"

"This is not true, Dmitry," said Sergei, his voice taking on a panicked tone.

In the distance was the sound of approaching sirens. The gun battle was only moments old but the cops were already on their way. Armed cops.

Shelley risked a sideways look at Dmitry, and saw the expression on the Chechen's face, a mixture of anger and betrayal.

But no surprise.

"It *is* true, Sergei," said Dmitry. As he spoke he shifted his aim from Shelley to Sergei. "You told Karen that you hated your brother. You told me that you hated your brother; that you had only contempt for his actions in Moscow. But you don't hate your brother, do you, Sergei? You have his picture in your wallet."

Over the way, Sergei's face hardened and Shelley saw where the roots of his deception lay. He thought again of the old masters reusing their canvases. How the past stayed underneath all those layers, yet at some point would make its presence known again.

"Yes, Dmitry, you are right," said Sergei. He had cast aside all pretense now. "And you were right before. Family is what matters. The Kravizes had their time. Now it is time for the Vinitskys to lead."

Shelley's bead on Sergei had never faltered. And so he saw what Dmitry did not: an almost imperceptible sideways movement of Sergei's eyes as he indicated to Bennett. A movement that said, *Kill him. Kill Dmitry.*

Shelley's finger tightened on the trigger, ready, knowing he had to fire before Sergei but also that he had to time it right, he had to be sure Bennett had shifted his aim or he would blow the back of Shelley's head off.

The moment seemed to hang in time.

And then it happened.

All four weapons crashed together. Only Dmitry failed to find a target, his shot going wide. But Shelley's round hit Sergei dead center in the forehead, blowing out the back of his head in a welter of blood and skull and brain matter, throwing him backward at the same time, Lucy crumpling safely to the deck. Bennett's two rounds were clustered at Dmitry's heart, opening holes in his T-shirt and sending him staggering back before he dropped to the tarmac.

And Sergei's round hit Shelley.

He felt it like a heavyweight punch to the shoulder and threw out a hand to support himself as he was thrown back, twisting to the side at the same time, landing bodily on the ground.

How badly am I hit? came the thought. But his next instinct was to protect Lucy, and he pulled himself to his knees, raised his SIG to take aim at Bennett. *Why hasn't Bennett opened fire?*

And then he saw why. Bennett stood in the same spot, Glock held loosely in his hand. He was looking down on himself to where a dark, gleaming patch of blood was spreading slowly across the groin of his navy suit trousers.

As Shelley watched, Bennett's legs gave way beneath him, and he, too, sank to his knees so that they faced one another, both wounded by the same round—a round that had passed through Shelley's shoulder and into Bennett.

The sirens were getting closer now.

"Drop it, Bennett," said Shelley. His finger tightened on the trigger, and for a moment he almost . . . but no. His finger relaxed. "Drop the gun," he said, but realized Bennett had no intention of discarding his weapon. Instead his head dipped, and he pushed the barrel of the gun into his own mouth. "Bennett, don't," started Shelley. "You don't have to—"

But he never got to finish that particular sentence.

EPILOGUE

TWO WEEKS LATER Shelley and Lucy maneuvered their battered, injured bodies into the Saab, complete with crutch for Lucy, and made the drive from Stepney Green to the Drakes' house in Ascot.

Arriving, they drew up in front of brand-new gates, where Shelley approached the keypad and out of sheer curiosity punched in Susie's birthday for the code. No way would it still be the same, he thought. Not after all they'd been through.

The gate clicked and began a slow swing open. Shelley shook his head. "Fucking idiots," he said, and rejoined Lucy in the car.

"What is it?" she asked.

"Nothing."

"'Fucking idiots,' you said. Not exactly the toughest bit of lip-reading in the world. Who on earth were you calling 'fucking idiots'? Not our hosts, I hope."

Shelley grumbled something non-committal and eased the Saab onto the driveway. Being back brought mixed emotions.

Lucy, on the other hand, was paying her first visit to the Drake home, and she gawped through the Saab's window. "Whoa," she said. "Big house."

"Yeah, big house," agreed Shelley.

"Must be difficult to heat."

"Never known it cold, to be honest."

"Oh, well, that's a relief. I was thinking of launching an appeal."

Apart from his Jag and her Porsche there were no other cars on the drive; evidently the Drakes had cleared their diary. When Shelley and Lucy buzzed at the front door it was opened by Guy and Susie together—apparently joined at the hip all of a sudden—and they were led through to the lounge.

As they sat and waited for drinks to appear, Shelley mused that the last time he'd been in this lounge it was filled with the Met's tech guys, as well as DI Phillips, who'd been convinced Drake and his men were lying to him. Which of course they had been.

Since then the police had proceeded with varying degrees of exasperation and disbelief, with the dust from the investigation yet to settle. Shelley and Drake received an occasional call from Phillips, being dogged, the way detectives are supposed to be, but that was about as far as it went. The police didn't like bodies turning up, of course. But the fact that the bodies had belonged to Chechen and British gangsters had sucked a sense of urgency out of the investigation.

What's more, Claridge had informed them off the record that there was no intention of pressing charges for anything that had happened at Foxy Kittenz that night. Nor, indeed, anything since. If there ever was a hook, Shelley, Drake, Lucy, and Susie were off it.

And then one afternoon Drake had called Shelley.

"Same number, huh?" the millionaire had said.

"Told you so," Shelley had replied, and for a while they'd chewed over the events of a fortnight previously, with Guy expressing his dismay at the treachery of Bennett's crew, and finally—"At bloody last!" Lucy had said later—thanking Shelley for everything he'd done.

"I didn't do it for you," he'd told Drake.

"I'm well aware of that, Shelley. But thank you anyway. Something else I want you to know: I'm making reparations to the kid who was hurt the night we raided the cam place. He'll be well looked after, that much I can say."

Rich-guy solution: throw money at the problem. But, as far as Shelley knew, the kid had made a complete physical recovery, and no doubt he wasn't going to turn his nose up at a bit of financial help.

And then Drake had asked if he and Lucy would be able to come to the house, and Shelley had been about to tell him to take a running jump when Drake told him the reason for the invitation. And now, here they were.

Susie greeted them both effusively. "My savior," she told Lucy, who demurred.

"Actually, you saved *my* bacon," she said.

"Really?"

"You kicked the car door, remember? Throwing off the guy's aim. Nifty move."

"Even so, it's because of me you need this," said Susie gravely, indicating the crutch.

"Not for long," Lucy assured her.

"And how is the shoulder, David?" said Susie, turning to Shelley.

"On the mend," he told her.

She took his hands. "My lifesaver," she said, and gave him a kiss on the cheek, bringing her perfume back into his life. "How can I ever thank you?"

Lucy could think of a way, but Shelley had made her promise not to say anything. "You and your bloody pride," she'd fumed.

Small talk out of the way, Guy collected the urn and all four of them left the house, crossed the front lawn, and passed into the field beyond, where Emma used to keep her horses. There they gathered in a semicircle, Susie at the center, and bowed their heads.

"I knew this is where you'd want to be, sweetheart," Susie said. She upended the urn, a mother saying farewell to her daughter, and they each said their silent goodbyes.

A short time later Shelley and Lucy took their leave, and at last Shelley put the Drake house behind him for what he dearly hoped would be the last time.

For a while they drove in silence, until Shelley cleared his throat. "Luce," he said, "I've got something to tell you."

"I see," she said quietly. "It's like that, is it?"

"It's a bit like that, yeah."

"Okay, but before you go on: are you leaving me?"

"Can't I just—"

"Just answer me that: are you leaving me?"

"No. Absolutely not. God no."

"Then I think I know what it is."

"Look, why can't I just—"

"Did you sleep with her?"

That was it. The question lay between them.

"No," he said at last.

"But . . . okay then. Did you *want* to sleep with her?"

"There was a moment outside the hospital where I wanted to put a bullet into Bennett. But that's all it was. A moment. Like an impulse. Half a second later I knew I didn't want to do it."

"Because it was the wrong thing to do? Or because you didn't want to do it?"

"I didn't want to do it *because* it was the wrong thing to do."

"And you're saying it was like that with her?"

"There was a kiss, Luce." He saw her flinch and the sight was like a knife into him. "But that's all it was. That was the impulse. Half a second later I knew I didn't want to do it."

"Because it was the 'wrong thing to do,'" she parroted unhappily.

"Yeah, but what made it wrong was the fact that I loved you— loved you then, love you still. More and more every day."

They drove a while in silence.

"You know what this means, don't you?" she said at last.

"What?" he replied, fearing her reply.

"It means you owe me brainstorming, Shelley. A lot of bloody brainstorming."

ACKNOWLEDGMENTS

My thanks of course go to James, as well as our brilliant editor, John Sugar, and copyeditor Alison Rae. Also my agent, Antony Topping, and Dave Taylor. "Do a good show, all right?"

—A.H.

ABOUT THE AUTHORS

JAMES PATTERSON is the world's bestselling author and the world's most trusted storyteller. He has created many enduring fictional characters and series, including Alex Cross, the Women's Murder Club, Michael Bennett, Maximum Ride, Middle School, and I Funny. Among his notable literary collaborations are *The President Is Missing,* with Bill Clinton, and the Max Einstein series, produced in partnership with the Albert Einstein estate. Patterson's writing career is characterized by a single mission: to prove that there is no such thing as a person who "doesn't like to read," only people who haven't found the right book. He's given over three million books to schoolkids and the military, donated more than seventy million dollars to support education, and endowed over five thousand college scholarships for teachers. The National Book Foundation presented Patterson with the Literarian Award for Outstanding Service to the American Literary Community, and he is also the recipient of an Edgar Award and six Emmy Awards. He lives in Florida with his family.

*　　*　　*

ANDREW HOLMES is the author of the acclaimed thrillers *Sleb, Nobody Saw,* and *Bloody Kids,* as well as a previous Shelley adventure in collaboration with James Patterson, *Hunted.* He can be found on Twitter at @holmeswriter.

JAMES PATTERSON
RECOMMENDS

HUNTED

If you're looking for a quick, suspenseful read, then I've got the book for you. In this first outing by former Special Forces officer David Shelley, the stakes are high as men from the streets are lured to the English countryside for a mysterious game like no other. Shelley decides to go undercover to shut it down once and for all. But this game is anything but fun, and not winning could lose you your life. My detectives are used to being the hunters—searching for criminals in the most dangerous situations. Shelley is about to learn what it means to finally be the hunted.

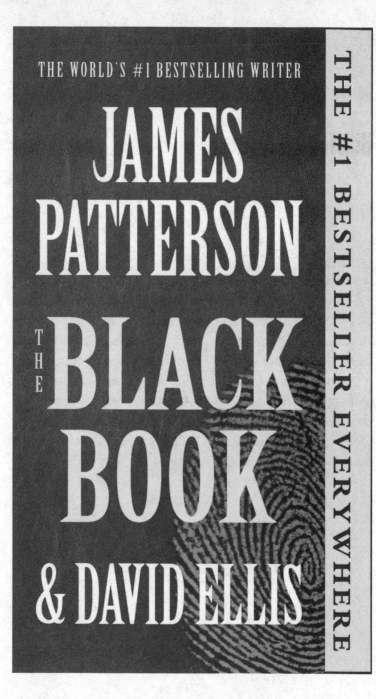

JAMES PATTERSON

THE BLACK BOOK

& DAVID ELLIS

THE BLACK BOOK

I have favorites among the novels I've written. *Kiss the Girls, Invisible, 1st to Die,* and *Honeymoon* are top of the list. With each, I had a good feeling when the writing was finished. I believe this book—*The Black Book*—is the best work I've done in twenty-five years.

Meet Billy Harney. The son of Chicago's chief of detectives, he was born to be a cop. There's nothing he wouldn't sacrifice for his job. Enter Amy Lentini, an assistant state's attorney hell-bent on making a name for herself—by proving Billy isn't the cop he claims to be.

A horrifying murder leads investigators to a brothel that caters to Chicago's most powerful citizens. There's plenty of evidence on the scene, but what matters most is what's missing: the madam's black book.

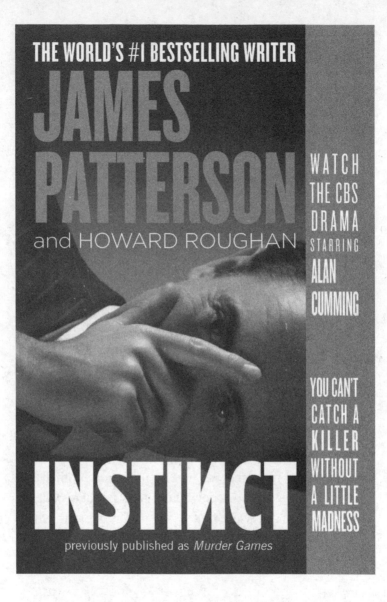

INSTINCT

Like many of you, I'm a true-crime fan. Whenever I see a profiler at work, I always wonder: Can knowing how a criminal thinks turn you into one? So I created Dr. Dylan Reinhart, who literally wrote the book on criminal behavior. When a copy turns up at a murder scene and the NYPD recruits him to help, Dylan has to go deep inside the mind of a very twisted killer. What happens is more shocking than any tabloid story. Pssst—the book is now a TV show called *Instinct,* and it stars the very talented Alan Cummings.

For a complete list of books by
JAMES PATTERSON

VISIT
JamesPatterson.com

Follow James Patterson on Facebook
@JamesPatterson

Follow James Patterson on Twitter
@JP_Books

Follow James Patterson on Instagram
@jamespattersonbooks